GONE |

GONE | ELISABETH SHEFFIELD

FC2
Normal / Tallahassee

Published by FC2 with support provided by Florida State University, the Unit for Contemporary Literature of the Department of English at Illinois State University, the Program for Writers of the Department of English of the University of Illinois at Chicago, the Illinois Arts Council, and the Florida Arts Council of the Florida Division of Cultural Affairs

Address all inquiries to: Fiction Collective Two, Florida State University, c/o English Department, Tallahassee, FL 32306-1580

ISBN: Paper, 1-57366-108-2

Library of Congress Cataloging-in-Publication Data
Sheffield, Elisabeth.
  Gone / Elisabeth Sheffield.-- 1st ed.
    p. cm.
  ISBN 1-57366-108-2
  1. Inheritance and succession--Fiction. 2. Mothers and daughters--Fiction. 3. Maternal deprivation--Fiction. 4. Loss (Psychology)--Fiction. 5. Missing persons--Fiction. I. Title.
PS3619.H464 G66 2003
813'.54--dc21

                                    2002014233

Cover Design: Victor Mingovits
Book Design: Lisa Savage and Tara Reeser

Produced and printed in the United States of America
Printed on recycled paper with soy ink

Acknowledgments

I am grateful to Patricia Ackerman, Stephanie Sheffield, Sarah Gerstenzang, and Melanie Sheffield Montgomery for their intelligent and helpful responses to this project. I am further indebted to Melanie Sheffield Montgomery, and David Montgomery as well, for invaluable research assistance. My gratitude goes also to fellow writers Jeff Solomon, whose smart and theoretically informed reading was most useful for the final draft, Greg Bills and Jeffrey DeShell. Jeffrey DeShell in fact deserves particular thanks, for providing an emotionally, intellectually, and creatively supportive space in which to write this book.

Finally, I would like to thank Brenda Mills for her astute editing, as well as all her other help, Lisa Savage for the fabrication of the faux auction pages, and Ralph Berry.

Credits

Pages 12-15: Juju's recollection of her little cow is inspired by an anecdote in *Human Life*, the memoir of the 19th century clergyman, pacifist, abolitionist, and suffragist Henry Wright. See pp.93-187 in *Growing Up in Cooper Country: Boyhood Recollections of the New York Frontier*, ed. Louis C. Jones. Syracuse University Press, 1965.

Pages 86-89: Dixon Ryan Fox's description of the restoration of the Hooperville countrystore is modeled on an incident recounted in Louis C. Jones' introduction to *Three Eyes on the Past: Exploring New York Folk Life*. Syracuse University Press, 1982.

The mannequin depicted in the "Online Auction" pages was supplied by Tony Goffredo of Everyone's Hair, Inc., in Boulder, CO.

To my mother, Patricia Ackerman

Gone daddy gone...I don't know why you suggested that I come here. OK. You're right. You didn't suggest anything. You can't. There's nothing behind those deepset hooded eyes but the void yet the mouth mumbles as if saying a rosary while the fingers fumble with the edge of the sheet counting invisible beads.... But you were an atheist, weren't you? Forgive me. Your mouth mumbles as if it isn't saying anything your lips expanding and contracting as rhythmically as the oral cavity of a fish. Is that better? Less judgmental more objective and scientific? I hope so because of course you're no more culpable than the carp trapped beneath the ice of the Otsego no more accountable than the sleet that smears the windows of the Lakeview Lodge for the Aged as I sit here by your bed.

Still I can't help feeling that you owe me something. You're my granddaddy after all the Big Fish who spawned us all with a sweep of his mighty tail. And so it stands that I'd swallow Juju's hook and line if not the sinker about how *your grandfather has something he wants to pass on to you before he dies... Remember the old painting that used to hang in his study, the one of the young girl watching over a herd of cows in a field dotted with buttercups?* Why shouldn't I believe her why shouldn't it be a Winslow Homer an early American gem to make up for the one

I lost when you banished us to LaLa Land? Fair is fair or at least square cuz that painting's got to be worth a mint. So give me a home where the Mohicans once roamed where Abner Doubleday invented a pastime where mapletree sap flows thick and sweet where boys and girls play in the woods until the owl gives a hoot and Mommy hollers time to hit the hay. And if I can't have that I'll take a check.

Ms. Amber Bowersox
RD #1
Cooperstown, NY 13326

31 August 1998

Dear Ms. Bowersox,
    I'm admiring the photographs of you and your lovely
cow in the "Scenes from the County Fair" page in the <u>Star</u>
(which I still subscribe to even though I now live in the City,
"because you can take the girl out of the country, but you
can't take the country out of the girl"). "Relaxing between
events at the Junior Livestock Show" the caption beneath
reads, utterly failing (as words so often do) to capture the
complexity of your mood. While my own language will no
doubt fall short as well, let me attempt to describe what I
perceive. I see a young woman no more than fourteen years
old (and while girls mature earlier these days, I'm guessing
fewer than a dozen red roses have bloomed in your white
nylon panties), a young woman at the very threshold of the
biological destiny she can either take up or turn her back to,
but for the moment simply lying in the straw, her head
cushioned by the velvety shoulder of her recumbent Holstein
(which, according to the accompanying article, has received
"a bouquet of blue ribbons" for both conformation and milk-
production). And it may be a trick of the light shifting
through the canvas tent in the background, light which
outlines the left side of your face against the dark neck of the
cow while leaving the right side in shadow, but it seems to me
that your emotions are deeply divided.
    Even as you bask in the glory of bucolic accomplish-
ment, you also feel trapped. Your life seems as dim as the
inside of a barn or a convent, a dull sanctum within which the
days flow one into the next, circling through the seasons like
milk streaming through the tubes of a milking machine. Then

you remember the show you saw on television last night, the one about the woman lawyer with the pencil thin legs and slippery looking hair, flirting against evil in a world of tinted glass, reinforced concrete, and steel. And like a prince contemplating an escape with a sexy commoner, you dare to imagine a future other than animal husbandry.

Perceiving all this, I'm writing to persuade you against taking such a rash step. For once you forsake the farm, you can never truly return. Oh sure you can go back, clean stalls until you reek of hide and dung, pitch hay until your latissimus dorsi scream. But the odor that clings to you will have become as impersonal as exhaust fumes, while the ache in your muscles will be no different than the one you feel after working out on the lat machine at the gym. You'll no longer belong where you are, Amber, nor anywhere else, and you can't know what it feels like to lose that sense of "belonging" until it's gone and every place has become interchangeable with every other, like cartons of homogenized milk. Only then will you come to appreciate the rich and faintly gamy flavor of farm life. Only then will you come to realize, like the husband who understands too late that his wife was actually kinkier than his mistress, or the nun who misses her dirty habit only after she's kicked it, that the tie to the land is a turn-on, a restraint that paradoxically permits release.

I know what I'm talking about, Amber, when I speak of the discreet charm of the farm. Sure I never actually lived on one, but I once owned a cow—a wee wild and tawny thing with long slender legs like a dancer's that could clear a five foot wrought-iron fence in one grand jeté. My daddy found her for me. He was a doctor himself, but he came from old New England dairy folk (ask your grandparents if they remember drinking Vanderzee Milk) and had always yearned to revisit his pastoral past. When I told him all I wanted for my tenth birthday was a cow to call my own, he couldn't have been more pleased. The next day a carpenter began unrenovating the renovated stable at the edge of our property,

un-painting, de-varnishing, un-plastering and de-insulating,
turning the cushy guesthouse cum game room back into a
true-to-life tumbledown wreck fitted with four stalls and a
milk room.

Daddy bought my cow a day or two after the stable was
finished, from a farmer out in Cherry Valley who said she was
a fine animal of "old-timey stock," although a "bit high-
strung." Nimbleshanks, the old fellow had called her, and
tried to throw in the bug-eyed calf fumbling at her udder. But
Daddy told him we only wanted the one. I still remember the
first time I saw that limber little minx, on a muddy spring day
back in '52. Daddy had put a pair of blinders on her and was
trying to coax her to walk down a heavy plank he'd leaned
against the bed of the truck he'd borrowed from a patient, but
she didn't want any part of it. The more Daddy wheedled the
more she stiffened her knobby knees, the more he cajoled the
more she dug in her cloven hooves. Finally he lost his cool
and started to jerk the rope. And at last she came, only not
down the ramp but over his head—sailing over him like some
dusky swan. Yes, Amber, like a swan she sailed over his head,
neatly alighting just two feet away from me onto the only dry
patch of ground in the barnyard. It was as if elegance incor-
porated had flown off the back of a flatbed truck, as if a
windfall profit had landed at my feet, though I'd made no
initial investment. But truth be told it wasn't until some
months later that she completely took over my heart.

After that my father didn't want anything to do with that
"insolent mammal," despite the fact that he was the one
who'd chosen her out of all the cows in the county. He
padlocked the door to her stall, then told me I'd better not
forget to milk her twice every single day, once in the morning
and again in the evening. So each sunrise and sunset I'd have
to coax the wild little witch to let me put my pail beneath her
belly and pull my stool up alongside her flank. And more
often than not she'd kick my bucket over before it was half
full so that now whenever I drank milk I'd see my glass as

half empty, though before the advent of Nimbleshanks I'd
been as cheerful as any normal girl. The worst, however, was
when she'd escape the barn because, as I've already indicated, that cow could fly like a bird. Not only could she clear
tall wrought iron fences without even grazing her belly but
she'd appear to hover for a second or two over the palisades,
as if inviting evisceration. Sometimes I'd chase her for
hours—tearing up through the woods behind the stable to
Grove Street before charging down into town dodging cars on
Main, then on to one of the side streets floundering in
flowerbeds, trampling trellises and knocking over birdbaths
while Nimbleshanks herself hardly touched the ground, let
alone anything else. I'd curse and scream that I never wanted
to see her "damn brown face again" and yet could not stop
chasing her, like a balletomane following some hair raising
"pas seul," until finally she'd end the performance with a
deep "révérence"—at which point I'd run huffing up to her
side and slip the halter over her head.

The "pièce de résistance" came one evening out in the
barn. For the first time ever it seemed as if I'd be able to fill
my bucket in a single milking, as Nimbleshanks stood quietly
in her stall, meek as a young girl in a confessional. Not a
sound, not a movement but for the occasional swoosh of her
tail, the delicate twitching of her moist pink nostrils in the
vespertine air. And then in a snort, sweet repose was broken—with a single well-aimed kick she'd knocked the bucket
over sloshing the front of my blue jeans with her warm white
liquor. For a long moment I just stood there, watching the
steam rise up from darkened denim. For a long moment I held
myself back, until finally restraint gave way and there was no
recourse—I had to unbuckle my belt. What else but to yank
the leather strap from round my slender waist, and wield it
with one hand as I needed the other to hold up my baggy
dungarees while I drove her into the corner of her stall? What
else but to bring that strap down again and again over her
withers her crops her barrel her ribs her hips her thurls

because I'd allowed her tricks to go without recompense for too long? Yes, it was as they say "pay back time" though even still I made sure all my lashings fell below the neck because I knew that every welt gained by that dear brown face would be my loss.

Then all at once she dropped to her knees. And there she was, hind legs straight and forelegs bent so she appeared to be bowing, big sad amber eyes gazing up at me out of that austerely delicate face—just imagine Audrey Hepburn with her shorn head and nun's habit in <u>Robin and Marian</u>, though perhaps that one was before your time. But even still, you must get the picture, and I ask you what was a girl to do but drop her arm in forgiveness?

From that day forward, whenever I began to unbuckle my belt, she'd drop on her knees and remain there until I'd emptied her of milk. I couldn't whip her when she was in that position, but I could and did treat myself to many a frothy cup as I filled my buckets with her flow.

With warmest regards,
Judith Vanderzee

Gone daddy gone... And not just you and my pops but Mommy, Anna and maybe Juju too. And Heidi won't tell me anything. But Juju must have sent that letter from somewhere even if somewhere could be Anywhere USA. Yes she must have sent it from somewhere and didn't the nurse at Lakeview say Dr. Phinney might have an address. People say that's where your aunt stayed the last time she was in town.

So here we are Dr. Heidi and I sitting in the arsenic and old lace living room that used to belong to her parents, each of us at one end of an ivory silk sofa clotted with crocheted antimacassars. Anna and I used to argue what they were for she said to keep Franky's greasy scalp off the upholstery I said so Pious Peg could just grab one off a chair and throw it over her fat face on the way to mass. But Ma and Pa Phinney have cast off the burden of the flesh and even Heidi looks like she's lost a pound for every year since the last time I saw her. Or maybe it was always just water weight and she shed it in tears over Juju. Ein lämbchen Oma called her, a fat little lamb. Die wölfin gobbled her up and then spit her out again.

The drapes are drawn even though there's still some light outside and the pink shaded lamps at each end of the couch surround us with a rosy glow setting the stage for feminine intimacy and maybe even a true confession or two. Only the cushion between us is empty and we're positioned at an angle and distance no doubt diagrammed in the *Guide to Good Manners* sandwiched between volumes of the *New England Journal of Medicine* in the built-in bookcase beside the fireplace. So I lean back a little and extend my legs lifting one four inch platform boot on top of the walnut veneer coffee table. I see her looking at it the pink-rimmed nostrils of her snub nose twitching slightly to the accompanying tap tap of her navy and Kelly green flats. I could tell her what I learned when I tits and assed for Intro to Drama: Oedipus to Willy Loman, that it's a cothurnus. But she wouldn't know what I'm talking about and besides we're not here to act tragic or make a scene. All I want is an address a telephone number. Or an e-mail account. That's it. I don't need to know why she's still putting up with Juju's crap. The only psychodrama I'm interested in is my own and that's only for as long as it takes to scalp my ticket.

How was your grandfather today? Did he know who you were?

She's slipped on the same concerned face you used to wear for your patients it's better than a white coat. But I can see behind the professional compassion I can see she hates you for all those years of coming home from school to an empty house because her mother was filling yours. Such ingratitude you'd say. If you could. After all wasn't it a step up for the scullery maid from Schenectady when she became Doc Vanderzee's housekeeper? A step up that prevented the brilliant but sickly Franklin from having to step down as the circulation of the Otsego Journal grew smaller and smaller, that allowed him to continue to sit in his editor's office sailing away from lumpen wife and daughter on the Mayflower of his imagination? Yes I'm certain she can't stand you as she stares at me, waiting for an answer.

No.

So sad to see a brilliant mind break down. Not just brilliant but broad. Years ago, he saw past my spotty record and still

awarded me a partial Vanderzee to attend the Life Sciences pro-
gram at Cornell. If it hadn't been for him, I couldn't have gone.

Something's baking somewhere, something sweet and spicy and good. But underneath I'm sure that's rancor I smell seeping forth like the scent of sour milk from a carton long past its expiration date the curdled odor of too many motherless afternoons that not even a full scholarship to Cornell could have masked. I push back deeper into my corner of the sofa folding my hands over my stomach shifting my gaze to the coffee table. A dark-faced woman with thickly kohled eyes looks up at me from the banana yellow cover of *National Geographic. Nepal's Women of Grace.* What was she thinking when they took her picture? Give me back my soul you fucker.

So sad. I'm sure he'd be so proud to know where you are—is it UCLA?

No it's a small private school. No need to tell her what one. *You wouldn't recognize the name.*

Still, an English professor. Although I've heard that the salaries for Ph.D.s in the humanities are ridiculously low.

She doesn't need to know that ABDs make even less that I was dead in the water with a moribund dissertation on Sylvia Plath a thirty-three-year-old adjunct instructor at a commodity college that I read so many run-on sentences over the past two years that I can no longer punctuate.

Well you won't have to worry about money when your grand-father dies.

Bitch. She's got to know Juju must have told her you've never given us squat not even college tuition for Anna yup no Vanderzees for Vanderzees neither full not partial cuz as your father has shown me, easy money weakens the will to succeed.

She's looking down picking an invisible piece of lint off her fairisle sweater.

Although to be honest with you, that might not be for a while. This illness—and we're not even sure it's Alzheimer's, only an autopsy can determine that—can drag on for years.

Sort of like you and my aunt?

She winces. Touché even though it was a stab in the dark a stinkbomb in the night cuz I don't know much about their relationship—we were already living out in LaLa Land. Yeah I got her good and now listen to her squeal. No that's coming from somewhere else.

Oh there goes that awful kettle.

Saved by the bell she pops up from the sofa and trots over the dark stained floors. Sounds of hostessing come from the kitchen sounds of drawers sliding out and back like shuffling feet the refrigerator door squelching open a minute later smacking shut. Of course she doesn't want to think about my aunt it was probably deeply shameful to her doing what they did. There's no way she could've rationalized it. No way Peg's mandatory Sunday morning masses at St. Mary's nor Franklin's optional snippets from Poor Richard's Almanack early to bed early to rise makes you healthy wealthy and wise could've justified those nights no matter if they went to bed at sunset and got up with the first peep of God's creation. She doesn't want to think about my aunt doesn't want to think about the games they played. I can just see them Juju of course would've been Franklin Phinney ye olde New England man of letters Heidi her own mom the illiterate Irish maid servant he'd plucked off some upstate city street even if she was already a doctor by then she'd be into playing bottom: Please sir, can you help me read this list sir, it's victuals for me missus. Why I'd love to young lady. Just give me your address book I'll tell her, my lips are sealed. We'll never talk about Juju or the love that dare not speak its name let alone its telephone number. Just let me write it down.

But lo what's this Heidi Ho's back in the ring again lightly balancing two cups and saucers a large steaming silver teapot a cow shaped creamer sugar bowl a pale yellow plate of freshbaked sugarcrusted gingersnaps and a huge stinking block of cheddar all on a silver tray.

Stella would you mind taking this for a moment while I clear the table?

I would. The smell of that cheese revolts me. But if I want to get out of here with Juju's number I should probably start acting nicer. So swing your boot off the table Stella stand up and take the goddamn tea tray. Man it's heavy. Solid silver no doubt an heirloom from the Phinney side and then there's the added weight of the full teapot the cookies and the monstrous wedge of cheddar. And yet little Heidi carried it in as if it were a styrofoam stage prop. Feeble Franklin's strong-armed daughter. She must've got her muscles from her ma.

Remember when I used to babysit you and your poor sister? Back then you were the sensitive one. And such a strong gag reflex, my oh my. When we walked past the garbage cans in Pioneer Alley I'd have to hold my bandana over your nose, she says as she plucks Nepal's woman of grace and *Neuroscience* off the table and drops them into a red velvet armchair. Then flashing her caps at me she lifts the tray from my hands swings it through the air and slaps it down on the coffee table. Saucers rattle the pile of cookies shudders but nothing breaks or even spills. Anna had the weak stomach not me I just didn't like things that smelled bad but who cares we both know I'm not here to talk about what a puker I was as a kid.

And she must know I'm not interested in chit chat because this time she takes the velvet chair opposite the couch instead of sitting down next to me like before. I add two heaping teaspoons of sugar to my tea swirl it around then up the ante with a third. Seems like I always crave it when I've had a lot to drink the night before. A vortex forms in the center and a little tea splashes over the rim and onto the saucer. I wonder if she remembers the time I made her cry. Anna and I were drawing pictures and so I drew her and when it came to her body I grew fascinated by the curves that were swirling out onto the paper from the felt tip of my magic marker, curves that seemed to be pulled outward and downward by the scalloped borders of the lovely garden spread out beneath her. There was nothing personal finally in the proportions I presented to her—but she didn't seem to understand that I was only submitting to the spirit of the picture. Honest injun Heidi, I didn't mean to be mean.

But oh baby it's all gone now—that flabby potato white flesh that hung from her bones weighty as fruit about to drop yet never falling only dragging her down. Now she's Nepal's woman of grace, rare and sparc as the Himalayan air. Light as air but strong as steel a self-sculpted triumph of modern design a celebration of the victory of aesthetics over comfort of aspiration over upbringing of karma over dharma. Oh baby how hard it must've been for her not to succumb to a bite of soft white bread slathered with mayo before bed not to tarry at the invitation of her sagging mattress in the morn how hard it must've been instead to drag her spandexed bod through the streets of Cooperstown at the ass crack of dawn. Especially after Juju left her.

She holds out the yellow plate of cookies: *Here, have a gingersnap. You used to be crazy for sweets.*

I sweep a pile into my lap and hand her back the empty dish. Her eyebrows nearly merge with her hairline. It's not that I don't care about aesthetics—I've just never been a minimalist.

We sip and crunch in silence. That is she sips and I crunch as the cookies crumble the way cookies do littering the wide front of my sailor pants with crumbs. I wonder if it's still snowing outside if those big wet flakes of spring that get caught in your lashes and sting your eyes are still falling from the sky. I wonder if she's gotten over Juju. God that cheese reeks. I should say something.

I'm sorry about my aunt. But I didn't have anything to do with it—I was just a kid the last time I saw you.

She watches me eyes bright and absent as a sparrow's even cocking her head slightly so that I half expect her to fly at me and start pecking wildly at the crumb-covered canvas of my pants. I want to cross my arms up in front of my face but instead put my hands on my knees and lean forward. Try again.

Are you sure you have no idea where Judith might be or how I can get in touch with her? It's important, she wrote that my grandfather has a painting for me. But when I spoke to his lawyers today they acted like they didn't know what I was talking about.

No I don't.

That's it. Three small units of sound. In school I learned each word is meaningful cuz of its difference from the others. Truth be told they sounded the same to me, three puffs of breath as slight as bird tracks in the snow hop hop hop. Fuck her. I look down at her slender tapping calf-skin covered feet and see them sinking into mud a black ooze a primal tarpit see her bones etched in ancient shale. Yeah cuz I wish bygones could be bygones wish that anachronisms weren't wheeling about the room scaly wings churning the air. Swooping down out of nowhere like Juju did that time she came to California after my mom left. Not a word? Not a word? She kept asking staring at Anna and I with goggly blue eyes running her palms over hips draped in a pair of flowery palazzo pants that afterwards Oma said must have cost a pretty penny. After she'd gone Anna asked what the hell was that about. And Oma said it was obvious you'd sent your trusty spy to confirm my mom hadn't headed back to Cooperstown, to make sure she wasn't going to spring out of some local dump just when you thought the streets were safe again for Sunny Jim.

I've got to call the hospital about some tests I ordered earlier today. Can you see yourself out?

She's risen to her full five feet. Full fathom five my granddaddy lies. If not yet then soon. She leaves the room and I hear her feet skittering over wooden stairs scrambling up somewhere far far away. A door slams at the top of the house as I button up my leather coat in the vestibule. This is it I guess. I'm barking up the wrong tree or maybe the right one but there's no use if she won't come down nothing I can do nothing I can do but turn this knob and go. Man it looks cold out there. Far far away...

Stella, wait.

I turn around and there she is clutching a mashed black cardboard box to her flat chest. There she is peering up at me a little smile on her lips a wink of gold at the apex of her ear. What is it a ripple of wire threaded through the thin rim of flesh—is it new or was it there all along? Icy air slithers up the back of my coat it must be seeping in from under the door.

She left these.

And now she's stepping forward thrusting the box out so that I can see the words scripted on the top: *Fredericks of Hollywood.*

I take it slowly lift the lid with one hand. What no leopard print peekaboo panties no black vinyl sex police caps with shiny matching corsets and night sticks that double as dildos no chaps or Chippendale bikinis not even a naughty nurse outfit or milkmaid's costume complete with milking stool—what a disappointment. Instead there's a bunch of loose letters a slovenly tumble of sealed though unstamped envelopes of all different colors and sizes all addressed in Juju's spidery handwriting *Amber Bowersox Jacqueline Funk Aubrie Rathbun* names I don't recognize but *Dr. William S. Vanderzee James S. Vanderzee Barbara Salzmann* and what's this *Stella Vanderzee* I know all too well. So now it's revelation time Inspector Stella cuz golly gee whiz these pages could not only bare her smelly maybe even still warm secrets but they might sneak a peek at yours and Daddy's dirty skivvies too the unmentionables that Oma said my poor mother would never talk about. But do I really want to know? No I really don't give a fuck about what happened in this goddamn town all I want is that painting. She can keep this box of trash. I close the lid start to hand it back. Stop. Start again. No. Because maybe there's an address somewhere in the jumble, some way to track old Juju down.

I tuck the box under my arm feeling the contents shift and slide as I turn to go. But now I feel a tug on my sleeve she's grabbing at me with her little paw and my heavy leather coat suddenly feels as thin and flimsy as nylon. She's close enough so that I can see the pinkish skin around the coil of gold wire in her ear.

Knowledge is a treasure, but practice is the key.

Her grip on my coat turns to a gentle push as the door at my back gives way.

Ms. Jacqueline Funk
38 Elm St.
Cooperstown NY 13326

18 May 1999

Dear Ms. Funk,

I understand, having seen you pluck a paper petal off a sign tacked to the bulletin board at the Ugly American Food Emporium yesterday, that you seek a babysitting job. Please don't be alarmed, by the way, that a seeming stranger knows your name. In fact, I'm not really a stranger; your grandmother and I were brief but fit friends in the fifth grade and played naughty games after school every day with the lilli dolls my father had brought back from a plastic surgeon's conference in Frankfurt. (Lilli, by the way, was Barbie's saucy German source, shamelessly plagiarized by the founder of Mattel.) But then one day my papa walked in as Lilli Eins was grinding Lilli Zwei into the parquet floor with her molded plastic pelvis and spoiled the fun with a lecture on the principles of sexual reproduction. And while that was long ago if not far away, I think your grandmother remembers, that the stiff little nod she gives me when we see each other on the street (rarely, since I spend most of the year down state these days) alludes to Lilli's ramrod charm.

Anyway, Jacqueline, it is as a stranger who is not really a stranger that I would like to offer you some very good advice. I expect, of course, nothing in return: my words will help you to help yourself, and that shall be reward enough. Sweet Jackanapes, if you must work (and at this point you might ask whether you truly need the last recording of the three blond brothers, or whatever trifle it is that you're saving for), then let it be as a paper girl or a burger flipper or an ice cream server— anything but a babysitter. You probably think I'm crazy, my Jeune Fille. What's so terrible about babysitters, you're wondering as you read this. And to be sure, the babysitter seems to have nothing of the gothic authority of the governess, the bleating negativity of the nanny. So passive she'll work for less than the minimum wage, so permissive she'll tolerate the trespasses of children and parents alike, she's beloved by all. When the babysitter comes, the poptarts pop and the potato chips fly, bedtimes become pillow fights, televisions flicker all night like fairy fires, we all drink cola instead of milk and even bring out the rum. Yet this sweet indulgence, this effervescence of tolerance presents the gravest peril—for within it, boundaries disintegrate and rules decay, children sink and parents swim, suspended only by parlous fantasies. And it's the babysitter who is perhaps the most endangered of all, as she permits herself, during those long lax hours of sucking sour balls and reading romances on the couch, to entertain notions she might otherwise have never had.

The advice I have just given you, Jackstraw, is based on solid experience, for I was once a babysitter myself. Of course this was long before you were born, back in the early days of a profession that arose in response to the nuclearization of the American family, in the aftermath of WWII. By the mid 1950s (and I imagine that seems like an aeon ago to you, who probably had a diaper rash the day the Berlin wall collapsed), all the grandmothers had flown away to Florida and if the Smiths wanted to stay up all night drinking Fish House punch at the Joneses, well then, they had to pay the girl next door to keep an eye on the kiddies. For the first time ever a young woman could put money in her pockets that hadn't been filched from daddy's, and I can tell you those were giddy days. Which is not to suggest that I used to steal from my father. No, for he was always happy to unfurl a crisp fiver from his roll. All I had to do was ask. But I was tired of asking. I wanted bucks of my own, a cigar box of crumpled sweat-stained georgie boys under my bed like all the other girls had, and so early one summer Saturday I made

signs out of a dozen sheets of the thick monogrammed
stationery I'd received for my fourteenth birthday, and thumb
tacked them to trees all over town.

For a week my signs were spattered by sparrows and
smeared by rain, and not once did my powder blue princess
phone ring with a reply. Until finally, at noon on the following Saturday, my father called home from the hospital to
announce that his new nurse, who'd recently moved to town
from some godforsaken dairy farm outside of Troy, needed a
sitter for her daughter. Mrs. Salzmann was expecting me at
3:30, he said, before she left for her evening shift. Thus it
came to be that a few hours later I was standing on the
warped front steps of a little tarpaper-covered house, the
white Brooks Brothers shirt I'd lifted from a hanger in my
father's closet (all the girls were wearing the shirts in the
family that summer, if not the pants) sticking a bit to the
small of my back after the hike down into town and then up
the hill again over the railroad tracks to the end of Grove
Street, my shoulder aching with the weight of the straw beach
bag filled with balloons, bottles of bubbles, comic books,
crayons, my old lillis, and my brother's discarded matchbox
cars…any and everything I'd been able to think of to help
keep the tiny tot entertained until her bedtime, when I'd be
able to curl up on the couch with a supple, leatherbound
edition of Cleland's Fanny Hill (also nabbed from my dad).

Three or four times I rapped on the hollow plywood
door. No answer, though from within I could hear strains of
guitar music and a chorus of baritone voices. I tried to peer
through the dirty diamond pane in the top of the door, but it
was curtained off on the inside with dun-colored cloth.
Pressing my cheek to the glass, I could hear words: "Oh
what's that you say, mother, we've got beans in our ears
beans in our ears…"

Rap, rap, rap, again, but still no one came—nothing but
"beans in our ears beans in our ears…" I started to bang the
"wood," to pound with my palms, and would've gone so far

as to kick with my saddleshoe if I hadn't been sure the cheap plyboard would splinter with the blow. And now the light had begun to dim and a breeze to frisk my starched white shirt. A storm was gathering, and as I looked over my shoulder and saw how the light had begun to rustle over the rusted black Willy jeep parked at the end of the street, conjuring up a lurid red glow, how the trees that loomed beyond had begun to shimmy and shake, birds shuffling from branch to branch, I realized that if I cut through the woods I could probably get home again in half the time it had taken me to reach Mrs. Salzmann's tarpaper shack. Yes, and if at that moment lightning hadn't blazed the sky white as my stolen shirt, followed by a sky-rending crack of thunder, I would've sooner left than stayed.

I had raised my fist to resume pounding when, before my knuckles had even hit the wood, the door swung open. "OH WHAT'S THAT YOU SAY WE'VE GOT BEANS IN OUR EARS, BEANS IN OUR EARS..." Oh what to do but face the music, and I stepped inside, pushing the door against the wind until it latched. As the song of the legumes pulsed in my ears, a sickly gas, which I'd later discover seeped from the oven in the kitchen, its scent mixing with something like sour milk, monopolized my nose. At present, however, I was clearly in some sort of living room. A brightly painted watercolor sign with an intricate but nevertheless amateur border of flora and fauna on the opposite wall asserted that "HOME IS HEAVEN FOR BEGINNERS," and I remember thinking (I must confess) that heaven was then hardly worth the effort. What a dreary place. Low stained ceiling, buckling gray linoleum with an odd hump in the center like the shoulder of some buried beast, plywood front door flanked by gnarled bamboo fishing pole and battered wicker creel, two additional doorways hung with blighted ivy-patterned curtains, three warped windows with silvery crosses of electrical tape memorializing the cracks in the panes, white elephant sofa only half-hidden by a soiled mustard satin quilt so that

clumps of pus-colored batting oozing from the defunct
upholstery were clearly visible, no television set just a
wooden radio with a mouse-sized hole in its black grill cloth
roaring "BEANS IN OUR EARS BEANS IN OUR EARS,"
from a rickety stand.

And then lightning flashed again and suddenly there
were no beans in my ears, only the rushing of the wind and
the drumming of the rain on the tarpapered roof overhead.
There was nothing to do but make a run for it as soon as the
storm let up. For not only were there no babes to be sat
here—clearly, there was no money to be made. Best to wait
outside on the porch, I decided. Anything would be better
than sitting in this dump. I turned to leave.

"Mmmmmphhh."

I slowly swiveled round. In the doorway on the other
side of the room, a doorway which no doubt led to the even
more squalid interior of the house, stood what appeared to
be a human being. I say "what appeared to be" because the
only clearly human attributes of this creature were two
rather thick white stockinged legs which ended in feet shod
in scuffed white leather oxfords. Above the pudgy knees, all
was a shifting amorphous mass of white like some ghostly
essence struggling to materialize—only this was no ecto-
plasmic phantasm but a being all too solid and real. No,
there was no getting away from it, no getting away from the
warm whiffs of flesh and blood and talcum powder as the
thing writhed inside a tegument of what appeared to be
nylon tricot. No getting away from it, as suddenly a head of
silky dark hair popped out and then immediately afterward,
two plump pale brown arms. Then the head swung forward
and flipped back so that the mane of hair fell away from the
face. And now I saw two large eyes, pupils ringed by thin
circles of babyblue, set above cheeks soft and round as
yours, my Jacko'lantern, only these belonged to a mature
woman, and not to a young girl. She smiled at me with
sweet full lips as she pulled a rubber band from her chubby

wrist, leaving behind a bracelet of red, and used it to secure
her long hair back in a ponytail.

"Hallo," she said in a voice clotted with some sort of
vaguely Germanic accent. "I am Beata Salzmann and you
must be the daughter of Doc Vanderzee. Welcome."

Escape was out of the question, now that the woman had
seen me. If I left, she would tip off my pop, who would then
want to know why, after finally hooking a babysitting job, I'd
decided to let it go. I could already see how his face would
look when I explained—how the nostrils of his Roman nose
would flare like trumpets, how his shapely patrician lips
would purse up as if to launch a projectile of spit. But of
course the only expectorate I could expect from his lips
would be verbal: "little snob," he'd no doubt call me. And
this epithet would be flung with all the force of his twenty
years of "selfless service" as a reconstructive surgeon to the
citizens of Otsego County. Having noted the ironical effect of
the quotation marks in the last sentence, Jackpot, you may be
thinking that medical doctors are richly rewarded, both
financially and socially, for their so-called "selfless service":
indeed, is it not the prospect of prosperity that saves the
Hippocratic from becoming the Hypocritic? Thus how could
my father fault me for failing to leap at the chance to spend a
surely profitless night in this rathole? The fact, however, was
that he could and would, and further, that his disapproval was
far drearier than stained ceilings and leaking upholstery,
much harder to bear than the smell of cooking gas and sour
milk. I'd sooner parade through the streets of Cooperstown
wrapped in nothing but that soiled mustard satin blanket than
see my father's lips mew up with displeasure, than hear them
spew out those two damning words.

"My daughter is in her room," Mrs. Salzmann said,
pulling up a short zipper at the front of the garment (which I
now realized was her nurse uniform), so that the nylon pulled
snug across her large breasts. "I will show her to you and then
I must vamoose."

Oh joy! The brat was in bed, and it wasn't even four
o'clock yet! As I followed Mrs. Saltshaker through one of the
musty curtains out of the room and into the back of the house,
I imagined curling up on the couch with my pilfered <u>Fanny
Hill</u> (next time, perhaps, I'd snag something by that Marquis
de Sade) until she returned at midnight, the mustard satin
quilt pulled over my legs (in the future, I'd have to remember
to bring a cotton thermal blanket from home). Sure the pay
would be lousy, but I had the whole night to myself. A night
free of my brother James' pranks and pratfalls, of our housekeeper Peggy's motherly pats and milky ministrations, and
best of all, of my father's cold sweet kiss, which he invariably
planted on my brow upon his return from evening rounds, and
which I longed to refuse and could not, anymore than I could
deny myself a midnight fudgescicle from the freezer. In fact,
as she led me through the kitchen past the stinking stove and
an icebox the color of a nicotine-stained tooth, I even had the
happy thought I might lose a few pounds on this job (which is
not to imply that I was overweight, Jackie-O, but simply that,
like most teen-age girls, I aspired to the svelte ideal of
magazines like <u>Mademoiselle</u>—an ideal, by the way, that you
might try to emulate yourself. I saw that package of Little
Debbie cupcakes you were clutching in your chubby paw as
you read the advertisements on the supermarket bulletin
board).

Off the kitchen ran a short dark hallway with a door on
the end (later I learned this led to the in-house outhouse) and
a door on either side. Stopping in front of the door on our left,
which was an inch or two ajar, Mrs. Salzmann said in a low
voice: "You must keep the rope short and not be afraid to jerk
it now and then."

I followed her into a room that was only marginally
brighter than the hallway, the single light source being a
square foot of glass set high up in the wall like a window in a
gas station bathroom. Against this pane beat the rain, big
drops smearing the vitreous surface and running into each

other in a filmy wash through which the weak day glow wavered, casting a dim and unsure illumination on the bed beneath. How odd that it was in this tentative light I first saw Barbara Salzmann, since I knew for certain, as soon as I set eyes on her, that I loved her.

Only her close-cropped head on the pillow was visible, her body being covered by layers of white sheet and dun-colored crocheted blanket. And what a head it was. She had inherited the framework of her mother's broad Nordic features, only in her case this framework had been honed and refined, the rugged and rather masculine planes and abutments smoothed and scaled down into a hard polished little jewel of a face, set off by short mink-dark hair. Never before had I seen child with such a strong square jaw, such a firm chin, such high and prominent cheekbones, although finally, it wasn't her excellent bone structure that captured my heart, but rather the feathery black lashes that fluttered against her warm olive skin, as if poised to flit away.

"Bad Barbara, get out of bed," Mrs. Salzmann said, yanking the covers back from her daughter's body.

It was then I saw this was no small child, no tiny tot, but a nearly full-grown girl, albeit on the smallish side, with breasts straining the thin knit of a wife beater, and well-spread hip bones jutting above the elastic waistband of a pair of washed-out pink pajama bottoms. Slowly, insolently, the black wings lifted, revealing large light eyes like the mother's, only they weren't blue, but an orangey yellow like the fiery bourbon my father smacked his lips over each evening, calling it "an acquired taste," and their gaze was slightly askew. Later I learned that the right one was false. But at the time I had no explanation for those strange amber eyes, and I must admit, Julep dear, that for a moment I was taken aback, not just by their asymmetry, but also by their hue, for don't the colors orange and yellow conventionally warn us to slow down and take heed? Only for a moment, however, did I pause—no longer than a deep breath and a swallow.

Bad Barbara raised herself on one elbow, twisting her pink pajamed hip so that the waistband buckled, showing the welt the elastic had made in the flesh just above her navel. It was like a miniature road and I imagined running one of the matchbox cars in my totebag over the grooves in her skin, then drove the thought from my mind as it simply made no sense (back in those times, my little Jalopy, young people were considerably less aware of their sexuality than they are now). Returning my eyes to her face, I saw Barbara blinking up at Mrs. Salzmann, full lips parted: "I'm sorry, Mother, what did you say?"

"You heard me, you tricky girl, sleeping when you should be awake, awake when you should be sleeping. You stay up all night doing god knows what making strange things in your closet maybe sneaking out the door and into the woods, then all day in bed. However, now this nice young lady, this Miss Judith Vanderzee daughter of Doc Vanderzee, is here to make sure that you don't lie down until it is time, and that when you do, you stay there."

As if to emphasize this last point, Mrs. Salzmann leaned over the bed and gave Barbara a sharp slap on the bottom. Then she stood up, tossing her ponytail, which had fallen forward as she bent down, out of the way—only instead of tossing it straight back over her shoulder, she'd thrown it around the front of her neck like some absurd fur stole. Lacking the props of grand dame, it seemed she had to affect them, and indeed her exit would've been queenly if the tip of her white oxford hadn't caught on the wooden cigar box lying on the floor by the bed, sending her tumbling into the door where she managed to catch herself with a hand against the frame. Pausing for a moment, but without turning around, she said:

"Miss Vanderzee, please let me know if she gives you any grief."

The moment her mother was gone, Barbara sprang from the bed and closed the door. Then she stooped down to pick up the box. Raising it to the dim light of the window, she carefully examined the exterior. The brand was "EL PRODUCTO" and the box appeared undamaged, although even if it had been this seemed of small concern. After all, for most girls it was the contents that mattered. Then again, maybe for a girl like Barbara, one who had so little, this brown cigar case with its gold seal specifying "FOR REAL ENJOYMENT" was a genuine treasure. Yes, I thought, it is the box itself she holds dear, and I waited for her to open it because I knew the best part of the "EL PRODUCTO" design belonged to the interior: in the inner side of the lid the manufacturer always glued a gold-rimmed image of a woman in a long scarlet dress sitting on a park bench with a lyre beside her, a mirror-smooth lake in the background and a peacock in the foreground.

But when she finally opened the lid, I saw no trace of the image of the woman in the red dress—for the inside of the case was completely covered by a lining of ginger-colored fur. Yes, my pretty Jack-in-the-Box, it was lined with some sort of animal pelt, which had been cut, trimmed and glued to the thin wood with such care and expertise that it appeared organic, as if in the darkness of its penetralia, the box had cultivated its own secret fleece. Barbara stroked the furred recess with her finger, then gazed crookedly up at me through those wing-like lashes:

"I made this," she said.

"Very nice," I replied, at a loss for words. And what could I say, after all? Although my father had a shelf full of art books at home, I'd yet to be exposed to Joseph Cornell's boxes, let alone Lucas Samara's. And neither, of course, had Barbara. Yet somehow in this fallow bungalow, this HEAVEN FOR BEGINNERS, the demonseed of art had taken root.

Later she showed me her other works and works-in-progress, most of which were "sculptures" consisting of strange contrasts and congruencies of ordinary objects and materials—toothbrushes and tarnished silverware, pesticide canisters and peanut shells, shellac and papier mâché— although there were drawings as well of queerly voluptuous little women, dancing over newsprint in hoof-like spiked heels. All of these, she told me, she had created in her bed-room closet, where she often worked the whole night long at a table made out of two milk crates and a sheet of plywood, beneath a dangling 60 watt bulb. In fact, it was in Barbara's closet that my father's Brooks Brothers shirt remained when I finally left the Salzmann shack early the next morning. And when I returned three days later (thanks to my pop, Mrs. S only worked the evening shift every third night), it was from that same closet that the shirt emerged, transformed.

She'd rigged the garment to a frame of twisted coat hangers so that it was stretched flat, the sleeves standing straight out at right angles to the sides before dropping limply at the elbows. Across the back she'd painted "MY POPS IS TOPS" in what appeared to be red nail polish, then she'd lightly shellacked the whole, giving it a wet-looking gleam (which anticipated the work of George Segal, but without that fatal nostalgia for the human form).

Holding the stiffened shirt in front of her torso, so that her head seemed to rise up out of the collar, she fixed me with her crooked yellow gaze: "You can hang it on the wall. Or you can fly it."

I chose the latter. And so as soon as the last rattle of the Salzmann's Willy had disappeared in the distance, we navi-gated the shirt out of the house, dipping and turning through door frames and around corners, down the porch steps and up onto the slope of the lawn behind the house. A breeze dabbed and batted at the thing as we carried it—Barbara holding the collar end while I held the tails—to the uppermost part of the slope and laid it button side down on the grass, while over-head the moon dangled in the still light sky, giving off a pale galvanic glow. The dark border of the trees rising up behind her, Barbara dug the pockets of her baggy dungarees (which were fetchingly gathered around the waist with a maroon and navy-striped silk necktie) and produced a ball of string and a long darning needle wrapped in felt. As I held the shirt to the ground to keep it from blowing away, she used the needle to pull the string through the fabric a few times, securing it around the flat frame of twisted hangers in between, then with her fingers nimbly tied the loose end in a square knot.

Handing me the ball of string, she raised the stiff and gleaming shirt over her head and told me to start running down the slope. So I took off, and as I leapt over the lawn lightfooted as a lamb or the cow that jumped over the moon, I felt Barbara release the shirt, felt it rise sharply and catch on the breeze. I let the ball of string in my hands unfurl as the air carried the shirt up up up as my heart swelled and rose sailing on an updraft carried by the liquid current of the sky. And then suddenly there was a tautness, a tug, and a terrible sense of release. As the string fell and tangled around my hands I watched the white shirt sail away over the dark treetops, the loose sleeve ends flapping like wings, away away come again another day. And that, my dear Jackalack, is why I recommend that you find another profession—lest a similar deprivation befall you. Sure you'll go home with a few dollars in your pocket, but in the meantime you'll have lost the shirt off your back—not to mention the heart that was pinned to its sleeve.

Warmly,
Judith Vanderzee

Say what St. Mary's it's already seven o'clock? I wonder if you can hear them ringing up there at the Lakeview Lodge for the Aged and if you can, do you think they toll for thee? Ding dong the wicked doctor is almost dead as I descend Heidi's icy steps one hand on the railing the other holding Juju's box. Almost dead or at least half which alas is not the same as half pregnant. This could drag on for years she said. Then again when you're dead you're dead there's no going back as I walk across the lawn the snow's brittle skin breaking like communion wafers beneath my boots. Gramps is it true what the Catholics say about how it turns into the body of Christ in your mouth? Of course not—that would be against the laws of nature. But once Anna and I followed Peg Phinney to her church tailed her all the way up to the altar. Afterward we scampered back down the aisle with the papery discs encrypted in our mouths praying they wouldn't turn into Jesus before we reached the street. It was too late though Anna said cuz she felt a tiny kick just as she was spitting hers out.

Discretely the new old-fashioned street lights flicker on casting kilo-watts of quaintness over hardfrozen spring slush. Last night the bartender at the Pit told me they're genuine replicas of 19th-century stagecoach lanterns. He also said that the last year you were head of the Chamber of Commerce Beautification Committee they called you the Great Icemaker because you somehow pushed through an ordinance banning shovels snow blowers and road salt. No doubt this accomplishment owed something to the oriflamme of the Glimmerglass Opera—a triumph your supporters had waved in the faces of the naysayers for who would've thunk the Met would agree to a farm team so far upstate? Yes it's amazing the way you could make your drunken hallucinations of Siegfried ringing out across Otsego Lake of village sidewalks glittering like the hero's sword a collective reality. Apparently in the latter case you claimed to have been inspired by sepia-tinted photos of snow-bound Cooperstown at the turn of the century but more likely it was a vodka suffused episode of Northern Exposure (everyone knew you stayed up all night at that point slaloming the channels of Finlandia). But then you had to resign cuz you really were losing your mind and in the meantime the rest of the committee seeing as how the people in this slick white-coated simulacrum are real how they slip and fall and break their legs and only get up again with legal assistance, said yea to salt. It's too cold however for the salt to do its job. Too cold and so the crystals glitter dully on the ice like broken glass and I wish they were cuz I'd take off my platform boots and dance bleed all over your frozen synapses until you remember. Remember. Just a quick thaw is all I need enough for you to tell me how to get what's mine and then I'm outta here.

Outta here just like those geese honking overhead they must be flying south for the winter. Or is it the other way around? Yeah now I remember they go in the fall come back in the spring but then it seems like it's a little early. If I was a goose I'd stay down in Florida or wherever it is they fly to at least through spring break what's the rush why come back here and freeze your feathers off if there's no good reason?

Main Street is dead but then it always was after 5:00 from November through April. The only difference is all the "We'll see you May 1st" or "Back with the Sun" signs in the windows of the baseball boutiques and olde tyme shoppes. No doubt this hard-nosed acceptance of economic reality this new willingness to cut losses and take a long winter's nap has something to do with the decline of your influence. As the Pit guy put it: your grandfather had some nice ideas but most of the free mulled-cider at the Winter Carnival got sucked up by the locals.

Anyway being that it's still April we've got the entire second floor of the Tunnicliff Inn to ourselves. I've taken to feeling so comfortable that I can start unbuttoning my sailor pants on the way up the stairs. Eight buttons across the top six down each side three on the inside—makes you wonder how sailors could get into and out of each other's pants so easily. Still two more sets of buttons to go but no more steps and at least no. 7 is already open. Maybe some of them just waited with their pants off waited with their portals open for the hot spray of salt against their asses the spasm savage as a shark bite.

Sssssss KLYNK. Sssssssssssss KLYNK.

Just waited all afternoon the pipes of that damn radiator hissing and clanking how can he stand the noise?

Stella.

Gotta piss. Don't look at him.

Sssssss KLYNK.

Yeah gotta piss like a big dog gotta piss like Moby Dick and so I plunge past him dirty clothes tangling about my ankles like seaweed or clinging lovers plow past him sprawled on the bed my hand still fumbling with my buttons fuck clasping Juju's box under my arm until at last I reach the door. As I pull it closed behind me, the flap of my pants falls open. Exposing the dick I don't have.

I pull the flush stash *Frederick's of Hollywood* under the claw footed tub and open the door to his stare. His eyes silently summon me from the other side of a sea of crusty socks stained underwear greasy foil wrappers crushed milk cartons dented Sprite cans Rolling Rock sticky Ron Rico crushed cigarette boxes barbecue sauce smeared pages of the MLA job list busted dreams broken hearts and other mistreated organs. Then again maybe I do have a dick cuz when I imagine his twenty-one year old chest beneath the thermal shirt, hard hairless and cetaceously smooth, what I feel for him is a desire as huge slippery and cunning as a white whale. Although if it weren't for the sex I'd dump him.

He stares at me with big cow eyes.... No doubt at this point you'd object Gramps if you could. My dear child, you are mixing metaphors. And though I could argue that surf and turf make a tasty combo you'd undoubtedly be right—cows don't logically follow from sailors sharks sea salt and whales. To be sure your once pre-eminently rational mind is now as riddled with holes as the moon and your famous analytical detachment has become nothing more than the remoteness of senility. Of a brain fallen sadly out-of-orbit. But at one time you probably would have pursed your lips at this sloppy proliferation of language this muddy swirl of words obscuring the clarity of meaning. Then again you might've perceived how my style perfectly mirrors my theme: the protean form of desire the shifting shape of lack beneath the conjurer's white scarf. Lift the silk and you'll find something else entirely. A rabbit a dove the body of Christ a papery wafer. Or maybe nothing at all.

Hey, I've been like...waiting for you all day.

What can I say?

Sssssssssssss KLYNK.

He's scratching his arms and chest the comforter pulled up over his legs and lap all four white down pillows behind his back. The money belt where he keeps his points cookers and cottons lies at his elbow zipped shut the *Last of the Mohicans* he bought at Augur's books covers his crotch. Looks like he's not letting himself have any fun or maybe it's just already over.

I sit down by the door beneath the red-printed *No Smoking Please* sign an ancient black rotary telephone squatting beside me on the damask-draped table. Shit only half a pack of flattened cigs left at least the lighter I stole last night from the bartender is full. I take a long drag and look around the room at how the green of the lima walls deepens to pea in the worn satin comforter which in turn is accented by pale shades of carrot and corn in the throw pillows and fake Kirman carpet. Someone didn't eat their vegetables.

You should be grateful. I let my gaze take refuge in the black gape of the fireplace.

Oh, but I am.

That's not what I mean. What I'm saying is that you should be grateful to have a fuller acquaintance with the emptiness of wanting.

No answer. Don't look. But I do. He's staring at the pod his feet make in the expanse of the pea-green spread. His face is the face of a kid who doesn't like what's on his plate.

Sssssss KLYNK. Sssssssssss KLYNK.

OK enough of that goddamn radiator. I get up walk over to the wall next to the bed, wring the knob shut. Over my shoulder: *Listen Skip if you don't like it, leave.* Skip town. Skedaddle.

I stand up look down at the bed. His eyes get shiny carbon slick like the eyes of a cartoon fawn. Rubbed out with a number three pencil because we're in no mood for tears. But I can't shut his mouth:

That is bullshit. What you said about the emptiness of wanting.

All of a sudden his sentences are bejeweled and sparkling the pinprick American "i" reset with a long gleaming "ee", the terse "s" with a lavish eastern sibilation. You are so inappropriate I want to tell him. Like silk in a slum like a live cow in a supermarket bleeding opulently all over the shiny white floor. So inappropriate so ridiculous with your silly American moniker perched like a too-small baseball cap on the velvet folds of Serkan Yavasogluari. But I don't. Not because I hesitate to hurt his feelings but because I know he'd take my meanness and turn it into something rich and rare, wring out a perfumed oil and label it Essence of American Bitch Goddess.

I love you Stella.

Well this is pretty heavy even though he's put his jewels away and the phrase is uttered almost lightly in the most stream-lined of American accents unencumbered even by beachboy diph-thongs. Undoubtedly to spare me the weight of it all. He's such a gentleman why every time we fuck and he's on top he asks is this OK am I hurting you are you sure even though I bet I've got at least ten pounds over him.

Yes that was pretty heavy he never dared to say anything like that before. Gotta shut him up but how? Maybe with the telephone cord. Weird how it's just like the one that used to crouch on our kitchen counter. Like a slick black toad. I should try calling myself twenty-two years ago: Hi little Stella I've got this yucky boy following me around what should I do? Well big Stella try this...

You know Skip every time I hear those words my gorge rises and I can taste the rancid heat of hard salami, feel grease clog my throat as if it is 1977 and I'm a kid all over again.... It was after my mom left my dad cuz he was screwing the babysitter and everyone else in town. According to the custody agreement he could have us every Saturday: pick-up at 11:00, delivery at 6:00. One day he said We're gonna get something special. Herkimer county cheddar and some out-of-this-world hard salami, from Colbert's Deli and Corner Market in Cherry Valley. Man, this salami is so good that Randy Colbert gets up at the crack of dawn every Saturday and drives all the way to Utica to buy it from 80-year-old Giuseppe.

I love you cats my pa says as he unties strings and unwraps white paper over his lap, and I'm not sure if he means Anna and me or the salami and cheese. Or maybe Randy and Giuseppe. Then he sets the white paper with the long dark turd of salami and the waxy block of cheddar on the dashboard. I love you and you'll love this he says as he begins sawing off disks of salami and wafers of cheddar with his Swiss army knife. I don't think so Anna mumbles as I accept a little sandwich of salami and cheese. I don't think so she says tears running down her face as Dad growls try it, you'll like it...

He told me he's been a veg since he was ten years old that he wouldn't touch meat with a ten foot fork but he's eating my story up, a little smile on his face hugging his knees to his chest. He's pathetic like a cow eating hamburger what he'll do to make me love him. I'd never let myself sink so low.

I love you.

Pathetic. I walk over to the window and plop down onto the gold-velvet cushioned seat. Turning my back to him I draw my legs up beneath me and press my hands then my cheek against the cold panes. Spring snow is wafting through the air again...like on the day she left. You were in St. Thomas no doubt playing doctor with one of your nursies on the beach while my dad was already at Vanderzee's Wine and Spirits, intoxicating the town. And so Anna and I stood alone in the doorway and watched her disappear around the bend of Leatherstocking Street big March flakes fleecing the back of her ratty mink jacket. Two little lambs shorn of their momma yet secretly proud she'd managed to escape her stall that she wouldn't put up with his shit anymore that soon she'd be joining the pack of village divorcees with their loose swinging breasts and flowing gray-streaked hair those women who ran with the wolves. Besides didn't she come back a few days later? Sure and then she led us away to the basement apartment on River the little holler in the hillside where Anna and I used to stand on the dresser jelly glasses pressed to the ceiling of our bedroom trying to pick out the words of the man and woman fighting upstairs. River street where the little lambs turned wild living like muskrats for seven months on the banks of the Susquehanna the damp seeping through the walls the wind blowing through the willows until finally Oma rescued us in her big Country Squire carrying us off to sunny Santa Monica. But for months we lived like wild animals dining each night on the fish our mama caught in the river and along the lakeshore cuz he wouldn't give us any money for groceries. Yeah that's what Oma said and what other explanation could there be for the constant fishy taste in my mouth? What other reason for why we ate nothing but bass pike perch trout sunnies and walleyes when she could catch them and muddytasting bullsheads and suckerfish when she could not for an entire spring summer and part of a fall? Yeah and so while maybe that was bologna about the hard salami surely he's to blame for the fact that even to this day I can't stand fish.

A long quivering sigh the wind in the willows comes from the direction of the bed and I look over, wish I could help it. He's staring up at the ceiling running a hand through his hair. His weird two-toned hair. The first three inches extending from either side of the center part are blond while the remaining three are dark brown. He claimed once that it just grew that way. What kind of chump does he take me for?

Come here. He lifts the blankets in invitation, pats the mattress. He's shivering how can he be shivering he's wearing a thermal shirt.

Then again how can he not be there's not an ounce of fat on him nothing but muscle and bone bound in olive smooth skin. And it would be so easy to warm him to slip under the covers with him to cook something up beneath magic white sheets. So easy to bury my nose in the sweet garlic of his armpit to savor the scrambled egg of his breath. Try it Stella you know you'll like it.

I slip off the window seat and walk across the littered floor to the bathroom. *I love yooou* he calls again as my hand is on the knob his voice insistent as a cow lowing to be milked. Mooo moooo as the door creaks shut. Booo hoooo cuz one of these days I'm just gonna strip the bed and then he'll see. Then he'll see there's nothing there.

Nothing there as I sit crouched in the filling tub hot water surging over my feet drowning out the last of his voice. But that doesn't mean he won't keep believing like they do on that show we watched the other night in the motel room in Ohio.

The one about the two FBI agents who soberly probe the paranoid fantasies of pop culture I can't remember what it's called
but it's been on for a while and I bet you secretly watched it
every week wishing they would come and investigate the aliens
who were taking over *your* brain. Anyway I imagine you've
seen it an early episode about extra-terrestrial spacecraft that
ends with a close-up of the guy's soft bovine features as he
explains how people can continue to believe in UFOs despite
all the evidence to the contrary: Because all the evidence to the
contrary is not entirely dissuasive. Cuz I love yoooou…
Moooooo…

Where are all the towels he must've taken them: *Skip, could
you bring me a towel?*

No answer. I wonder if he's mad yeah I bet he is and now
he's trying to tell me I'm not at your beck and call you can't just
snap your fingers you have to clap your hands too. He's fed up
in his own little way it's more than he can swallow I'll have to
teach him his stomach is bigger than his eyes. Yeah so open
wide. Someone needs to oil those hinges. Gone?

Yes he's gone money belt and all the covers thrown back
leaving me with nothing but the imprint of his hard young body
in the mattress. Ooooh baby's playing the big leagues now trying to get me to follow him thinking I won't be able to resist
reading this sign of his absence and tracking it back to his presence. But I don't need to—I can imagine him perfectly sitting
down in the Pit sucking a Bud like a calf at a teat. What I do
need is a buzz and I can get that right here in room no. 7.

My tickets to heaven are in my duffle bag by the bed, a
bottle of Hells Bells and a half-full photo cannister of pot. Naked and dripping I fish them out along with my pipe then
scoot back to the loo. At the sink I pour myself a big tumbler of
rotgut remembering how you said you always used the finest
bourbon in your mint juleps how you'd quote Voltaire as you
shaved the ice: The good is the enemy of the best. But then
what does that make the worst? I take a hefty swallow and then

pack the dugout of my trusty bat hitter with pot. Oh take me out of the ballgame take me up to the clouds...

And now I'm ready feeling good and lightly anesthetized. Numb enough to face Juju's needle and so I slide *Frederick's of Hollywood* out from under the draining tub. Putting the lid aside I set the box on the vanity. I kneel before it on the tiled floor, letting my hand hover over the richly-colored envelopes—over eggshell aubergine crimson oyster mushroom mocha lapis poppy terra cotta celadon citron tangerine lime heliotrope peacock. So many beauties, where to begin? Probably with the one to me or even to you if I want a current address. Oh but look at this lovely pale chartreuse addressed to *Barbara Salzmann*.... What business could a snob like Juju have had with Barb the Rube what could the city puss want with the country mouse? Rhetorical questions. It's all too easy to imagine my mom providing some sort of perverse entertainment for Juju a toy to lure into town and bat around with manicured paws. But what do I care let bygones be bygones let the cheese alone. Sure, the past is for chumps and I'm not gonna get caught. I've moved on.

Barbara Salzmann on flamboyant pricey-looking stationery that she must have bought in the city. Wonder what she was thinking as she scripted that fat busty *B* though it's not hard to guess: that bimbo my brother married. That bimbo with her dairyfine dimples and homegrown hair wholesome as oats a good egg sunnyside up. Yes that simple *B* says it all hence *arbara* huddled nearly illegible in *B*'s shadow, goslings under mother goose's breast. But then why does *S* rear up like a snake scattering *alzmann* across the remainder of the envelope?

I get up and take a couple more swigs straight out of the Bells bottle. To protect against venom. Then I kneel back down in front of the vanity glance at my face in the mirror. How pale and somehow cut-off it appears as if behind a diving mask as if it's time to take the plunge. As if it is time to slide a bobby pin under the flap to break the seal of the envelope, time to pull out the folded sheet of citron spread it out on the vanity and begin

to read. *Dear Barb* as far away somewhere above the surface
metal rasps, a key turning in a lock. Behind me hinges creak and
I stuff Juju's letter back into its envelope.

Hey watcha readin'? A love letter?

I sit back and look up at him the tiles hard and cold beneath my ass. He's leaning against the doorframe a smile flickering about his lips his thumbs hooked in his pockets just below
his money belt.

I doubt it. Wonder what he would say if I let him read it? Is
it possible that he's not the idiot I've made him out to be? Better
to offer him drugs:

Wanna bat hit?

No. He steps forward, gently stroking his arm. *Why doncha
come down and see if you recognize any of these weirdos down
at the bar.* Flash of white teeth: *then I'll ask if I can borrow some
money.*

He's swaying slightly. Or maybe it's me. Maybe we're both
swaying slightly like fronds of kelp in a warm ocean current.
Maybe those are tears spiralling round the tiny sinkholes of his
eyes maybe he's high or not high enough. And maybe I'm too
stoned or not stoned at all cuz when he extends his hand I
decide to go with the flow and take it. He pulls me up—a feat
which always amazes me—and we stand face to face his warm
eggy breath filling my pores. He touches the little scar that floats
in the space between my lip and my nose. I turn my head.

OK why not? But give me a few minutes to get ready.

I rifle through my duffle looking for the perfect outfit for a
descent into the Pit something spiffy to go spelunk my dim memories of little Anna and baby Stella toddling from lap to lap collecting boozy kisses. The piss yellow crushed velvet scoopneck
patterned with mesh figures like ancient runes. Perfecto. It's only
a little sweaty-smelling and looks terrific with my navy blue sailor
pants. Plus the mesh is great for netting old men's eyeballs. Maybe
tomorrow I'll bring you my catch to keep you company in your
deathbed: Here's lookin' at you Doc.

Sure and as I pull this shirt over my head I can already feel them two big dark eyes clinging to my body like limpets. Sure—except for once he's not looking at me. Instead he's sitting in the window seat his chin resting on his knees gazing out into the soft snowy night. In the shadows of the window alcove he's beautiful. In the shadows the silly two tones of his hair have darkened into one while the streetlight brings his profile into relief against the panes. He looks as remote as a figure on an old coin…suddenly too valuable to throw away. But I know it's just a trick of the light and the chemicals coursing through his body…a momentary and completely artificial self-reliance. He has nothing to give to me…. He's needy as a beggar greedy as a baby and I'm too young to be a mom. Light bulb: what if I don't come back to room no.7 tonight? What if I just leave him at the Pit and drive away in the early hours of the morning?

But if I bring my duffle bag with me baby'll get suspicious and start to cry. Besides it's too much to lug around all night. Just pack light a voice whispers in my ear. And maybe it's my mom's cuz I remember how she stopped using suitcases when we were living out in LaLa Land how she'd toss a pair of panties a toiletries kit a box of charcoals a couple of gum erasers into her battered old creel on her way out the door for yet another three-day fishing trip. Ha. Over those two years she packed lighter and lighter until the last time when all she took away with her was the empty creel. Yeah I guess it's just a matter of establishing priorities and so I sweep all of Juju's letters off the vanity into my green suede knapsack. Then I pull on my coat and hoist the sack over my shoulder. One last swig of Bells afore ye go.

Ms. Sayra Fant
16 E. 68th St.
NY, NY 10028

20 June 1997

Dear Ms. Fant,
   I hope I've spelled your name correctly. "Fant" of
course was easy. It's right there on the gold plate screwed just
above the mail slot into the glossy black door. One simply has
to squint a little to close the distance between wrought iron
bars and gleaming brass. Of course squinting cannot deliver
the mail, and so the postman keeps a little key to the gate, a
key which he'll twist by rote in the lock with one hand, as he
holds this letter in the other, checking the addressee. And
perhaps he'll puzzle for a moment as I did; in fact, I've had to
take a phonetic stab in the dark at your first name, translating
the sounds pronounced by your parents, brother, and nanny
into a single written sign. Initially, I thought what I was
hearing might be a southern pronunciation of "Sarah," but
then the distinct upper east side intonations of the man and
woman you call "Mama" and "Daddy" (who presumably go
by the names etched in the brass, "Tobias Fant" and "Hinda
Olli-Fant") refuted that theory. "Sayra" it must be.
   Actually, it occurred to me as I wrote that last sentence
that your surname is not necessarily "Fant." It is possible
you've been saddled with "Olli-Fant" instead. Then again,
I've observed that the mother tends to shoulder the burden of
hyphenation alone. And from what I've observed through the
palisades, yours could no doubt carry another syllable as
easily as the computer bag she slings over her shoulder each
morn. What a woman! A veritable virago trumpeting orders to
the nanny even as she's stepping out the gate, an amazon.com
warrior suited in gray micro-fiber and a pachydermatous
mien: such a contrast to you, my soft-voiced Sayra of the

fuzzy brown ringlets and spindly limbs. One surname seems too cumbersome, let alone two. A single soft syllable would be enough, just a bit of verbal gauze to embellish your slight being. "Say." Or even as I sometimes hear your little brother call you, "Thay."

Although I have a feeling you don't care for "Thay." And it is true there is something a tad viscous, even sticky about that one. Thus when "Zackie" pleads, "Thay, pleathe hold me," sliding his pasty paw into your light brown hand at the 72nd Street entrance into Central Park, you wince as if you've touched goo (and perhaps you have, as I've seen him use the same paw to wipe his ever-seeping nose). Say, I sympathize. For even if his palm is dry, does he need to cling to you, when he's got the nanny on the other side of him, her strong brown fingers (only a couple of shades darker than yours) wrapped around his doughy fist? Clearly he lacks even a spark of independence, as do so many children these days. You on the other hand, despite your fragile appearance, possess a certain tensile strength. I see it when you adhere to your book, despite the screams of your brother and the other children spinning on the tire swings at the 77th street playground, despite the stare of that "weird old lady" sitting on the bench across the way. And I see it when you suddenly look up and shoot me with one of your ocular rubberbands. Ouch! But I don't mind—in fact I find something piquant in the sting.

Yes, I delight in those smarting glances, each of which rebounds upon my youthful self as I recall how I too hated being stared at while I was reading. I especially hated being stared at by my brother, who was just as helpless as yours, Sayra, and even more vexing because he was older and thus should have been a source of knowledge and stimulation rather than a drain. Yet I recall only the drain, glug glug glug, always taking never giving, as he sucked off my superior intelligence. Glug, as I'd be immersed in my German primer, <u>Die Lesestücke Für Die Kinder</u>, and he'd sidle up to the sofa,

mutely begging me to decipher <u>Dick and Jane</u>. Glug, as he'd
get in Swann's way, falling to his knees before me with a
cracked beaker in his hand dripping some dubious mixture onto
Proust's masterpiece in the original Parisian (a three-volume
Moroccan leather-bound set from my father's library that
would now be worth a considerable sum if he hadn't ruined it
with his sulfurous jissom), until I agreed to "help" him with his
chemistry set. Glug, as he'd lurch out of the garage with the
manual to his Triumph, having spent a half hour trying to
locate the spark plugs, stagger over to where I lay in my bikini
on the patio, my face shaded from Plato's sun by <u>The Birth of
Tragedy</u>, and silently drop the greasy pamphlet onto my legs.

To be honest, however, it wasn't really the intellectual
beggary that irked me so. After all, one does not lose one's
genius by giving it away, and in sharing mine with my
importunate brother I gained a small philanthropic satisfaction. No, what I truly resented was being wrested, time and
again, out of the theoretical world of books into the dull
reality of practice (especially when so often the practicum
required first undoing the mistakes of my muddle-headed
sibling). For in the world of books, there was no downtime,
no dithering, no wasted data nor meaningless digressions. In
the world of books, I only had to read to instantly comprehend, my progress through the millenia of human knowledge
and experience unimpeded by the protoplasmic baggage and
mental stumbling blocks that had hindered the writers and
thinkers whose work I now consumed. I could absorb the
distillations of genius without lifting a finger (I speak figuratively, of course, since one still has to turn the page), oblivious to the distant clatter of Peg Phinney, our housekeeper, in
the kitchen, to the snipping of the gardener's hedge shears in
the topiary beyond the window. Thus it was my favorite
pastime to lie for hours sprawled on the satin counterpane of
my bed, intent only on the flow of words into my brain—
until, of course, the moment when James would step into my
room and break the current with his mute presence.

You may be wondering why I'm telling you all this, little Say. Well, first I want you to know that I understood the other day when you told the nanny you'd "rather read," after she asked if you'd keep an eye on Zack while she used the park rest room. It's only natural for a girl to feel this way, especially such an intelligent one. (Was that <u>The Sound and the Fury</u> I saw you reading the other day? My oh my.) Given such a snot-nosed and snivelling alternative, why would you not "rather read"? Why not, indeed?

But even as I want you to know that I understand your preference for books over your brother because I've "been there," I have another, higher purpose: to inform you that there's more to life than what's between the bindings. Oh Say, I was just like you as a girl—a fair biblioflower, a foolscap orchid whorled with veins of bookish wit, thriving in my intellectual hothouse and yet secretly yearning for some experience beyond the glass. Just like you, even though I can imagine your nostrils flaring darkrose over this claim. How could that old bag in the baggy pants (which actually aren't pants but a harem skirt I picked up in Constantinople) think she once resembled you in any way? And yet I did. Just like you I longed to touch surfaces more responsive than the page, to hear whispers more sensuous than rustling paper, to smell perfumes more pungent than bleached wood pulp, to taste flavors more exotic than my own saliva: in short, I longed to live. But if you insist on differentiating your case from mine, I'll grant you this—mine was more dire. For I grew up in Cooperstown, NY, one of the most beautiful places in the country, a spot described by its founder as "Nature's pleasure park," a "region of ro-mance" where the rough-hewn work of the glacial forces that shaped the Appalachians suddenly acquires formal symmetry and grace, as if some vision had flashed deep within those ancient ice crystals, some future Kodak moment. And yet I could not see a thing, let alone hear, touch, smell, or taste it.

Rather than feasting on the world, I starved on the word. Instead of plunging into the genuine Glimmerglass cupped in

its chalice of dark forested hills, I read about it in The Pio-
neers (thirsty reader that I was, I'd drink anything—no matter
if Cooper is not a vintage that improves with age). Oh sure I
knew, in theory, that I lived in Paradise. But in praxis I dwelt
in the middle of nowhere, far from the bustling hobs of
Manhattan, Paris, and Berlin, the places where all the books
worth reading were cooked up. Thus when I looked up from
my page to cross at a corner or enter a shop (for I carried my
reading with me wherever I went), what I saw was the sticks,
and the taste in my mouth was straw.

     And then, one day, life tore the book from my hands. I
was fourteen years old and had recently started babysitting
two nights a week for the daughter of one of my father's
nurses. I say "babysitting," although truth be told, Barbara
Salzmann was only two years younger than I and already
physically as mature, if intellectually and emotionally less
evolved. Indeed I saw myself as guide rather than guardian, a
curbing influence on that headstrong and more aboriginal
spirit. It was late afternoon in mid July, the end of a long hot
day that I'd mostly managed to evade by reading in the air-
conditioned sanctuary of my father's library, but was now
forced to yield to as the sweat slithered over my ribs and the
mustard satin quilt that hid the wreck of the Salzmann sofa
stuck to the backs of my thighs. My charge was sitting
Indian-style on the linoleum-covered mound in the center of
the floor, a mound formed by the stump of a tree the original
builder of the house had apparently found easier to cement
over than uproot. I'd been reading to her from The Last of the
Mohicans, with the idea of giving her a head start on the
eighth grade English curriculum, having recently discovered
the poor girl had only made it through the seventh with the
help of a special, after-school "story hour" spent on the lap of
her teacher, Mr. Peterson. But Barbie's thoughts were clearly
not on Cooper as she gazed out the window with its silver
cross of tape over the crack in the pane, pert chin raised as if
she listened to some distant yet crucial pulse, the drumbeat of

blood summoning her home. I closed the book and let it fall to the floor. If she stood up and walked to the window, I would see the penny-sized moon of white panties glowing through the hole in the back of her cut-off dungarees, but she remained perched atop her mound like a dog guarding a bone. Then suddenly she shook her head, turned, and looked at me—her slightly lopsided amber gaze (for the right eye was false) glowing through strands of black hair.

"I'm bored."

Understandable. I admitted that Cooper's aggressive use of the passive voice and hacksawed characters failed to engage. However, I went on to say (albeit somewhat hypo-critically), he held an important position in American literary history, and further, his descriptions of nature were consid-ered to be unparalleled.

"Let's go out," she suggested, unfolding her legs and splitting them over the mound as if she were straddling the back of a small elephant or maybe a bison.

Sure, I replied, our little public library was open for another hour. Or perhaps we could catch the late afternoon show at the local movie theater, a bit of fake French fluff I'd already seen with my father (who'd called it a bon bon for m&m eaters), though I'd rather enjoyed the part where Maurice Chevalier sings "Thank Heaven for Little Girls."

"No, I want to do something outside."

Something outside. Something under the bulging gray sky that at any minute could pour its contents upon us like an enormous slop bucket, although rain at least would sluice away the mosquitos. And what would we do? What stories do stones have to tell? What philosophy professes the moss? And if a tree falls in the forest, who cares if anyone is there to hear it or not? Besides we'd gone outdoors a few weeks earlier, when I'd watched Barbara demonstrate a homemade kite. Granted the crude construction of textile, wire, and string had flown rather well, but wasn't it time for me to put my foot down and reel the girl in? I stared down at the cover of The

Last of the Mohicans, a garish illustration of a bare-breasted
Chingachgook, dark cheeks slashed with blue war stripes,
black locks bristling with feathers. Then again, it was possible that too strong a hand could break the thread of trust I'd
established between us, a tenuous one at best given the
difference in our backgrounds and temperaments.

Yes, Barbara was made of very different stuff than I, a
doctor's daughter, descendent of generations of wealthy
globe-trotting Kant-quoting gentlemen farmers, both a
princess of the ivory tower and a citizen of the world. Her
ancestors were illiterate German peasants, simple folk who'd
settled a hundred years earlier in the mountains of Taborton
east of Troy, New York under the divine guidance of their
lettered and mildly diabetic parish priest (whose sweet tooth
had ached to set sail ever since he'd read about the American
sugar maple in Nordamerikanishe Fauna und Flora). In their
backwoods reclusion, her people had retained old world
customs and superstitions, decorating their walls with fraktur
and hanging "A-drags" over the cross-roads on Friday nights
to drive away witches. At the same time, they'd been infused
with a certain new world wildness, with something of the
darkness of the forest, a wildness and darkness that was
particularly apparent in the women, whose minds were as
independent as their skins were uncommonly brown. Thus
Barbara's mother, Beatta or "Batty" Salzmann, though she'd
only recently joined the Basset nursing staff, often challenged
my father's orders. And not only would she challenge him,
but she'd draw her support from her years of assisting her
mother, a famous "rag doctor" in Taborton, rather than from
her recent medical training in Albany (which had in fact been
paid for by the profits from Uta Salzmann's "practice").
Fortunately for Batty, my father had so far taken a charitable
view. Indeed I'd heard him speculate to colleagues, eyes
twinkling, that the Taborton folk had "absorbed the ways of
the matriarchal Iroquois whose spirits no doubt still roamed
their hills."

Barbara was no longer straddling but crouching, rocking on the rubber soles of her white-sneakered feet, queer goldish eyes glowering through lank brown locks. Suddenly I felt her otherness as I'd never felt it before. If I said "no" she'd surely just slip out the door as soon as I turned my back and dash over the weedy lawn into the woods, PF flyers disappearing into the darkness like white rabbits leaping back into their magic hat. And then where would I be? How would I explain to Mrs. Salzmann that her wild child had slipped my lead? And worse, how would I be able to go home and crawl between warm dry sheets knowing that Barbara tossed and turned in a bed of rain-slicked leaves, with nothing between the rifling breeze and her rose petals but the transparency of her thin wet t-shirt (not to mention the opportunity presented by the hole in the back of her cut-offs)? Better surely if I said "yes," better if I followed her into the wilderness rather than taking the chance of her venturing forth without me, better if I shared her mattress of moldering foliage than let her sleep in the woods alone. With a sigh I gave in. But where, exactly, did she want to go since "outside" could be understood as just about anywhere?

"It's a surprise," she answered. Smiling faintly she stood up, grubbed in the pocket of her cut-offs and pulled out a red Swiss army knife. With her nail she dug out the larger blade, shaved it lightly over the surface of her thumb, then did the same with the small one and the tiny pair of scissors. What was she testing them for? My stomach flopped as I envisioned her eviscerating some convulsing bass for our supper, then quieted when she failed to gather up the pole and wicker creel that stood in the corner by the plywood door, and instead slipped through the ivy-patterned curtain that screened her mother's bedroom off from the living room. Perhaps she had nothing more in mind than an hour or two of frolicking in the forest or splashing in the lake. However, when she returned a few minutes later with two folded white sheets in her arms, it became clear that she was indeed

planning for an extended encounter with nature, although a
single sheet for each of us hardly seemed adequate protection
against the night damp and the mosquitos. Surely we needed
more substantial bedding, sleeping bags, and even a tent if we
were going to spend the night in the woods? But when I
suggested going back to my house and looking in the basement for more gear (for I remembered once hearing my father
tell a crony that my mother, who'd been fatally hit by a car
while I was still a toddler, had not, even before her death,
been "a happy camper"), she merely stared at me, wooden as
a Cooper Indian.

Nevertheless, as we stood a half hour later leaning
against the rust-flecked iron railing of the stone bridge at the
end of Main Street, watching the soft jade waters of the
Susquehanna river flow beneath us, I felt I was on the right
path. For though perspiration had plastered my thin cotton
blouse to my back and ribs during the hot trek through town,
the straw beachbag that was cutting into my shoulder held not
only the two folded sheets, but also The Last of the
Mohicans. The latter item I'd been prepared to leave behind;
it was Barbara, much to my surprise and delight, who'd
stashed it in with the sheets at the very last minute. I could
only conclude that my influence was already having some
cultivating effect on her savage spirit. And what of the two
large darning needles and spool of cotton thread she'd taken
from her mother's sewing basket just before we left, which
now made an incongruous bulge (the needles sheathed inside
the spool) in the right pocket of her cut-offs? Well, no doubt
she meant to slide off her shorts and secure that niggling hole
between the back pockets, as she sat listening to me read to
her on the mossy bosom of the Susquehanna.

At the same time, as I watched the water slip away
beneath us, liquid jade lightly gilded by the sun filtering
through the willows and maples on the bank below, I found
myself wondering about that "right path." What was it really
and would it be so terrible to be lost? For as I listened to the

river's susurrous flow, something was loosening within me. Something was loosening, a paradigm shifting perhaps, as the scents of wet clay and cattails twitched in the breeze. And then suddenly I felt the never before acknowledged knot between my shoulder blades, the coil of constant concentration, go slack. What if Barbara wanted me to read to her and I refused? I was imagining how I'd put it, maybe in terms of how sometimes it was right to lay our books aside and listen to the murmur of nature (for maybe moss did have a philosophy, if one only gave moss the chance to profess it), when Barbara tapped my shoulder.

"Let's go, or there's not gonna be enough light."

Enough light left for what I didn't ask, but simply followed as she stepped away from the railing and started walking back toward town. At the point where rust-bespeckled iron abruptly gave way to unadorned stone wall, she stopped. After casting a searching look at the stark lime facade of the Ryan Fox house that stood just beyond the wooded slope down to the river (an unnecessary precaution, for its owner, our local historian, had undoubtedly left for cocktail hour at our local tavern), she placed her palms on the stones and kicked her legs over, landing lightly on the other side. Leaving me to make my own way over the wall (impetuous child!), she went leaping down the embankment, foliage swallowing her denimed behind.

When I at last emerged from that sloping thicket, my penny loafers having slipped and skidded the whole route, so that my russet locks were bedizened with bits of bracken and maidenhair fern and my ankle socks were fringed with burdocks, I found her sitting with her back to me on the grassy swathe that runs along the river's edge, her legs folded to one side her head cocked to the other. I strolled across the lawn intending to sit with her in contemplation of "Beldame Nature" while enjoying the symphony of cicadas, but the moment I dropped my straw tote on the grass beside her, she was off. What to do but pick it up again and trot off after her

along the bank? No time to stop and smell the flowers as I
kept sight of her retreating back, although I did manage to
snatch up a few visual bouquets—a cluster of white hydran-
geas in the shade of the wooded slope to my right, a few
spears of purple heather along the bank to my left, a gaggle of
golden rod and black-eyed susans in the meadow beyond as
the grassy swathe curved toward a little stone foot bridge
ornamented with crenellated stone turrets. No time to stop
and feel the wind in the willows (if there'd been one) as I
stepped onto the stony span and saw a white pennysworth of
underpants disappear into the weeds on the other side of the
river, although I did catch an earful from two ducks squab-
bling in the reeds below. No time but the time of that little
white moon, the bouncing ball that was guiding me through
Nature's lyrics, teaching me words I'd never found on any
page, words I'd never found 'til now.

On the other side of the bridge, I found myself standing in
a sort of herbal corridor screened on one side by lanky grasses
and weeds and on the other by brambly hedges. No sight nor
sound of Barbara, only the suddenly tuneless drone of the
cicadas and a small white butterfly or maybe a moth flitting
over the gravel scattered along the narrow path. However it
seemed to me that she'd veered to the left as she vanished into
the vegetation, and if that was so, then there was no way she
could have gone but straight along the river, since the tangle of
nightshade and blackberry bushes running along the right of
the narrow graveled path presented a formidable green wall,
blood drops of nightshade manifesting the capacity of thorns.
No way but straight as I ran lightly over the stones intent on
my goal, though even still I could not ignore the tall grasses
and queen anne's lace lashing playfully at my legs, the blackberry brambles plucking at my hair, the mosquitoes murmuring
in my ears as if to reinforce the lesson I'd only so recently and
tardily learned, that the world is alive.

At last I came to a break in the hedge, and as I stepped
out of that vegetal aisle, wiping the sweat from my eyes with

the hem of my blouse, a view of a spacious sloping lawn rose up before me. Rows of maples towered down the mild decline spilling long purplish shadows like velvet trains over the grass, and for a moment I forgot my quest as I stood in awe of their grandeur. But then I caught the chalky white of Barbara's t-shirt and sneakers streaking through the darkened trees at the top and recalling my assignment, charged the slope.

I found her crouched before a grassy knoll, a knoll that I immediately recognized as a local curiosity called the "Indian Mound," though I'd never approached it from this vantage point. Indeed I'd only visited the spot once before, "folklore fishing" in the company of my father and brother James, and then we'd entered through a nearby gate in the stone wall, having come via the sidewalk that runs along outside the perimeter of the park rather than trekking over the river and through the woods (which is not to imply that I regretted the route Barbara had shown me). Without turning, Barbara read from the stone plaque embedded in the grass at the base of the mound, in the halting singsong of the primitive reader:

"White man cheering!
We near whose bones you stand were Iroquois.
The wide land which now is yours was once ours.
Friendly hands have given back to us enough for a tomb."

At the closing syllable of "tomb," she slowly swiveled round on her haunches, an appeal in her amber eyes, a mute inquiry. I tried to pretend I didn't understand the question, as if she were a panhandler speaking in a foreign tongue. But I did. How could I not, given my newfound appreciation for "the wide land," an appreciation which Barbara herself had taught me? And so I had to answer truthfully the question her eyes seemed to imply—that the transaction had not been an equitable one. I sat down on the grass, my back against the mound as I gazed down through the rows of maples standing like sentries over the soft rich jade of the Susquehanna. Yes, I had to admit that "enough back for a tomb" didn't quite seem a fair exchange, an idea that hadn't occurred to me earlier when our father had smilingly read the plaque to us.

Then again, as Barbara scrambled up the hillock over my head kicking a scrap of sod down into my lap, I had the feeling that something was a bit off; this was not the poem I recalled from that earlier visit. Yes, it seemed unlikely that the white man had been "cheering." Kneeling, I saw that she had indeed misread, that she'd mistaken what was meant to be a forgiving salutation for a bitter description: the first line was "White man greeting." And while her mistake could in part be attributed to the fact that time had amputated the tail of the "g" and lopped off the top of "t," it seemed to me that the girl still had far to go—that if she read more she'd realize that "White man cheering" presented a tonal discrepancy. Such crowing exultation simply did not match up with the charity of the "friendly" and no doubt Caucasian hands which had given back enough for a tomb (as well as engraved the stone).

My stomach rumbled, and suddenly I realized how perilously close I'd come to forgetting my pedagogical responsibility. For we couldn't stay out here—sooner or later we'd have to return to civilization, where knowing the philosophy of moss would not put supper on the table. Oh Say, sure I'd learned something that day from Barbara and her woodsy ways, had learned something of the "wide land"—but she had still more to learn from me if she was going to graduate from high school and even someday, perhaps, go on to college. Yes, she needed to improve her reading skills, to better comprehend the twists and turns of connotation, the complications of context, or she'd forever stumble along in a mess of misapprehension and no doubt end up cleaning other people's houses like old Peggoty, who couldn't read without moving her lips.

Time for a few more pages of Cooper, I decided, and then we'd head home and see what scraps Batty Salzmann had left for us in the icebox. But when I reached in my straw bag to pull out the paperback, I discovered it was gone, along with the sheets. It seemed that Barbara had already taken it, that the ill-educated but industrious girl had decided on her own initiative to pick up where we'd left off. No doubt she'd already spread the sheets out on the grass and was waiting for me to join her. I clambered up the mound digging in the toes of my slippery-soled loafers, crawled on all fours across the grassy top. Looking down over the side, I saw Barbara sitting right under my nose with <u>The Last of the Mohicans</u>. But instead of reading the book, she was slicing out the pages with her jack knife.

Say, imagine my horror. She was destroying a book— the most barbaric act imaginable from the standpoint of devout literati such as you and I. It's surely no wonder then that at that moment I considered leaping down, snatching the knife out of her hand and thrashing her. Slapping her cheeks both fore and hind until red glowed through that soft fawn skin like flames illuminating the sides of a wigwam. But even as my hands tingled in anticipation my mind argued that violence was not the solution, that fighting fire with fire only speeds the conflagration. And then all we have left are the charred bones of what might have been. No, a thrashing was not the way to tame the tiger-eyed girl—only reason would awaken the potential within that savage heart.

Well that I didn't give in to my first urge. For as my palms ceased their throbbing and I found myself admiring how swiftly and neatly she was disemboweling Cooper's novel (only a thin sheaf of pages remained, perhaps fifty), I began to consider her action in a new light. Rather than expressing contempt for literature, perhaps this dissection showed her newly born love for it as well as a nascent critical ability. Indeed this "ripping apart" of <u>The Last of the Mohicans</u> could be seen as a kind of primitive literary criticism. And if I disapproved of her methodology, I had to admit I concurred with her judgment. My duty then was not to punish her, but instead to guide her toward more refined forms of literary analysis. I scooted down the bank beside her just as she was gathering up the excised pages, having first shuffled them like a pack of cards.

"Here," she said handing me half the stack along with one of the two sheets which had been lying still folded on the grass beside her. Then she pulled the spool from her pocket, unwound a long piece of thread, cut it with her knife and gave me that and one of the two large darning needles as well. Feeling a bit foolish, I stood clutching my sheet, pages, needle and thread, while she spread the other sheet out on the grass off to the side of the mound. Then again, I also recognized, as she went on to moisten a length of thread with her lips and then to guide it through the eye of the needle, that one of the duties of any caretaker and educator is to know when to play along. Yes, it's part of our role to recognize the finer points of a good mud pie, to know how to sip with dignity from a tiny cup of tea—this is the only way to gain our charges' trust.

"Okay, you can make the stitches big since we only have about forty-five minutes of light left, but try to keep the rows straight," Barbara instructed as she knelt down and with two long and rapid stitches basted the top edge of page 86 of The Last of the Mohicans to the end of the sheet. Next to it she tacked page 338 and next to that 17 and so on, her hands darting like hummingbirds over the fabric forming a kind of fringe across the top of the sheet. Within minutes she'd reached page 2 and the end of the row, at which point she turned to me and asked, rather cheekily: "Don't you know how to sew?" Somewhat taken aback but resolute in my plan to improve the girl, no matter how ridiculous I made myself in the process (though I'd only put thread to needle once before, with rather painful results), I spread my sheet on the grass and set to work.

Twenty minutes later the sun had ducked beneath the hills leaving nothing but a blush of western sky, and my sheet with its three crookedly stitched pages of Cooper was as

blood spattered as any virgin's. Barbara in the meantime had
not only finished fringing the sheet from top to bottom with
beautifully stitched horizontal rows of paper but had gathered
a pile of small rocks from somewhere which she'd used to
weight down the corners of her creation, as if in anticipation
of a breeze, though the air remained still and hot. "Here," she
said, taking thread and needle from my hand.

The light was at its lowest ebb, had washed the trees, the
wide and sloping lawn, the Indian Mound and Barbara's skin
in bluish gray when finally the two sheets were fully feath-
ered with The Last of the Mohicans. Against the dim expanse
of grass the squares of white Cooper-ruffled fabric appeared
both bright and vaporous, like some sort of spectral duvets.
As the icy diamond of Venus chipped the darkening sky
above and a chill crept up from the river below, I imagined
wrapping one about me, imagined lying out all night under
the illegible stars and the cold comfort Barbara's strange
sheet would provide. A shiver ran down my spine even as I
promised myself we'd hit the books first thing in the morning.

But as it turned out, the sheets were not for our use.
Having chucked all the corner rocks but one into the darkness, Barbara clambered up the mound first with one sheet
and then the other. Then she shook them out over the top, as
if she were making a rather large and unwieldy bed. Stretched
out and spread end to end, the fringed sheets covered nearly
the entire upper half of the oblong mound, and if they fell a
bit short lengthwise I had to admit that there was still something mesmerizing about the effect, something awesome, and
even a little sad, like the breast of some great white bird, a
snowy owl perhaps, lying on its back. Taking a bit of broken
twig from her pocket, no doubt collected while I'd been
stumbling along the banks of the Susquehanna, Barbara
pounded it with the retained rock into the corner of the sheet.
With the half moon looking on and my wholehearted ap-
proval (for though I'd never heard of Cristo, indeed it would

be at least a decade and a half before he emerged on the
scene, I'd begun to sense that there was something inspired in
her wrapping), she secured all seven remaining corners in the
same fashion.

    At last stepping back from her work, she took my hand.
But she didn't say a word. And somehow I knew she couldn't
say a word. Yet if she was nothing but a dumb artist, that
didn't make her ineloquent. For as it should be clear to you
by now, Sayra, words aren't everything. No words aren't
everything, and as Barbara pressed my hand and the chill
rising up from the river quickened into a breeze, I listened to
the dry rustle of 564 paper tongues and understood.

Naturally,
Judith Vanderzee

P.S. What philosophy professes the moss? None, it just is.

Then there was the time she lost it in the lake—the night we drank all those bottles of cold duck.

Ouch! I can't see a damn thing. Help me Chubs play Antigone to this hapless Oedipus, give me the succor of your firm young hand.

Yeah and everybody took turns diving for it the next day. Remember Bucko how you bobbed up with a big gob of seaweed and muck in your hand bellowing I found the eye! I found the eye! But it was just some brat's marble. Or was it a Sunday putter's golf ball?

Oh Dixon you're such a charmer the way those classical allusions just fall off your tongue like pages out of a cheaply glued book. But I can't see any better than you can in this fog.

Just follow the street lights.

What street lights, Madame Boyd?

Then follow Spotty's yellow pants. Where'd you get those godawful things Spotwood? You look like a duck.

I like to look like a duck.

What I heard is that she once lost it at your place Chubby. Seems she wrapped it up in a piece of kleenex and put it on the dressing table hoping to get some shut-eye after an all nighter at the Boyd Estate. When she woke up it was gone and the crumpled tissue was on the floor in the butler's pantry by the cat's dish. That's what I heard Chubbadub.

According to local lore it also once ended up in the Fish House punch.

Local lore my ass. You put it there yourself Dixon. That was back when she was still living with Jimmy but had already started wearing that patch. You naughty man you found that eye in their medicine cabinet and then you dropped it in the punch bowl when nobody was looking. And you were so pleased with yourself when she knew who did it when she said I was keeping an eye out for you Dixie...

Ha ha Chub.

I found it once. A big fish took it and was keeping it inside him. But I caught him and took it back.

Sure you did Spotty. And I bet that fish offered you a wish if you would just let him keep that eye.

No he didn't offer me a wish. But do you want to know what I would have wished for if he had?

No!

A thick white mist is wafting in from the lake, blotting out heads, fragmenting torsos and limbs but leaving voices intact so that they can still lampoon my mom everyone taking a stab driving home what a freak she was what a joke the one-eyed hoe from Hicksville. They think they can say anything say that she was already wearing the patch before he left her as if it were a choice an affectation when they know damn well it was after. One day the eye was just gone daddy gone, I don't know how but I do know when. When she couldn't afford another. You must've seen her on the street Gramps, could have given her the six hundred for a new one but the patch stayed over the empty nest a black reproach you obviously chose to ignore.

Someone's got to know what crap this is know what really happened why my mom wore that fucked-up scrap. I grab Skip's arm pull him back putting another layer of fog between us and them now blocking off entirely their convulsing bodies the sight if not the sound of laughter. His eyes are gleaming big wet bambi eyes his lashes beaded by the fog. He can smell the confidence coming I can tell by the way his nostrils are dilating, nothing worse than a vegetarian anticipating spilled guts. So never mind. But now I've gotta give him something.

Chubby, the woman with the poufy white bob, her real name's Charlotte and she's loaded. Her dad Chip whose real name was Charles used to get wasted with my grandfather, but now he's dead and she's the last of the Boyds one of the founding families of Cooperstown. The original Boyd got rich buying up land cheap then renting it to poor farmers in the 19th century. His real name was Charles but they called him old Null and Boyd because he'd revoke their leases when the hops were ready and get scabs to harvest them. Old Null and Boyd I admit I made that up but the rest I heard from Oma so it must be true.

Chubby. Sounds like a cartoon, Chubby the Teletubby. But she's got bucks? My father used to say that in America your name could be Son of a Bitch as long as you have money people take you seriously. What about the rest of these loons? Like their fearless leader the baldie in the red sport jacket who looks like Captain Picard? And the ancient dude with the troll-do, where'd he escape from? A key chain? And why are they all hanging with the 'tard over there in the yellow sweats?

The rest, as if I've got the inside story. Sure I remember Chubby Boyd was the classic old money lush Bucko Bielaski the avant garde new money lush as well as my dad's best drinking bud Dixon Ryan Fox that must be who he means by the troll hairdo some kind of historian and professional folklorist as well as amateur bartender who used to hang out with you mixing drinks and recounting stories or was it the other way around. And Spotwood Boyd was just a poor fuck, the misbegotten son of some minor or disinherited Boyd offshoot and backwoods bimbo like my mom but even dumber. But they're like people I met once at a big well-supplied party, faces parceled out by the flash of strobe-lights, gestures indexed by the steps of a chemical reaction and then forgot left behind like a half-finished drink a jacket a glass eye. Bits and pieces of somebody else's life when you see them again on the street or at Starbucks as if time itself was a drug flooding the synapses breaking the circuit of experience. Meaningless snips and snaps like Juju's letters all jumbled in my sack, like the salad that was once your brain. And I bet you think I shall never get it put together entirely, pieced, glued, and properly jointed. But the reason Sylvia couldn't do it was that she couldn't see the full picture, the big Ted in her head. I on the other hand have got the gestalt—the three of you against my mom.

So where we going?

Beats me, Skippy. I was in the bathroom doing a bat hit when you made plans with these people.

I did not. Big Bird said you ready to go? I thought you knew.

Where are we going? my boy calls into the whiteness.

The fog rends open surrenders a brief glimpse of Chubby Boyd perched on Bucko Bielaski's shoulders her mushroom cloud of thick white hair glowing, the wool of his blazer that was scarlet back in the bar now congealed to black. It's like I've stumbled on something that's none of my business a crime I know nothing about. I shouldn't be here don't belong in this town gotta go as soon as I get that painting.

Good question Chubby, where are we going?

The Bump, Bucko. I told you before but you were too busy studying the menu at the Pit.

Forgive me, I was considering the Belle du Jour, the new resident's wife. Imagine that little pot au feu, left to simmer day and night while Dr. Boy is at the hospital....

You can't get in. Every night a man comes and he puts a big lock on the door.

I have a friend with a key, Spotty....

Ahhh Chubby's mysterious friend. Does he go bump in the night?

Now tell me Dixon, as a historian, would you have been considered a wit in days of yore?

Skip rolls into me a soft smack against my shoulder. *Is this Bump place an after-hours club?* he asks breathing his sweet scrambled breath into my ear.

A car passes taillights two red eyes swallowed up by the mist, five seconds ago, ten, a minute and it's as if it never drove by. Should I explain how the Bump was your baby? How Chip Boyd had appointed you curator of the early American art collection at the Fenimore House but you weren't satisfied with fostering another man's brainchild? How you wanted a brat of your own conceived out of your conviction that a museum should show not just what people produced but how they lived? How according to Oma you were lunching at Ed's Diner in Dedham MA one day back in '48 and spotted the boarded-up building through the picture window? How after you finished your slice of boston cream pie you asked who the owner was and it turned out that old Ed had inherited it from his grandfather? How you paid for lunch and a late 18th-century tavern all with one check? How you then had it trucked piece by piece to Cooperstown and refitted together just a hop skip and a jump across the road from the Fenimore House? How that was the start of the little hamlet of Hoopersville which grew building by building to include a blacksmith's a print shop an apothecary a lawyer's office a general store a plain little church? A cute-as-a-button colonial village although apparently you always told everyone that cute was not the point. This was no Disney diorama no Epcot fabulation—this was reality, history as it happened, happening here and now. So you hired a staff to plough the fields to milk the cows to churn the butter to scutch and hackle the flax to show not only the tool but the hand that holds it. And you encouraged plagues and scourges sour butter and rough cloth because the good old days were not so good. Rumor even had it that you fed the cows the lupine that brought the spring of crooked calves, cuz modern life wasn't sufficiently malevolent. But who cares that's all history and I ain't a teacher no more.

No, it's just some old dive they're breaking into.

Along the lake road up the hill past the golf course where Anna and I used to do furtive cartwheels after you stopped paying for the club tumbling down to the shore where only members could swim but who cares because we're marching on the other side of the road beside the low stone wall over the wooden gate hey ho into *the story of how the plain people of yesterday, in doing their daily work built a great nation where only a forest had stood.* Why tell Skip that the words etched in the brass plaque are yours these words that will clang for decades to come like the loud laugh that speaks the vacant mind? Ha. But maybe your influence lives on because as we stumble toward the olden days over the frozen knuckles of last year's lawn away from the craft exhibition barn where you once offered Anna a summer job at the looms instead of the college tuition she'd written you for the fog suddenly lifts.

As if someone has drawn a curtain thrown a switch Hoopersville appears before us—the buildings lining the sides of the dirt road like a gauntlet all dark under the bright full moon except for one where windows pulse a lurid light. And my heart starts to pound. I stop breathe deep take in the smells of cold manure and warm animal bodies blowing through the village from the livestock barn crouched at the edge of the woods. Breathe deep before I realize what I'm breathing before I can stop myself from hearing what Oma said, about how you asked my father why buy the cow Jem when you can get the milk for free? Time for some air freshener.

Time for a toke and so I tap Skip's arm to get him to wait while I dig out the bat hitter. Yes time for a toke time to mist my brain with memory repellant cuz I really don't want to think about all this shit—tomorrow I'll find that painting and then hit the road. But in the meantime where's my pot could I have left it back in the room, how am I going to forget this crap without it? My hand still rooting in my sack I look over at Skip. Maybe he remembers what happened back at the hotel whether I picked it up or not. Maybe but probably not as he gazes up at the moon one hand shading his eyes as if he's looking into bright sun the other hooked on the precious pouch where kanga keeps his roo. No I don't think so. Forget about where he was or is his mind is already springing forward, will there be a bathroom a closet someplace to go get fixed?

Nothing to inhale but frozen earth and cow shit. Nothing to hope for but free booze as Bucko and Chubby break loose from the other two start running toward the lighted tavern Chubby's white pouf bobbing her laughter pealing over the icy fields. *Giddeyup Bucko, giddeyup.* The door of the Bump Tavern opens and I see a dark bell-shaped figure standing in a wavering light as a familiar voice exclaims *Chubs! Where have you been?* Chubby slides off Bucko's shoulders and wraps herself around little Heidi Phinney. Arms circling each other's waists they sidle indoors awkward as a twoheaded calf as the beast with two backs. But what do I care about how the animals pair off? It's not my ark.

No it's not my ark as the air is suddenly filled with honking blackness roiled by a rush of wings and I cover my head with my hands press my elbows over my chest because there's no phonebooth to take cover in. Why didn't they go south like they're supposed to what are they still doing here in the dregs of winter? Maybe they can't get out maybe they're stuck boomeranged back each time they try to leave by some kind of avian nostalgia addicted to the way things were trapped in the town that time forgot. They try to fly away but then they've been laying their eggs here for generations and once you leave you can't go home again. Better to stay put to settle down each night on the splintery docks at the country club fluffed up against the cold lake wind than to laze anonymously under the southern sun drinking from the fountains of Florida malls.

The last goose honk fades over the golf course but now a new sound rises behind me: *chubaboom, bababoom, bababoom boom boom...* I turn to see him squatting on the dirt path over his open pouch jacket off thermal sleeve pushed up snaking rubber tubing around his arm. Chanting *chubaboom, bababoom* in his own private room his own narrow little nirvana.

Not now Skip not in public and I snatch up the pouch, zip it shut and jam it in my pack. Then on second thought I fish it out and toss it back into his lap—it's not my burden.

Ok he mumbles blinking up at me like an animal in its pen a baby in his crib roused by the flick of a light switch. Looking at me like what now I'm awake is it time to eat? What am I doing with him? Time to end this miserable affair. But how? I wonder what you'd say, what you said to my father. Just do it Jimmy, tell her that the marriage is over. Time to end this miserable affair time to git along little doggie your misfortune is none of my own. Time to git along and maybe tonight's as good a night as any—maybe I'll dump him at the Bump. Yeah let them drink him under ye olde trestle table, then leave him there. Cuz he's history…

And so is Heidi heidi ho who greets us at the tavern door in some sort of colonial whore's gown her face and cleavage washed red by the coal heart of an iron lamp like the ribcage of a small vertebrate. She's been rummaging in grandma's attic looting the matriarchal war chest and no doubt sees herself as a bombshell from days bygone with a madder red neckline swooping beyond the frontier of her tan, madder still lipstick blasting past the borders of her lips. A bombshell but the only explosion was inside her head an explosion that shot her out the backdoor of her Phinney heritage into the wilderness of the Puritan psyche.

You must be freezing. She stands on tiptoe to set the lamp down on the mantelpiece of the enormous fireplace just to the left of the door. That gaping maw you had reconstructed brick by brick. I heard once that you had each brick numbered with chalk so that it could be refitted in the exact place it occupied in the original. But then the mason left the bricks out in the rain.

Alas. Heidi's hand falls on my shoulder grasping the strap of my backpack and her smell—an odd mixture of bayberry pine human sweat and something like caged ferret—wraps around me like a bear hug. Clutching my strap she ushers us over to the fireplace and it's a relief when her paw drops away and she steps back.

What you two need are noggins of winkum. The train of her red dress sweeps the wide planks of the floor as she sails off in the direction of the bar where Spotwood and an old woman holding a fat tabby cat are sitting on bar stools. Chubby and the rest of the crew are at a long table nearby and Spotwood's voice rises over the noise of their banter: *If a fish gave me a wish, you know what I'd wish for?*

I look at Skip standing in front of the fire and wish that he'd stop shivering. I wish that he would stop shivering and staring at me with those big black calf eyes. I wish that he would just do something. Why doesn't he go shoot up? I imagine picking up the poker holding it over the flames until it glows red as a valentine pressing it against the inside of his arm. Would he cry? Would he hit me? Would he knock me down and hold the iron rod against my flesh? The ten foot long fireplace is big and hot enough to roast a cow or a person and I think about what it would be like to slowly turn on a spit your skin crisping up the fat oozing out beading dripping away like desire until nothing is left but blackened shards and downy piles of ash. What am I doing with him? What am I doing here with him?

And now Heidi's back pushing steaming wood and tin cups of something that smells like brandy into our hands.

Drink up. Doctor's orders. She leans toward Skip her lips pulling back from her sharp white teeth.

I hold my cup under my face feeling the vapor imbuing my pores, watching Skip back away. From behind a scrim of steam he asks: *I don't suppose you have a bathroom here?*

She tosses her head flashing the thread of gold in her ear and points: *Through that door behind the bar. You can't miss it.*

And now he's whispering *I'm sorry* as he slinks off hunched over his cup like a beggar who's just received a free bowl of soup. He'll probably dump it down the toilet. Not that I can blame him for that it's probably some cheap little schnapps, nothing left but syrup and sour breath after the alcohol boils off. Still there's nothing else to drink us beggars can't be choosers I'll give it a try. *Mmmm.* Not bad, not sweet at all yet fruity like fruit with teeth apples that bite you back. I wish he would I hate the way he keeps saying sorry. I hate how he keeps trying to get me to play the martyr game, how he asks me not just to exonerate him but to pretend that his addiction is this cross that I have to bear. I hate the way he keeps telling me that I should leave cuz I deserve better, cuz as long as he's on the junk he can't give himself to me fully. Why can't he understand I only want him partially? Why can't he understand the junk is his charm? Yes the junk is his charm, or as Siggy puts it somewhere the appeal of the addict is that of cats and birds of prey, the appeal of inaccessibility.

He disappears through the swinging doors and I drink to Freud feel the brandy burn down my pipe then fan out diffusing through my tissues. Basking in my own glow I turn back to Heidi watch the coal in her lamp sputter and spark and see that it's not really coal but some sort of wood. *Isn't that a fire hazard?*

Sure but hey, that's half the fun. This whole building could go up in flames just like that—the wood is so dry that it would probably burn to the ground in an hour. People talk about the burden of history—as if history was this huge crushing weight—as if it was a monolith a granite mausoleum. But history's lighter than that pack on your back Stella, lighter than a feather, slimmer than chance—a fire, a flood, a crazed tyrant, a broken test tube, a bottle of vodka—and poof, it's gone. Pooofff! she repeats waving the lamp for emphasis.

Puuffff! Did I hear someone ask for Puff? Spotwood calls from the bar. *Hey come on over and see Puff do her trick.*

Close up in the sputtering light of the beeswax candles set at each end of the polished oak counter I see that the creature sitting in the old woman's lap the animal I thought was a cat is a raccoon. Its amber eyes blink up at me out of its black mask and then suddenly it raises itself on its haunches and extends a small black hand.

Spotwood touches my elbow. *Puff wants to shake. Please don't hurt her feelings.*

I take the paw and give it a gentle shake but when I release my grip the animal doesn't let go. It clings to my finger with a warm dry paw that feels almost powdery like a surgical glove and stares up at me. Its mouth opens slightly and I see the glint of teeth.

She wants to kiss you Stella, Heidi says.

So I let the creature pull my hand to its snout. Soft bristles sweep my fingertips for just a second and then my hand is released. Great trick, I say folding my arms behind my back.

Oh but that's not a trick. That was simply courtesy. The old woman extends a jewel-knuckled hand to me. I take it lightly don't want to mangle her bones in the clutch of her own rings but she takes mine hard crushing it for a moment before dropping it. *Yes that was simply courtesy* and suddenly I recognize the voice if not the face—that rasping purr like a feather of Brooklyn caught deep in the throat of the upper east side. Yes the voice is familiar but even in the uncertain light of the candles I can see the bright blue eyes have clouded over like an old mirror and the thick white rope of hair that she used to wear twisted around her head has shrunk to a patchy crew. She must be at least 80 maybe 90 years old.

Duchess Semjanov. What a pleasure. Not. But I climb up on a bar stool anyway, sliding my pack off my shoulders cuz even though there's nothing in it but old letters the straps have started to cut. The raccoon in her lap stares at me and pleasure is not the word as I remember the photo sessions you made Anna and I endure—the hours of tortured posing in whalebone stays and stiff taffeta skirts the endless adjustments of flower baskets and fans the hounding questions meant to scare up an expression of startled innocence. Do you love your mama a lot? How would you feel if she died? All this captured on special antique film that turned the ruddiest tomboy's tan a pale 19th-century sepia making even budding radical feminists look languid as wilted roses. And you were so pleased with the results: if only my granddaughters could look like this all the time.

Stella you and your sister were among my best subjects, she says placing three fingers studded with amethysts rubies topaz and sapphires too big to be real on my forearm letting them rest there like some splendidly armored insect. *Among the best but don't think that means my portraits were about you*, she continues as her brilliant fingers lift flap back to her lap alighting on the head of the raccoon. *Once the shutter clicks that's the end of you. When I won the l'Oeil d'Or it was not for Doc Vanderzee's granddaughters but for two Edwardian girls who took their first breaths in a tray of developing fluid.*

OK OK it's time for Puff to do her trick. Spotwood reaches for the animal swings it up onto the bar. *Hey Bucko could I have a cigarette?*

Bucko stands up from the table the light of the fireplace polishing his pate playing over his scarlet sport jacket turning it molten and I must admit he's red hot for an old guy sexy in a last chance glowing embers kind of way. Wonder what it'd be like to toast my marshmallows there as he taps his breast pocket raises his eyebrows inquiringly as if he can't hear as if the noise level is just too high but then pulls out a pack of Salems anyway and tosses one in Spotwood's direction. And Spotwood actually snatches it out of the air with a neat flick of the wrist sticking it in the slit of his yellow duck fuckers. It's a guy routine a Huck and Jim Kirk and Spock Mel and Danny routine just like the one he used to do with my dad. Yeah gotta remember Bucko's a jerk and keep my mallows in their bag.

Spotwood picks the raccoon out of Duchess's lap and places it on the bar. It stands feet splayed claws grazing the polished counter its yelloworange eyes staring indifferently out of its black face its nostrils trembling faintly. Its eyes seem to say that the bar top could be a log in the forest or a large flat rock at the edge of a stream, that our pale faces could be the patches of light visible through the darkness of the trees. Yes it's all the same to Rocky Raccoon whether the white stick Spotwood draws out of his pocket and dangles in front of its muzzle comes from mother nature or the marlboro man. All the same to me whether I stand here and stare at this dumb animal stare at a cigarette or shoot myself in the head. Might as well have another shot of Heidi's hooch. Yup might as well when whaddya know Rocky swipes the cig with one black paw. Spotwood produces a lighter. Not a flinch as the flame leaps up—the animal simply takes a drag and then blows out a little cloud of smoke.

Puff the magic draaaagon, lived by the sea, the Duchess sings.

Wow some trick.

Oh but that's not the trick, Heidi says from behind me reaching over my shoulder to set her glowing red lamp on the bar. *That's just her reward.*

No sireee that is not the trick, Spotwood reiterates as he first places his cup on the bar and then starts rolling up the sleeves of an expensive looking chamois shirt which has gotta be a cast-off of the better Boyds. Heidi lifts her lamp dousing his skin with red light and then I notice a spattering of still redder spots on his left inner forearm spots the size of cigarette tips. Oh no I don't need to see this—I may be a bitch but I'm not really a sadist. I don't need to don't want to see this the degenerate pastime of a fallen Boyd the wormholes in the apple that rolled too far from the tree. Don't need to don't want to but then Duchess Semjanov's gripping my arm leaning into me and whispering *his mother had the exact same birthmark in the exact same place. If you connect the dots it's an X. Isn't that mysterious?*

Ok so it's not self-mutilation just a birthmark an opportunity to insinuate if his father had connected the dots he would've
brought a rubber to the trailer park but now she's hissing *watch
this* rings pressing into my cheek as she steers my head back to
the bar where the raccoon is taking a drag. It exhales its mask
lost for a moment in a cloud of smoke then drops the cigarette
into Spotwood's cup. There's a sizzling sound as the animal pulls
itself to its feet waddles down the bar and settles with its back to
us the ring-striped tail twitching like a cat's. Everyone starts clap-
ping and cheering: *Bravo Puff, Bravo! Good for you! Good for
you!*

    That's the trick?

    *Of course. It's easy to start smoking but not everyone can
quit,* Heidi says now standing on the other side of the counter
and reaching for my cup as Spotwood scoops the raccoon up
from the bar and carries it off somewhere. *More winkum?* she
asks even as she's already refilling it from a large silver thermos.
*This came from apples picked from the trees in my own yard.
Trees planted by the first Elijah Phinney over two hundred years
ago. Which is not to imply I assume they'll still be there next fall.*
She pushes the steaming cup in my direction drink sloshing onto
the wood but her eyes are not for me.

    I turn and there's Chubby standing behind me holding up
a tape. *Heidi darling, is there any way to play this?*

    Of course Heidi says dipping down behind the bar. She
surfaces, sets a dusty boom box on the counter. It's got a sticker
of the road warrior on its pocket door another stranger stuck in
a strange land. But I don't have to stay. Heidi drops beneath the
bar again as Chubby slithers up on the other side of me. Springing Mel Gibson she clicks in the tape pops the button then leans
over smiling her shriveled lips slicked with orange gloss like
ham hide under aspic: *This was a favorite of your mother's.* It's
like being between a rock and a hard place between a bitch and
a witch because if I move too far the other way I'll end up in the
Duchess's lap. I don't have to stay but I do.

Between a bitch and witch and now it's the witch breathing in my ear grazing my shoulder with her jewels: *She used to drop dime after dime in the Pratt jukebox, just to hear this song.* Between a bitch and a witch and worse in front of me as Heidi reappears holding a dusty crystal decanter half full of tobacco-colored liquid and two glass goblets as the boom box crackles to life sputters *pop pop pop* and starts spitting out the sounds of brass and tinny guitar strung together by a mucoid tenor: *She was afraid to come out of the locker, she was as nervous as she could be. She was afraid to come out of the locker, she was afraid someone would see...*

And now Heidi's pulling the cork. *Two, three, four tell the people what she wore!*

Pop!

It was an itsy-bitsy teeny-weeny yellow polka dot bikini but I never saw her in a bathing suit even at the club where Anna said she was supposed to take us to hang with all the ban de soleil bitches and their retinues of coppertoned tots and peeling au pairs because you said it would be good for my dad's business. Although it's true she was afraid to come out of the locker cuz the beach wasn't her scene she'd leave us to the lifeguard and go sit up in the clubhouse hunkered down in a corner with a gin and tonic eyes hidden by a pair of big black wraparounds.

Oh no Heidi not that again...I told you I wouldn't. I may be a sot but I'm not a fool.

...and in the locker she wanted to stay or better yet the bar buttoned up in that old mao jacket while all the other women pranced around in tiny tennis dresses, sarongs, sunbunnysuits, bikinis and even monokinis picked up on the Riviera for a few francs. A favorite of your mother's I don't believe it, it would've hit too close to home.

Well you don't have to drink any Chubby, but young people like to try new things.

And old ones too. Last time I had the most gorgeous dreams. Two, three, four stick around we'll tell you more.

New? You said you found it in a box beneath the counter of the museum pharmacy. So it has to be at least a hundred years old. It's probably poison.

But I don't want to know. *She was afraid to come out in the open, and so she sat bundled up on the shore* yeah because the ban de soleil bitches would've been paying snide compliments about chesty country girls and the zinc-nosed geezers would've ogled her, doffing their white yachting caps flashing her with their nasty bald heads. *Two, three, four tell the people what she wore!*

Chubby darling, put on your thinking cap. Surely you know that drugs lose their efficacy over time. Anyway, I've already tested it and it's fine.

It was an itsy bitsy teeny weeny yellow polka dot bikini and so she drank Oma said until she was completely soused because the booze flowed like water back in those days and when she was lit to the gills she could forget herself her inhibitions and insecurities.

Yes I assure you it's fine. The problem last time was all the bourbon you drank afterward.

Two, three, four, stick around, we'll tell you more!

I'll take a drop Dr. Heidi dear, those dreams were so inspiring.

...an itsy bitsy teeny weeny yellow polka dot bikini and over the years she got more and more depressed until in the water she wanted to stay.

In the water she wanted to stay...

Here Stella would you like to try a bit of laudanum? Heidi's holding out a goblet a half finger full of the brown stuff. Laudanum. Wasn't Chubby just saying something about *probably poison?* On the other hand it's still dope if not exactly my cup of tea and I don't think I can get through the night without some so what the hell *here we go from the locker to the blanket from the blanket to the shore, from the shore to the water...* Here's to you Mom, ugh this tastes like shit. *Guess there isn't anymore!*

An artist must take risks, the Duchess says holding her glass up twirling it so that viscous rivulets run down the inside. Then she clinks it against mine: *Here's looking at you kid, although that doesn't mean that's who I'll see!*

A tiny sip yeah this is truly awful poison or not the other stuff was much tastier though the afterburn is kinda nice like the sun coming out in my chest like poppy petals spreading swelling unfurling. Did she ever get this feeling did she ever relax after a couple of drinks or was she always uncomfortable always feeling out of place scurrying from the locker to the blanket from the blanket to the shore, from the shore to the water?

Yes an artist must take risks. The Duchess clinks my glass again then takes another big swig. Her vapor blue eyes slide over my face as if looking for and failing to secure a grip: *Young woman, what is your sign?*

My sign?

Duchess is inquiring about your astrological sign, Heidi says. Sneaky bitch hasn't poured herself any, though the bottle stands right in front of her.

Capricorn.

Ah, the goat. The goat loves the vine and also gold. He craves oblivion but also security. His home is his castle and his wine cellar is his moat. You're nothing like your mother but then I believe she was a Pisces.

I have no idea what she's talking about. You're nothing like your mother...who said I was? I can hold my liquor and she never could.

It was an itsy bitsy teeny weeny tiny yellow polka dot bikini, Heidi sings putting her arm around Skip who's just stumbled through the swinging doors. He smiles down at her glassy eyed then drifts away floats round the corner of the bar arms circling me from behind pressing his forehead into the back of my neck. *I'm so sorry* he murmurs into my hair like he's somehow let me down. As if I'm the one with great expectations.

What I want to know is how you can trust a man with hair like that. Chubby reaches over my shoulder fingering one of the black tips of his blond hair. And now she's taking his arm pulling him around me to her as if he was just another dish on her table the butter she didn't ask me to pass. *Tell me you sweet boy, how do you get it to do that?*

It just grew this way. He's letting her stroke his jawbone his eyes cast down lashes demurely fanning his cheekbones. Apparently butter thinks he knows what side he's buttered on, that we can hit her up for cash or maybe crash indefinitely in the Boyd guest cottage.

Oh it can't be that simple. But her tone implies that it is, that she's delighted with him this nutrasweet little California surfer boy imported from Izmir. She's delighted with him thrilled with what she's got before her a genuine first generation American born and raised in the City of Dreams. Oh isn't he adorable with his sun bleached roots he probably believes this really is the land of opportunity that everyone can become blond if they really want to oh let's make him recite the pledge of allegiance it's so cute when they sound like they really mean it. Yeah for her he's the real thing the honest immigrant good old country people just like my mom. A boy still bound up in idealism still encumbered with native beliefs and superstitions like a simple peasant maid perspiring in layers of petticoats too afraid to wear an itsy bitsy teeny weeny yellow polka dot bikini...

Simple Simon met a pieman going to the fair, the Duchess says sweeping the inside of her goblet with a bejeweled finger. She raises it to her lips daintly licks away the brown syrup then extends it. *Bucky dear, I was hoping you would join us...*

He takes her hand. *Simple Simon met a hymen and said I think I'll go through there. Said the hymen to Simple Simon, you bastard don't you dare,* he murmurs stroking the veins above the jewel dusted knuckles with his thumb. Don't you dare but then he uses her grip as a drawbridge wedging himself between us. His elbow presses against my breast as he holds his tin cup out to Heidi and he smells like Old Spice like you used to wear like Anna and I used to wear for years trying to smell like a rich old man until we realized anyone could buy it for a buck 99 at the supermarket. Still I'm smelling him, not just smelling but inhaling him and remembering that feeling I used to have around you of not having and never getting that only made me want more.

Which is how she must've felt like the little match girl with her nose pressed against the glass but then when they opened the door she fell on her face. But she couldn't go back again either couldn't go home. She was too fancy for Taborton, Oma said. They spoiled it for her so that she couldn't leave and couldn't stay couldn't be that simple ever again but then could never be one of them.

You know there's a Devo version of Yellow Polka Dot Bikini, Bucko breathes into my ear. *It's hilarious and also more interesting instrumentally with this demented xylophone warping the rhythm. But they leave out a lot of the lyrics and you lose the from the locker to the blanket from the blanket to the shore idea which is what made the song so emblematic back in 1960, the year it hit the charts.*

What bullshit but I play along anyway sucking in the sweet musk of Old Spice: *Emblematic of what?*

Emblematic of the atomic age, baby. This world of flux, where the ground is constantly shifting, where there are no certainties no fixed ideals no gold standard for our bucks in god we trust, just the finger on the button, no guarantees or quality control no past or future, just this endless game of musical chairs.

Oh so it's that old pomo yaddah yaddah I wonder if he's making a play for me even if he did say chairs instead of beds. It might be fun to succumb but then I'd just be giving him what he wants putting on a g-string and pasties and performing in the show.

The world of fluuux, the Duchess drawls craning around Bucko, trying to fix me with her floating gaze. *We all live in it we have no choice but the artist plunges in...kicks about...luxuriates in an exquisite uncertainty...* And now her lids are drooping her chin sinking to her chest. As her forehead sinks to the bar she's murmuring...*your mother...swam like a fish...*

Splash! Now what are you going to do with the body, Mistress Phinney?

Oh she'll be alright. Spotty will drive her home, help her find her way out of the deep end and into bed.

What about me Heidi's reaching across the bar saying something into Bucko's ear and I can't make it out it's like they're behind glass. Things are starting to get a little submarinish I really should get going. But wait, what's that word *painting* she's saying. And *Stella* or maybe *tell her.* And now he turns back to me: *I understand you're interested in early American art.*

How to put it? Not really, I'd just like to have what my grandfather meant for me to have.

Not interested? Why not?

Because it's boring. And primitive. Just like it's called.

Well, said Simple Simon, that's just my nom de guerre. Actually, I think you're mixing up the art of the academy with the art of the folk, and further, that you're misunderstanding the latter. Maybe we should hop over to the Fenimore House for a little art history lecture, babe. Let's go get the key from Dixon.

A little art history lecture heh heh well guess I gotta go with the flow stay a little longer and see what it is maybe Foxy's got the Homer stashed across the street. But where's my knapsack? Shit. Oh right, down here under my stool. Maybe I've had enough of that stuff. Whatever it is. Ok now I'm cutting loose, bye Skip, bye Chub. Bubbles of giggles trailing behind me. Like a fish, the Duchess said. She must've meant drink, even if she doesn't know how my mother died. Cuz if she'd ever seen her swim she'd know what Oma told me that my mom never had lessons at Boyd Gymnasium like Anna and I they were too poor never learned to do the proper strokes only enough to keep her head above water. Which is what I gotta do now. Stella just keep your head above water. So I won't drink anymore. But I won't drink any less. Ha. No I better not touch anymore of that stuff my legs already feel like they want to float instead of walk. Good thing Daddy Bucks has my hand is guiding me toward the table cuz otherwise I might just waft up to the rafters. And now we're sitting down on a wooden bench which should feel hard but is amazingly soft as if upholstered with sponges and here's old Foxy talking at us bushy tuft of white hair bobbing as he speaks.

As I was saaying slurp...it was 1947 and we were striving to recapture the typical country store of the young Republic. We'd found the building...an early 18th-century gem slurp slurp tucked away in the hills east of Troy still serving the locals as a kind of moonshine emporium slurp...

What's he got in his mouth? It sounds like he's rolling something around and sucking on it between words.

...acquired for a song, just a couple of c-notes played to the tune of cold hard cash slurp slurp, and had it installed across from the schoolhouse.

So, you'd, ahem, found the building. What next? As I recall, you went on to stock the shelves with treasures plundered from the poor folk of Otsego County.... Dixon, could you just shut up and give us the key to the Fenimore House?

Plundered is a strong word, Bucko. I think it would be more accurate to say collected. Yes, I'd stocked the shelves with historically relevant items I'd collected slurp during my explorations of the nooks and crannies of Otsego, sealed tins of chewing tobacco stashed by grandaddy on the shelf of an abandoned outhouse slurp, bolts of colonial calico squirreled away in the attic by some long dead maiden aunt slurp, spruce gum still produced by an old hard scrabble farm family outside of Hartwick because over the generations they'd gotten used to the bitter taste of bad luck in their mouths slurp slurp.

Skip's right he does look like a troll doll with that big thatch of white hair and wizened face.

But something was wrong.

Something was wrong I'll say something was wrong. Greedy old goblin he's talking about plundering people's lives as if that stuff didn't belong to anybody as if it was just there for the taking. The hills east of Troy that might've been Taborton and they got it for just 200 bucks just like they took away who she was and gave her practically nothing in return, nothing but an itsy bitsy teeny weeny yellow polka dot bikini. Yeah you took away everything and gave her nothing and that's why I'm not leaving until I get that Homer. Cuz it's not just money in the bank a recharge for my charge card, it's restitution.

Something wasn't quite right slurp and we couldn't put our finger on it and then one day the great man slurp, progenitor of the rather pasty looking young lady you just brought over to the table with you—you might try pinching your cheeks my dear for a bit of color or perhaps you'd like me to pinch them for you, heh heh slurp slurp—summoned me to his office for a chat.

The great man he must mean you my progenitor I wonder if it comes from Latin the same root as genital. If I was really educated if I'd gone to Johns Hopkins and not UC Cruz Thru if I was an ivy leaguer and pro dick like you I'd know.

It's possible I felt a bit intimidated since I was after all just a young man fresh out of graduate school then and not the eminent New York State historian I am now slurp...or perhaps I shouldn't have had Sam's chili special for lunch. At any rate, I farted. As the room filled with the aroma of my entrails, the good doctor exclaimed eureka! That's it, it's the smell that is missing!

Of course. The smell. How many times have I heard this story, old man? Five, ten, a hundred? Come on, hand over the key.

Yeah give us the key you old troll let Daddy Bucks show me my painting so I can take it back then go home and hit the sack.

Well excuse me Mr. Bielaski—some of us aren't as slurp sharp as we used to be. Anyway, I'm sure the young lady hasn't heard it. As I was saaaying, it was the smell that was missing and so we dredged our olfactory memories slurp each man pulling up the scents of the country stores that still existed in our respective boy-hoods slurp, one after another: fresh ground coffee, plantation tea, salt fish slurp, venison jerky, kerosene, ein bisschen cow ma-nure tracked in on customers' boots, sour milk and all the other glandular secretions slurp slurp that come to stiffen slurp the denim of the farmer's overalls. That afternoon we went on to gather the ingredients for this cocktail of rustic commerce slurp, and hav-ing procured them, the next day to distribute them about the store, a little more of this here a little less of that there, until the overall aroma seemed just right. The vesper bells of Christ Church where old J.F. Cooper sleeps his eternal sleep slurp were ringing when we at last closed the door and started off down the Lake Road back into town. And I'm not ashamed to say that as we walked I stumbled once or twice, intoxicated by the thought that we had brought historical interpretation one step nearer Truth.

Where is it? Is it in your pocket?

Let me finish, please. As I was saaaying, I felt we'd brought historical interpretation one step nearer Truth, a small step per-haps, a baby step, but nevertheless a step in the right direction, that direction being rearwards, toward the dark arsehole and abyss of Time where Truth hides slurp. The next day the store opened to visitors, with one of our villagers gotten up in full colo-nial regalia serving as the manageress. I'd had no time to indoc-trinate her in her duties, being tied up with the installation slurp of the smithy slurp that had just arrived from the hamlet of Vulcan, New York, and in fact it wasn't until late in the afternoon that I had a free moment. Well, let me tell you, I stepped through the door expecting a congress of yesteryear's stinks, and what I got was an autocracy of pine-scented air freshener. It smelled like a goddamned Adirondack Trailway's bus! Slurp! Nostrils twitch-ing, I turned to the lady of the establishment. Without any show of remorse slurp, she told me that the store had reeked when she'd arrived and so on her lunch hour she'd run into town and picked up four Air Wicks slurp, paying out of her own purse. No time to eat my lunch sir, all I've had all day is rock candy and a piece of that awful spruce gum.

If you don't stop talking I'm going to turn you on your top-knot and shake it out.

Your rudeness cannot distract me so you might as well wait until I'm done, Bucko.

Til he's done I'll have passed out long before then already I'm starting to see spots itsy bitsy teeny weeny yellow polka dots spangling his face.

To continue, later that evening over a glass of whiskey slurp I told Doc Vanderzee about the fate of our carefully concocted aroma. I'd expected anger or at the least annoyance, but not laughter. No, young lady are you listening, laughter is not what I'd expected from the great doctor who with the sponsorship of the eminent Charles Boyd, Esq. had conceived gestated and given birth to this museum. Heh heh so she thought the place stunk, ho ho hee hee. He laughed and laughed and then finally, wheezing and wiping tears from his eyes said: and why shouldn't she, that's a perfectly reasonable interpretation. A perfectly reasonable interpretation because why should she go along with our conception of the past? Why shouldn't she prefer her own sanitized version, why shouldn't she find that one the most convincing, given a world where every billboard and radio announcer tells us to clean up our acts, to brighten our smiles with Crest, wear Mitchum so you can forget a day, shave with Burma like the bearded lady who's now a famous movie star? Let me tell you young man slurp, the past is a question without an answer. Oh sure we can come up with answers, some of which are more interesting, being richer, more complex, more carefully constructed than others. It is not a given however that the public will agree. No we've got to educate them, to teach their palates slurp to discern that frankfurters are inferior to foie gras. Hee hee.

Frankfurters and foie gras question without an answer, what's he buzzing on about, isn't that from Sylvia? Except hers are plural, questions without answer, glittering and drunk as flies…man I'm really fucked. Gotta get him to stop and get the key so I can get my painting if it's here and go home. Bucko's vinegar isn't working better try honey.

Sir that's a very interesting story you've been telling about my grandfather and the country store. I'd love to hear more maybe tomorrow or the next day? But tonight I'm sinking fast in fact as soon as Bucko shows me his etching I'm going to crash.

And now I'm standing up amazing what the human body can do. Sure I've got one hand on the table for balance but the door's not far if I reach out at the same time I let go I can make it. Amazing what the body is capable of yes step right up ladies and gentlemen and watch the shit-faced woman walk the line. Step right up only they're both looking at me like they didn't understand a word I said Foxy's raking his tuft blinking at me with his goggle eyes while Bucko's got one hand raised like it's a game of mother may I. But I'm not playing I don't have a mother thanks to all of you just a stupid song.

I believe she said I look fetching.

Au contraire, I think she's through for the night. Forget the key, I'll just drive her back to her hotel.

Who said I'm through what about the Fenimore House? But he just looks at me eyebrows raised face all spangled the leopard finally shows his spots. He's not my friend. I'll just walk over myself, break a pane in one of those big windows and crawl through. Ha. Yeah and if the Homer's there I'll take it and if it's not I'll take something else a Grandma Moses or a Dead Sea Scroll whatever crap they have that looks old and valuable. Yeah I'm outa here watch me go only the floor's tipping better lean to the right so that I don't walk into the fire instead of out the door.

Made it. Course I knew I could, even when I'm totally crocked I can still get around I could drive if I had to especially now with the night air clearing my head. Man these stars are bright brighter than in Los Angeles like diamonds at the Gold

Coast Tiffany's the less you can afford the more they sparkle
Oma used to say. But they're the same damn stars. And I have
just as much right to be here as anybody isn't this where I'm
from where I was born where my roots are? Isn't that what the
cows down there are lowing, that this is where we belong tucked
away in our stalls? Yeah I can come back if I want to cuz there's
nothing in the way. I just don't want to. Don't need to. Still I
could if I wanted to Daddy-o—it's my hometown. Cuz there's
nothing you can do if I decide to park my ass here nothing you
can do if I decide this is it, there's no place like home. Just for
the hell of it of course cuz I can take or leave this place. Take or
leave it. And let the homegirls sing. So hit it girls: no place like
hooooome oooohm ooohmoo no place like hooooome oooohm
ooohmoo. Yeah listen Gramps can you hear it can you hear the
chorus rising above the fields swelling up over the town NO
PLACE LIKE HOOOOOME OOOOHM OOOHMOO can you feel
its sweetsour breath in your face its rubbery wet mouth NO
PLACE LIKE HOOOOOME OOOOHM OOOHMOO its massive
warm flanks pressing in like waves slapping you down dragging
you under under under NO PLACE LIKE HOOOOOME OOOOHM
OOOHMOO MOOO MOOOO.

Yeah there's no place like home to drag you down no place
like home even if you leave cuz home is where your heart is your
lungs your liver your spleen so she couldn't get away no matter
how many miles she went the past kept pulling sucking her back
until finally she gave up like Virginia like Edna like Sylvia let it
swallow her up like a big wet womb although in Sylvia's case the
womb was an oven dry as a bone. Still the principle was the same
asphyxiation by water or by gas the point is that there's no air
anymore. You've given up your breathing rights. She gave up the
air cuz she couldn't get rid of the past couldn't drown her sorrows
without drowning herself couldn't throw out the bath without
including the baby. That's why they never found a body only her
clothes lying in the sand a pair of jeans a black turtleneck that
nasty old fur jacket. Cuz in the water she wanted to stay.

What's that racket the geese are back. I thought birds were supposed to sleep all night then wake up early. Nature's alarm clocks. The honking must drive you crazy up there at the Lakeview, if only you could drown them out. And me too. But I'm not like her I won't give up my voice. Drag me under and I'll just rear right up like a sea monster like a bitch goddess like Lady Lazarus I'll rise again. Push me down and I'll not only pop up encore I'll climb your arm use your back to launch myself into the blue. Watch out cuz unlike her I got wings and I won't hesitate to use them to churn your holy ether mess up your pie in the sky with feathers and shit. Yeah just watch me flap better dive for cover cuz here we come again lifting up from the lake beating the moon out of the sky. Yeah better run for the phone booth cuz we eat men like air. Can you feel us I can feel us the night is seething with us fuming with our plumes racked with our cries yes I can feel us can feel the rush of our wings right over my head flying so low so low what the fuck what was that something just scraped my scalp. Fuck what was that and why is my hair all warm and wet. Christ I'm bleeding. Bleeding.

I'm bleeding those goddamn geese attacked me what if they strike again remember Suzanne Pleshette how she looked after they got her too horrible to even show with her eyes eaten out gotta run gotta run but where they're veering back behind me cutting off the Bump all the other buildings are locked hold your pack over your head for protection and think what to do what to do what to do. OK make a dash across the green it looks like there's some kind of tent behind the white picket fence that'll be better than nothing I'll pull the canvas down to protect my pretty face if they come after me.

Can't breathe. Hair sticky with blood. But no wings beating against the canvas no hissing outside. Safe in here. A good time to pull the air back into my lungs with a cig. Where's my pack? Can't see. Only feel. Packed dirt. Loose straw. Cold stone. Got it. Hope I didn't leave my Luckys back at the hotel. Nope, got them too. And matches. Lucky for me...mmmmmm... Oh, but not for this dude. It's too late for him. He's toast. No he's beyond toast, he's rock. What is it anyway, some kind of statue a human figure lying on its back in a bed of hay. Like the baby Jesus only he's huge. Light another match to see more. Wow a gigantic naked man a colossus his head's as big and square as a fifteen-inch teevee his dick's a porn director's dream. How weird why would they keep this here what does a bare-ass hunk of rock have to do with early American history they never took their clothes off back then. Man this cigarette tastes good. Just what the doctor ordered. My head will be fixed in no time.

They never took their clothes off back then that's what Anna said. Then she reached for his crotch. Yeah now I remember, you introduced us to him. Girls step right up, this is the Cardiff Giant, the Great American Hoax of the 19th Century. A one ton block of carved marble passed off to gullible Victorians as a ten foot petrified man. I dickered for three years with a fellow from Des Moines who was keeping the giant in his rumpus room. Look but please don't touch.

But now I've got you all to myself baby. And ooooh you're so cold. Sooo cold and sooo rough and that aftershave that eau de terre I just love a man who's not afraid to get dirty. What's that you said? Oh so sorry you can't say anything you're made of stone. OK let me guess what your line would be from that little smile playing around your lips, let me guess what's so amusing. Another drag first though to help me think, suck deep fill my chest like a room thick with smoke a theater on fire. Thick thick…but let's not panic I must've pulled too hard. Thick too thick… Can't stop hacking and something smells something's burning incense smoldering sweet like charred tamales is there a taco stand nearby? Not in this town.

Ouch what's stinging my toes needles in the hay yikes little flames springing up all around him dirty dancing like cartoon devils no angels to put it out. No cuz I'm outa here this is not the funny pages, it's a goddamn fire. Come on gotta get up stand but legs not working cramped up with cold. Oh jesus just roll. Just grab the pack and roll out the barrel here we go through the flap and over the falls, some people survived.

Sick. Sick to my stomach and flat on my back. The starry sky is spinning like the floor beneath a mirror ball only this ain't no party this ain't no disco gotta get moving before somebody sees the bonfire of your vanity they'll be out before long keep on rolling. Keep on rolling or maybe I can scramble make for those trees and hide. Keep on rolling but I'm not ready to get up just yet rest a minute feel the warmth behind us like when Anna and I used to lie on the floor in front of your marble fireplace heat massaging our silky heads arms folded across our chests as if we had every right to be there. Every right for every wrong so I'm going to lie here a few seconds longer on my back breathing the smell of burning hay basking in the heat of the Great American Hoax.

Ms. Aubrie Rathbun
18 Lake Street
Cooperstown, NY 13326

21 August 1994

Dear Ms. Rathbun,

Or "Brie," if you don't mind. I heard your friends calling you that yesterday on Baseball Hall of Fame Day, as you sat behind your folding card table outside the liquor store peddling cup after cup of lemonade to the disciples of Abner Doubleday, raising cash for the Catskill Climbers' trip to the Rockies. What an inspiring sight you were, so resolute in your selling as the August sun beat down on your little blond head, halting only to swipe your brow with a damp pink bandana, and never once looking over beyond the flag pole that stands at the intersection of Pioneer Street and Main, at the park benches in front of the Tunnicliff Inn. Never once glancing over at the sprawling boys studying you from beneath the brims of their baseball caps, for you knew that your dad would not only match but quadruple every penny you pulled in. Perhaps you remember me. I was your best customer: the panama hat woman toting the wicker creel, who kept gliding in and out of the House of Spirits, and who stopped at your stand each time she emerged. You might also recall that I never asked you for a fresh dixie—that always I simply asked you to refill the one I had. Then I'd set it in the darkness of my wicker box, so that I could add the miniature of "magic juice." Eight, nine, maybe even ten times I performed this ritual and yet never requested a new cup because I know every bit counts, even the nickel for each waxed paper container, when you're young and desperate to make a buck. Every bit counts, despite or maybe even because of the fact that your daddy is Robert C. Rathbun, Vice President of Susquehanna Savings and Loan, formerly Senior Branch Manager of Citibank in Great Neck, New York.

At any rate, I must say that "Brie" fits you to a Tee. The sound suggests a brash girl, a breezy bungee-jumping girl with natural blond dreds and bee-stung lips, a girl light and bracing as Gatorade yet also already overripe, like the cheese manufactured in France. Yes, there's something already spoiled about you—an air, maybe even an odor although I imagine if I were to take a sniff of your fingertips I'd detect nothing but cocoa butter laced with low tar tobacco smoke. (Yes, I saw you duck beneath the plastic tablecloth to take a few puffs of a Marlboro Light after the swarms had passed and you finally had a few moments to spare in between customers.) Something already spoiled about you despite the fresh biscuit brown of your tanned shoulders, so fetchingly set off by the straps of your white tank top. How to explain it though when you look so NEW, without a line or a droop in your taut flesh? How to explain what nevertheless seeps out of you, like methane from a corpse?

Something already rotten, as there is about any child who grows up rich in a small town. (Better if your parents had raised you in Great Neck. Back on the Island, in that bracing mix of sea air and auto fumes, you wouldn't have been able to fester so.) Yes, because I know, Brie dear, that you have never lacked for anything—you've lived a life crammed with creature comforts, sealed tight against want and worry. And within such close confines, the ego ripens like a cheese. Yes, it ripens, becomes replete with self-importance, rancid even, so you come to believe that the whole world is your own private cracker barrel, chock-full of goodies made especially for you. Thus you found it completely natural that by noon yesterday your cash box (a genuine teller's metal till, no less!) was nearly full with bills, that every baseball pennant-toting boy and his wallet-carrying dad ambling toward Doubleday Field should stop at your stand for a glass of your minute made lemonade, even though it was twenty five cents more per glass than the fresh-squeezed product of your rival round the corner, the sour-looking girl set up in front of Straws and Sweetes. Oh, and sure the fresh mint was a nice touch (I myself appreciated the way it spruced up my "magic mix"), but clearly it was not what gave you the edge over your competition—even you must have noticed the trampled green sprigs littering the sidewalks of Main Street after the hordes had passed.

Steeped in self, you exude a rich air of complacency. And like the ruinous odor of Danish blue, the peaty reek of single malt, this quality suggests a high price tag, an exclusive rot that people will pay through the nose to inhale. Surely that was the case with my brother James, who used to own the liquor store in front of which you set up your own drink-dispensing operation yesterday. There was no practical explanation for his success—he knew nothing about retail and scarcely more about alcohol, the proof having always been his principle of selection. Yet six months after he opened the doors of Vanderzee's Wine and Spirit Shop, the fellow up the street had been squeezed out of business. No, the reason James's booze business prospered had nothing to do with booze or business, given his wildly uneven selection, arbitrarily high or low prices, the dusty jumble of boxes in his display window, and faux expertise in fine wines. Rather, the store flourished because of James himself, because of the way he lounged behind his desk in the shadowy regions beyond the counter, his wing-tips resting on the ink-stained blotter as he held the funny pages up to his short-sighted eyes. Because of the way he waited, like a big reeking cheese sitting in the larder, for them to come to him. And of course every mousie in town wanted a bite. Yes every mousie wanted a nibble— but not everyone's a mousie and not everyone likes cheese. Both cats and babies prefer fresh milk to its caseated corpse, so I saw no reason to worry that snowy night I invited my friend Barbara Salzmann out for drinks and dinner on my daddy's dime, back in December of '65.

Thanks to a full-tuition "Vanderzee," Barbara had just completed her first semester at Pratt. She'd won her Vanderzee Scholarship after submitting a triptych of brightly painted cartoon-like scenes of barnyard butchery in lieu of the usual biographical essay. Given the fact that in the past the Vanderzee had always gone to a student showing scholastic rather than artistic promise, Barbara's triumph was unusual. Clearly, despite my father's claims that her unorthodox entry had been "tangible proof of a naïf ability worth cultivating" as well as "an impressive example of the folk-art technique of fraktur," she had not captured the scholarship with her triptych alone. Fortunately for her, Doc Vanderzee was a philanthropist of the feudal school, who could attach not just a face to the names of his beneficiaries, but also a personal history. Thus it was the girl's pathetic past as much as any nascent talent that had tipped my father's critical scale and won her the Vanderzee. In other words, Brie, he felt sorry for her.

This past was in fact illustrated in the third panel of the triptych, with a literalness which to my mind detracted from the piece as a whole (and I thought this at the time. Despite my fondness for the artist, pity did not, and never has, interfered with my critical judgement). Here a white bearded farmer who'd been shown in the previous scenes beheading chickens and garroting pigs, aimed a gun at a little girl with glowing yellow eyes. Beneath the image, which was rendered in the flat, highly stylized manner of German fraktur art, but with a certain raw energy that perhaps anticipated the work of Basquiat, Gothic lettering quizzed "Whatcha Looking At?" Well, it should be obvious, Brie, but lest you accuse me of begging the question, the little girl was Barbara, the bearded man her father, who'd shot her for giving him "the evil eye." As it had been beyond the ability of Barbara's grandmother, the famous Taborton "rag doctor" Uta Salzmann, to extract the bullet that had blasted through the girl's right orb and lodged in her left hemisphere, she'd been rushed to Albany Medical Center.

While Barbara was convalescing (she remained in the hospital for six months, one of those in a coma), her mother Beata (a.k.a. "Batty") enrolled in nursing school (the tuition bill footed by Uta's "practice") to avoid returning to Taborton where her husband remained at large, having defended himself with the claim that he'd mistaken the girl for a fox hiding behind a bale of hay. My father hired Batty Salzman shortly after she'd been dismissed from St. Peter's Hospital in Albany for ignoring the doctors' orders and instead relying on her own "rag" diagnoses (which she obtained by first laying a linen cloth on the afflicted part of the patient, pressing that same cloth to her own forehead, then removing it to "read" the disease "printed" in the fibers). In employing her, he not only supplied asylum (for otherwise the poor woman would've been forced back to Taborton, her babe exposed once more to the danger that lurked in the woods) but also a generous start-up bonus which covered the cost of a custom-made glass eye for Barbara, thus replacing the one so brutally lost.

But all that was long ago and far away. And so, it seemed, was the previous semester at Pratt, during which I'd traveled to Brooklyn as often as maintaining my place on the dean's list at Vassar had permitted, but not often enough to put to rest my fears for the girl, who though clearly talented was perhaps too artless for art school. All through the autumn months I'd been tormented by visions of her gift being trampled under the hooves of some horny young picasso or satyrical prof, who would mutilate it beyond recognition and then mold it into some disillusioned new form. But here she was back in Cooperstown, looking as fresh and untouched by her months in the city, as if she'd been born yesterday.

We were sitting at a table at the Tunnicliff Inn, that venerable establishment that stands on the northwest corner opposite the flagpole marking the heart of our little town. But not in the upstairs part. Not in the part that used to house the Lions Club annual Christmas party attended by the all male

members, their frosty maned mates, and velvet-suited cubs.
Not where old men still chomp fragile dinners—soft white
flakes of perch flesh, fluffy forkfuls of potatoes whipped with
light cream—with big expensive teeth. Not where tables
covered with sparkling white cloths dot the polished floor like
floes of ice.

No, it was down in the Pit, the warm soft underbelly of
Cooperstown where even today people, after a few numbing
drinks, expose their throats: I've been commingling accounts,
sleeping with my wife's sister, desiring a student in my
honors class, dyeing my hair after I told everyone people
shouldn't be ashamed to look their age.... All this offered
with a look that says I trust you, I'm giving myself up to you.
Hold me in your gaze and I'll buy you a bottle of beer or the
cocktail of your choice. Down in the Pit everyone is a baby
girl, a baby boy. Despite the fact that those exposed throats
are most always bitten, the confidences betrayed. Secrets are
too tasty to eat alone.... Within a week each one is public
knowledge; within two weeks it sparks as little interest as a
popsicle stick gummed to a sidewalk.

In the dark paneled-wood and brick interior of the Pit,
where after drinking a couple of Dave Zeller's parricidal
potions, even the most responsible adults would grow babysoft
about the mouth, diaper damp behind the ears, it seemed to me
Barbara was the most infantile of all. The most infantile of all, I
thought, as I watched the flickering light of the votive candle
that stood in a small glass bowl on the table between us play
hopscotch over the contours of her face, pooling with equal
liquidity in both the real and the false eye. Oh sure, she'd
acquired a certain superficial sophistication during her months
in the city, a polished look she had not possessed when she'd
stepped on the Adirondack Trailways bus three months before.
This she had achieved by discarding what she could (so that
beefy tee and grass-stained dungarees had been exchanged for
a skintight celadon-green cheongsam and black silk Nehru
jacket) while at the same time augmenting what she could not

(so that the vitreous cast of the false eye had been conferred to the real one, giving a glassy stare to both). However, despite this new sheath of ennui, this shellac of chic indifference, it was the same old Barbara underneath. This was clear to me as I watched her swirl her gin with a swizzle stick so that the ice tinkled against the sides of the glass, watched how the mask dropped and her face suddenly acquired an attentive look. And clearer still as she dropped her head to the table, slid the glass alongside her ear, listened for a few moments and then straightening up again said:

"I wonder what ice sounds like when it's growing."

"When it's growing?"

"Yes, when it's growing, when the ice crystals are forming. It must make a sound even if we can't hear it."

Yes, it was the same old Barbara, I thought, because only a baby would dwell on such minutiae, such tiny material particulars, the myriad bits of experience that the more mature mind bypasses, since cogitation takes place on a higher plane. Which is not, Brie, to depreciate Barbara's way of perceiving the world. Even then I recognized that something is lost in the conceptualizing shortcuts taken by the more evolved intellect, that doors are shut, pathways left unexplored in the leap to the upper levels of thinking. Even then I realized that Barbara's monocular, infantile stare was the gaze of genius (indeed, Barbara's reflections on the development of ice anticipated by 35 years one of the more original works at the recent Whitney Biennial, Brian Fridge's videotape of the ice crystals forming in his freezer).

Convinced, I took a sip of the Beefeater martini the barmaid had just brought to our table. Perfectly mixed. Perfectly stirred. Fiery to be sure, but with a fire that promised to soon defer to a more mellow warmth. I gave Dave, who was polishing glasses at the bar, a thumbs up (too bad, Brie, for your generation that he retired last year; you'll never know what a real martini tastes like), and then signaled again to the barmaid, a chlorotic looking young woman in rhinestone

spectacles which apparently did nothing to improve her
vision since it took me more than one wave to catch her eye.
When she finally sidled over, I told her that my friend and I
would like to begin with hors d'oeuvres—a dozen raw blue-
point oysters and two orders of escargot.

Cringing as if she expected me to swat her with the
menu, the young woman said she was very sorry but we'd
have to go upstairs if we wanted "upstairs food," since it was
only available in the dining room. Well Brie, I don't like to
abuse my privilege (I, for instance, never ran up a tab unless I
was certain my pop would pay, unlike you, $200 in arrears to
the proprietors of Danny's market after your father refused to
foot your "Naturade" bill), but tonight was a special occasion.
Indeed, the only reason I'd brought Barbara down to the Pit
was because it offered a cozier, more intimate atmosphere. So
I told the woman that if she cared to speak to Dave about my
order, she'd discover that the categories "upstairs food" and
"downstairs food" were more flexible than she might think.

A short while later the molluscs arrived, and also a
basket of linen-wrapped rolls. Someone had evidently taken
some trouble in the kitchen. The oysters were bedded on an
ice-heaped pebbled-glass plate, the anamorphic contours of
their shells accented by a purple orchid perched in the center
of the mound. Cradled by the delicate lip of the flower, and
also resting on the silvery clot of flesh within each shell, was
a pearl. No doubt plastic, but still it was a nice touch, as were
the two accompanying small gold-rimmed pebbled-glass
bowls bearing lemon wedges and a creamy horseradish sauce.
The escargot were less spectacularly presented, but nevertheless pleasingly, in blackware crocks, within which the tawny
cochlea floated in a buttery parsley-flecked broth. Approv-
ingly I noted the tiny silver forks, prongs offering additional
wedges of lemon, perched on the ledge of plate beneath each
bowl.

Barbara was staring down at her escargot, nostrils
twitching at the fragrant steam rising up from her bowl. I

wondered if she knew what to do with her fork, and took
another swallow of the elixir of the juniper berry, preparing to
introduce my novitiate to la dolce vita.

"You know they're just regular old snails," I said,
basking in the fire of the gin. "The same ones you can find
crawling round the roots of rose bushes and gliding up the
sides of garbage cans. It's all just a matter of context."

"I know," she replied removing the lemon wedge from
the prongs of her fork, "but context is everything." And then
she plucked a snail shell from her bowl with her forefinger
and thumb, speared at the cavity and pulled out a glistening
black morsel of meat.

I must admit I was disappointed. When you care deeply
about someone (and you can take the preceding clause in a
purely rhetorical sense, Brie, since you strike me as the sort
of girl whose attachments take shallow root at best), you
want, as Plato says in his "Speech to Pausanias," to share
everything with that person. In order to share this gastro-
nomic delicacy with Barbara, I'd anticipated that I would
have to overcome her natural culinary inhibitions, and further,
instruct her in the proper method of consumption. But as she
sat across from me chewing with evident discernment, her
fork poised in mid-air like a conducting baton between
movements, it was clear that she already knew a thing or two
about eating snails. Eyeing the celadon silk dress, which fit
her as if it had been tailored for her, I couldn't help but
wonder how she'd been able to afford that knowledge; while
the Vanderzee provided room, board and tuition, as well as a
bit of pocket money, it made no allowance for luxuries (and if
you're thinking that maybe she'd received assistance from
American Express, well, we didn't have credit cards back
then).

No allowance for luxuries, and yet the girl who'd grown
up in second-hand blue-jeans and discount tees was now
sitting across from me sheathed in shantung silk and exuding
the fastidious air of the connoisseur. In the flickering light of

the votive candle, the slubby fabric of her dress was both
brilliant and dull, the expression on her face both discerning
and simple. I raised my martini to my lips, swished the
expensive gin in my mouth. Oddly, the initial flame had not
abated; it tasted harsher on the third swallow than on the first.
I'd have to speak to Dave about this—while he was the most
vigilant of bartenders, something wasn't quite right on the top
shelf.

I was about to raise my finger and summon him over
when Barbara laid her little fork down on the side of her
plate, and, evidently warmed by her epicurean exertions, slid
out of her Nehru jacket. Twisting round, she arranged it over
the back of her chair. It was then that I noticed the label
sticking up from the back of her dress. I narrowed my eyes
and leaned forward: printed beneath (or more accurately,
above, since the label was upside down) "City Sophisticates"
was the additional information "100% pure acetate."

As she swiveled to face me, I leaned back in my chair. I
could not let her know what I had seen. "City Sophisticates":
the words summoned up some cheap little shop in the Garment District crammed with racks of deodorant smeared
dresses, seams already shredded from having accommodated
one pair of girdle-bound hips too many. Unpleasant as the
image was, however, I was glad for it, for now that I had a
better sense of where Barbara had been, I had a better sense
of where I could take her. Yes, and so when we returned down
state after the New Year, I'd meet her in Manhattan and we'd
stroll over to 5th Avenue. A frock or two from Bergdorfs
would blow my spring clothing allowance, but it would be
worth it to see the sparkle in her eyes when she felt for the
first time the caress of real silk, the delicate tickle of tulle.
Yes, what a pleasure it would be to see the Taborton tomboy
wrapped in a shellpink charmeuse gown, a collar of velvet
ribbon round her neck.

What a pleasure, I thought, as I sipped a fresh martini
(Dave Zeller having admitted it was not impossible he'd

mixed up the gins, since he worked more by touch than by sight). While I'd lost my appetite for snails, which indeed looked no different bobbing in their dark broth than the ones you could find floating in the metal basin of beer that our gardener set out amongst the rose bushes, the oysters still beckoned. I picked a shell from the iced glass plate. With my little fork I lifted the fold of glistening flesh and admired the subtle stringwork of the gills beneath, before taking the whole into my mouth. How wonderful, the chewy resistance of the meat even as it yielded its briny juices, washing my tongue with the wild taste of the sea. How delightful, the apprehensive expression of the girl sitting across from me as she stared at the remaining eleven oysters lying on their bed of ice. Plucking another shell from the plate, I explained that contrary to what she might have gathered from Fourth of July clambakes, bivalves, if properly chilled and prepared, could be eaten raw.

"Have you ever noticed how they look like eyes?" Barbara asked, resting her chin on her palms as she continued to stare at the molluscs.

No I had not, though to humor her I went on to note there was a long standing literary association between oysters and eyes, and then quoted from The Tempest: "Full fathom five thy father lies. Those are pearls that were his eyes."

"I'm not talking about pearls," she said, lifting her crooked gaze to meet mine. I recalled what a struggle Shakespeare had been for her in high school. "I'm talking about the slippery gray part."

Perhaps, I conceded, though it was an eye without pupil or iris. A blind eye.

"How do you know? Maybe it's looking at you right now."

While Barbara's whimsical view of reality was one of her most appealing qualities, as well as a source of her art, the conversation had become too irrational for my taste. Rather than replying, I took another oyster. Although edible it did not taste as fresh and spumy as the first, its faintly fecal flavor reminding me that the animal is essentially a bottom feeder, subsisting on the debris that floats down from above. I washed it down with a cleansing swallow of alcohol and looked around for the barmaid. It was time for the next course.

Unfortunately the Pit had begun to fill up. The "Zeller Cellar Dwellers," a.k.a. the "Troglodytes," had all taken their stools at the bar, while high-school friends of my brother, fresh from the old ski tow out on Pierstown Road, had claimed a large table as well as an adjacent booth on the other side of the room. Over the brim of my martini glass I surveyed the latter group, who'd managed to capture the barmaid and were besieging her with demands for hot toddies and fondue. I've never cared for the Gstaad look, those fanatically patterned sweaters with the pewter buttons made for thick cold-numbed fingers, the tight black ski pants designed to set off meaty buttocks, a look which well-suited my brother's friends who, although they'd only taken two tables, seemed to occupy half the room, filling it with raw wintry vigor. Indeed they'd extended the boundary of their table a good two feet, as the barmaid was forced to step over sprawling legs, to pick her way around the melted ice that had pooled beneath goatskin après ski boots. I actually felt a little sorry for the young woman, who looked more sickly and shrinking than ever, her rhinestones glittering feebly in the riot of rosy faces all bellowing their orders at once.

I looked over at Barbara and caught her studying the group. Seeing me looking at her, she dropped her eyes and returned to her escargot. I was glad that my brother, who'd been "broadening his mind" for the past year traveling through Europe with his friend Bucko (a procrustean folly financed by my father, who undoubtedly was trying to forestall James's inevitable failure to finish his bachelor's degree), was not in town, as his presence might have forced us to join them, at least for a round of toddies. For that would

have entailed following the traversal of stories about how
Patti once ploughed into shoulder-deep powder, about the
time Marky nearly met his mogul on the black diamond trail
at Sugarbush, about how Sandee had managed to slalom on
one ski round seven trees in a row, back and forth across the
two tables, sliding ever farther down the slope of stupidity.
And while I imagine that for you and your cohorts, Brie, such
tales provide entertainment, as well as a validation of the
purely corporeal pursuits you embrace (though in your
generation the oral recollection of these adventures has given
way to a video-recorded one), for my kind they only serve to
reinforce our disappointment in yours. Your inheritance is so
rich, my dear—you have not only the entire European intellectual and artistic tradition but also such native gems as Poe
and Pollock—and yet you choose to ignore it, preferring over
the printed page or painted canvas a blank wall of rock.

There was no compelling reason to join the ski club and
I was glad not only for my sake but for Barbara's as well.
Already I'd seen a blond buzz cut turn in our direction, seen a
blue gaze or two spear the air and it was clear to me the target
was Barbara; my own bookish mien discouraged such as-
saults. They were afraid of me, of my brains and, I should
add, my beauty (my flaming red hair presenting such a pretty
paradox with my cool white skin); but Barbara, whose
intelligence was less formidable and whose swarthy good
looks fell short of the Nordic ideal, would present no such
obstacle. No doubt they'd be all over her, the Viking horde, as
soon as we sat down at their table, trying to truss her up with
toddies and take her home.

Further, I wasn't entirely confident in Barbara's ability
to resist their attentions. After all, my brother's friends, two
years older than I, four years older than Barbara, had been
considered, despite their lack of scholastic achievements,
"the smart set" at Cooperstown High; to the singular eye of
the teen from Taborton they'd no doubt sparkled like
brilliants.

Fortunately James was far away, obviating any need to fraternize with his obtuse associates. He'd sent me a postcard from Corfu a few weeks before, a couple of ungrammatical lines, and now I imagined he was sunning himself on some secluded Greek isle. I could see him, sprawled alongside his old pal Bucko by the edge of the marble hotel pool, ignoring the rocky beach beyond where dark indigenous beauties collected thalassic leftovers. Rather, his attention would be on the streamlined blonde in the one-piece suit, doing laps in a lane that was no less definite for its boundaries being invisible. If it were anywhere but on himself that is, on his own sun-sanctified self. How easy to envision him simply stretched out over the flagstones like a king carved on a sarcophagus, dead to all charms but his own. Indeed my relief over his absence held no relation to my protective feelings for Barbara—of the "smart set" he was the one most stupid to her appeal. All the times he had seen her in our house, sipping soda in the kitchen, puzzling over her homework in my bedroom, he'd paid no more regard than he would've to Echo, my father's collie, and I was certain he'd pay no more now.

Giving up for the time being on the waitress, who had run off to the kitchen as soon as she'd finished taking my brother's friends' order, like a mole scurrying back to its hole, I drained my martini. Barbara was busy sopping up the escargot broth with a poppyseed roll she'd discovered in the breadbasket, seemingly oblivious to the two noisy tables on the other side of the room. If I were to carry my glass over to Dave for a refill, I could easily keep an eye on her from the bar. As I rose from the table, I asked her if she wanted another martini, or something else entirely, but she shook her head without looking up, amber eyes curtained by thick black lashes. Well, the urge to stay for a game of peekaboo was strong—I loved the moment she'd lift her lids, the lightning bolt of gold—but the desire for another drink was stronger. Brie, I should've played.

"Comin down pretty fast and thick out there," Dave commented, pointing with his elbow as he toweled off a beer glass, toward the stairs that led down into the pub. I slid onto a bar stool and leaned forward across the mahogany counter to peer at the gin selection—the last swallow of Beefeater's had left an aftertaste that undercut the experience of the cocktail as a whole.

"Wen up to take out the trash awile go. Couldn't sec two foot," he continued. "Remines me of the night your dad ran into the flag."

The troglodytes who'd been slumped over the countertop on either side of me sat up. I gave Dave a look that would've frozen any beer in the glass he'd just polished dry—but he didn't seem to notice. True, Brie, that my father's Bentley had been to the body shop on more than one occasion to get the dents banged out. I had no intention of defending these fender benders. Still, it seemed to me that Zeller was out of line. Surely he could pass over my father's irregularities, especially in the presence of the Cellar Dwellers. After all, if it weren't for my father he'd be leading the singular life of the mixologist, his existence tethered to the dim recesses of the Pit. But thanks to Doc Vanderzee, who was not only an esteemed reconstructive surgeon, but also the founder and director of the Farmer's Museum, Dave enjoyed the freedom of the press, as chief stereotypist for the Otsego Journal, the neo-colonial rag edited by Franklin Phinney. And now, I felt, he was abusing that freedom, disseminating information that was really nobody's business. So I told him, making my words as pointed as possible, that nights like this one, when safe passage out of the village had been suspended by the snow, reminded me how insular Cooperstown was, how people seemed to have nothing better to do than sit around and tell stories about each other. Then I said he could mix me another martini, or on second thought, maybe he'd better make that a Manhattan.

Dave reached for the shelves behind the bar, pulling down a bottle of good Irish whiskey. But instead of simply going about his business and stirring the whiskey with sweet vermouth and a dash of bitters, he gabbed on in the local patois (the most distinct feature of which, as you may have already noted, was its shortened syllables—a brevity achieved through the truncation of unnecessary vowels and consonants. In the last few decades this quaintly economical way of speech has all but disappeared, as the modern media has trepanned our once closed mountain culture. Or on second thought, maybe the patois has become so universal that we can no longer hear it, as the modern media has not only penetrated the folksy cloisters of yesteryear, but siphoned off precious regional resources and put them into general circulation. Certainly one can see the commercial motivation for such exploitation, as our lost local patois allows television and radio producers to fit more sound-bites into less air-time, and therefore to increase the number of advertisements in between. At any rate, I urge you to hold on to this letter, as what follows is a valuable ethnolinguistic record).

"Snow comin down like it had no place else to go and I told your pop I'd walk im home soon as I lock up—he'd never make the hill. But he insis he's goin to drive himself. Goin to set off like some kind of Peary into the blizzer when he can't even find the door. Had to let him out. Watch the white swaller him up…"

Dave paused, looked over in the direction of the stairs. The troglodyte on my left shifted on her stool, nearly tipping into me as she reached for her boilermaker and tossed back the last bit with a belch. Suddenly a coil of cold air shot down into the bar like a child's slinky toy, and one of the après ski crew called out "hey old buddy." But I didn't turn around, in order to set a good example for Barbara, who the last time I'd looked over my shoulder had immediately dropped her eyes and pretended to be investigating the oysters with her little seafood fork. It was important to distinguish ourselves from the villagers whose heads swiveled round every time someone new entered the bar, to demonstrate a downstate indifference to vulgar upstate ways.

Yes, it was important to distinguish ourselves, I thought, as the viscous voice of some Vegas crooner spilled out of the jukebox into the room behind me: "Baby it's cold out there." Most important, as the female vocals gushed after, "But I really must gooo…"

"Din't see him agin for a while," Dave resumed as he threw a dash of bitters into my cocktail. "But I heard he did his rounds the next day with a turb'n of gauze wrapt round his head like Lawri of Arabi. I did see the Bent for they towd it, front end kissin the concrit base of the flagpole. Cops of course recnized the car, though he parently 'left the scene' as they say. But even if they hadn't, they could've traced him home by followin the trail of red drops in the snow."

He stopped, threw a paper cocktail napkin down on the counter like a challenge.

I just stared at him, let him see in my face that I found his story perfectly ridiculous. On the jukebox, the woman was still pleading "I really must go," but the man's voice just ploughed right over her: "Baby its bbaaad out there, no fun to be had out there…" I was about to slide off my barstool, but then Dave slid a fresh drink into my hand, wrapping my fingers round the chilled glass.

I took a sip. Nectar. Still, I reminded him that at the beginning of his anecdote it had been snowing. Therefore wouldn't any trace of blood, assuming it was true my father had bled all the way back to Stagecoach Lane, have been erased by the snow?

"It stopped," he said, dropping a maraschino cherry into my drink, even as I was raising it to my lips. Whiskey splattered my face. I simply wiped the whiskey away with the back of my hand, for now that I had my drink I could rejoin Barbara. Indeed, I was about to slide off my stool when Dave commented, staring over my shoulder: "Almos can't tell that's a false eye. Jus a little crook."

Feeling that his gaze would follow me like tin cans tied to a fender if I walked over to her now, I decided to wait until his attention was occupied elsewhere. Well Brie, I shouldn't have allowed self-consciousness to divorce me from my desire—I should've gone back to her right then and there. Right then and there, but instead I waited, finishing my drink and starting another, as Dave filled my ears with a whole punch bowl full of nuptial nonsense, ladle after ladle of engagements, courtships, lovers' quarrels, patch-ups and permanent ruptures, until at last, leaving me to splutter over a story about how Batty Salzmann, after seven years as Doc Vanderzee's nurse, was suddenly "eatin apples agin" with a cheesemaker from Herkimer (this was rubbish, Brie. Both the apples and the cheese), until at last he turned his attention to a request for a pink lady from Patti Holden, an old girlfriend of my brother who was with the après ski crew. While he poked around in the bar cooler for an egg, making some presumptuous claim about how it took a "gent" to fix a good lady, I gripped my Manhattan and slid off my stool. Back to my baby as I took a big step out into the room

I almost dropped my glass.

The only reason I didn't is that every muscle in my body pulled taut a split second after it went slack. Strung tight by the height of my own astonishment, I just stood there and stared.

He had pulled a chair up next to hers and was holding an oyster shell aloft over her parted lips, as she sat with her head tilted back. Reading over what I've written (and you should know that the spatial interval between the last word of the previous sentence and the first word of the present one does not adequately represent the temporal gap. Please allow for a pregnant pause), I realize, Brie, that I need to clarify who I mean by "he." For while it might be obvious to a more perspicacious reader, I can't expect you to be so discerning. When I wrote "he," I meant, of course, my brother James. The big cheese. The funny-pages reading fool. Back from "Yerp" as Dave would no doubt put it.

I took another step and felt my knees wobble thighs tremble pelvis expand, as if bone and cartilage had suddenly been rendered into rubber, while at the same time my heart seemed to grow turgid to be pressing out and down filling my whole torso with a kind of gravid thrust. No doubt the liquor was taking license with my limbs, playing havoc with my organs, although under normal circumstances the bottle never got the best of me. Clearly it was a matter of mind over matter I told myself, taking a last anaesthetic whiff of whiskey before setting my glass down on a nearby table. Yes, it was a matter of mind over matter as I took another step clutching my stomach, and there was nothing the matter if I could just make it back to Barbara without exploding.

"Baby it's cold out there," the voice on the jukebox baritoned encore, its argument apparently rejuvenated by a new nickel. "I really must go," its soprano prey countered, and I wished she would. How I wished she would, but she showed no sign of leaving. No, there was nothing in her posture that indicated any intention of departing. On the contrary, her torso arced toward him like a wave swelled by the pull of the moon as she took the slippery gray nib of flesh in her mouth.

She chewed. She chewed and while I was too far away to make out the undulating movement of her neck, it seemed to me I suddenly felt a pulsing flow, like water washing over my skin, like sand running through my fingertips. Yes, I could feel her slipping away, could see him pulling her from me with all the crude efficiency of a pair of forceps, even as the jukebox insisted "Baby it's cold out there, no fun to be had out there."

And Barbara not only offered no resistance, having swallowed and raised her face to his, but went on to pluck an oyster from its shell, to roll the meat still dripping with its salinous fluid for a moment between thumb and forefinger, and finally, with an infantile smile, to press it to my brother's lips.

I think, Brie, that we'll let the curtain fall there—
although dinner didn't get beyond the hors d'oeuvres, the
show is over. Hopefully you've understood my theme,
because frankly, I find it too painful to continue. In lieu of
further elaboration, I leave you with the words of a famous
French philosopher: "No doubt you eat oysters innocently
enough, without knowing that at this stage in the animal
kingdom, the eye has already developed."

Watchfully,
Judith Vanderzee

P.S. Thanks to a bowl of borscht and a post prandial vodka, I
feel better now, if not inspired by the furor scribendi. (If, by
the way, you've had trouble with any of the vocabulary used
in the preceding sentence or above, I suggest a course in
Latin. I believe it's still offered at Cooperstown High, despite
the recent campaign of your dad and other local "Fathers for
the Future" to "bury the dead languages," because "kids
today need Spanish and Chinese"). At any rate, I find I am
compelled to offer you one final tidbit. You should know
James paid for the privilege of his droit du seigneur (a little
French would no doubt be helpful as well). For while the
world may have been his oyster, eventually my brother
discovered he was as capable as anyone of contracting
Hepatitis C.

Don't wanna open my eyes but something's tickling my nose. Don't wanna but I'm not dead yet gotta see the light or whatever it is that's crawling over my skin. Gotta see the light gotta crack my eyes. Still dark. Open wide. And see darkness break with a sunny smile a revelation of perfect teeth. Open wider and here he is leaning over me with his two tone hair hanging down over either side of his face like some kind of fucked up curtains or a bad habit. My Sister of Mercy.

Hey are you OK?

Am I OK? I pull myself up on my elbows and the peas and carrots decor of room number 7 swirls into focus. He's picked up the floor. Good boy. But I am not a good girl feel like I fell down the stairway to heaven like hells bells are ringing in my head.

What the fuck happened last night?

Well there was a fire. Somebody torched the Terrified Man. A fire truck came and hosed it.

Petrified Man. Idiot. But somebody means it wasn't me. Did I do it?

Whatever. Hey did you know it was some huge olden days scam? This guy carved a big statue out of marble buried it in a field then dug it up again telling people he'd discovered some ancient giant or maybe he said god. Everyone paid to see it. Suckers.

Goddamn there's that radiator hissing and clanking again don't they know my head is splitting. Gotta lay it back down on this nice soft pillow cuz I'm one too for drinking Heidi's shit last night. That's better. Yeah I'm a sucker too just listen to those pipes: *Ssssuckker, ssssuckker.*

We should come up with a scam. His hands press my temples.

Sure, why not? His fingers are cool. Soothing.

You could think of something—I bet you've got a million good ideas. And now he's stroking my scalp like he's looking for the secret button that'll spring the trap door. If I was her he'd actually feel something the screws beneath the skin the patch of titanium covering the hole in her skull. If I was her it wouldn't be worth getting inside. Not after the swap she made to be a Vanderzee. Shit for brains. But you're not gonna screw me. As soon as I've got the Homer I'm hitting the road.

What's this some kind of gray goo stuck in your hair. OOOOH nasty, it's bird shit.

It wasn't blood. Goddamn geese. Gotta get out of this town—find that painting and go. But how? Gotta think only now he's leaning over me again the dark tips of his hair nibbling my skin, his pupils expanding and contracting like fish mouths.

That Zeller guy collared me when I went down for breakfast this morning. He said your Visa isn't working anymore.

Christ must be maxed out. Can't deal with that now just gotta get him out of here.

Would you go buy me some alka seltzer? Take the back stairs so that Dave Zeller doesn't see you.

Sure. He kisses my forehead just one last taste to fill me up buttercup then he drifts off over to the chair rustling through something must be my clothes I don't remember taking them off. And now with my last five bucks crumpled in his pocket a smile on his kisser he heads out the door. I lift my hand uncurl my fingers: bye bye. *Click.*

OK where to start I guess all over again cuz last night was a bust a wasteland of opportunity got too fucked up. And now I've got a hammer in my head. Should've just stayed here and read those letters there might be something about what you did with the Homer or more likely a paper trail to Juju so I can track her down and ask her. Yeah even if there were no return addresses on the envelopes she probably mentions geographical details and landmarks inside crumbs of info that I can follow to her lair. Then I'll drag her out make her cough it up with the gin and olive pits grab my nugget and go.

So I'll just have to start over lug my knapsack into bed with me and start digging never mind my head cuz when the hoeing gets tough the tough get hoeing. Have to get up first though use the bathroom then look for the letters. Onward ho we are marching no we are swaying feeling a little dizzy better get down on the floor that's better we are crawling as to war. Crawling like last night only that was away I could feel the heat on the soles of my boots scorching my butt scrambling like a soldier for the trenches like a baby for its mommy catch me oh please catch me I know I'm just a baby and I can't make it alone. I swear I'll never touch that shit again. Someone must've found me maybe Skip lying on the ground and helped me home. Did I set it? Nobody knows, thank god.

These tiles feel good. Cool. I could just lie down here press my stomach against this floor all day. Then I could flip over and we could play checkers on it just color in every other square with magic marker or maybe even make it permanent a tattoo so I could charge people ten bucks a game with the Checkerboard Lady. Check her out see if you can beat the meat. How's that for a scam. Pathetic. Get up Stella off the floor and onto the loo.

There that's better got all those chemicals out of my bladder. Should've saved it though somebody could've got pissed on my piss. So what if it's poison can't be any worse than that shit they drink in Russia. OK Vladimir that's 1000 rubles a glass. Man

I'm hot this morning—two scams in two minutes. Only then I'd have to be drinking laudanum or whatever it was all the time.

I don't feel as bad as I did the pounding's already letting up as if peeing somehow eased the pressure in my head. And nausea's not really a problem let's try standing up again. OK a bit shaky but if I keep one hand on the sink I'll be fine. Yikes what was that in the mirror a terrible fish Sylvia would say. Or worse. I look like some kind of pasty mutant a piece of Chernobyl fallout maybe I don't feel so bad but I look like toxic waste. Good thing I don't need to see anybody but my faithful dog Skip today I'll just stay in bed and read those letters think about where to go next.

Now where'd I drop it? Maybe in here if I used the bathroom before I crashed. Nope. Must be out in the room. Legs still feel a little weird a little rubbery but they work and that's all that matters just like the pervs say about their blow-up dolls. How do I know Juju's not fucking with me? Maybe this is all a big joke like that one you used to tell about the boy whose father promised him a pony if he shoveled away the pile of cow shit behind the barn. About how the boy kept digging and digging because somewhere under all this shit there must be a pony. Hardee har har. But somewhere under all this shit maybe under my coat nope maybe under these blankets nope maybe under this underwear nope there must be a knapsack. Somewhere it has got to be somewhere and even if this is all some ghastly gag that was her handwriting and there must be a clue in one of those letters I can use to find her. Find her and confront her maybe threaten to sue for something like breach of promise for inflating me with great expectations just to watch me pop. For letting me think I'd find a pony under all the shit instead of just a pin.

Somewhere it has got to be somewhere. The Homer too for that matter. Yes and so why be paranoid why shouldn't she be mine the cow girl in her field of buttercups surely I'm entitled to a piece of the pasture. And Juju knows it knows she's mine my inheritance my birthright knows I've got the Vanderzee nose and I'll sniff that painting out sooner or later. So she's just work-ing me for her own twisted purposes seeing how far I'll go like that time she came to California and we went to the Chinese Theater. Did you know darlings that if you can follow the foot-prints of the stars without missing a single one your fondest dreams will come true? A ploy so she could slip into the bar across the street as Anna and I teetered and tottered on the cement wishing we could go back that things could be the way they were. Her big face laughing through the glass when the French man refused to forfeit the feet of Jerry Lewis. Go away leetle girl, the King of Comedy belongs to me.

What's that a loud angry man's voice in the hallway...*runnin a business not a shelter*...now another *Ok ok that's cool.* That's Skip's smooth as balm to the first: *understand your position...grandfather's loaded though...collateral?* Footsteps right in front of the door quick behind the bed I'll slide under if he busts in: *She got last night on collateral. Against better judg-ment. How do I even know she's the Doc's granddaughter? How do I know yer not a couple of California schemers?*

Dust on my lips. They don't vacuum under the beds here. Maybe I should say something holding my head high like Eliza-beth Taylor on the way out: whatt a dumppp. On the way out fuck where are we going to go? All I've got left is the Discover card Zeller wouldn't take it sorry young lady but we've discov-ered some problems with Discover. No offense. Will anyone? Heavy feet stomping away fee fi fo fum is that the floor trem-bling or is it me. Good he's gone. That's Skip's key turning in the lock.

Have you seen my knapsack?

Seen it?

Seen IT. My knapsack. You know the leather thing with the. straps. When you were my student in English 100 I'd put your papers in there.

No. He slumps down on the chair next to the phone and bracing his elbows on his knees pushes his hair back from his forehead, holds it there pulling the smooth slope of his brow even smoother. Earnest boy. A good egg despite the bad habit.

No Stella I haven't. I remember you had it when we left here last night but I don't remember you bringing it back.

Oh fuck. FUCK!

What? Why fuck?

Why FUCK? Because that knapsack had half a hav a hav a hav a… Whoa easy there that's not helping gotta pull myself together. Calm down. Breathe deep. *Half a million dollars in it.*

Your knapsack?

No! The Homer. Maybe more yeah I'm sure I could've sold it for at least that much, at least after the show of his work at LA COMA last year. Mausoleum quality those are the magic words to get the old folks to shell out the dough.

I'm sorry Stella but I don't get it. What does the knapsack have to do with that painting you're supposed to get from your grandfather?

Never mind. Just tell me where you found me last night.

Under a tree. After the fire trucks came. Everybody was standing around watching the Terrified Man roasting like a big kebab. But the smoke was making my eyes sting. So I walked off into the trees and there you were lying with your head on a rock.

Are you sure it was a rock? Could it have been my pack? God I hope I didn't leave it in the tent I don't think so I'm sure I remember the weight of it on my back as I crawled away. I'm sure.

Maybe. If it was, the old lady might've picked it up.

The old lady?

Yeah you know the one with the buggy eyes who passed out? But then she woke up. She kept looking at me watching me. Later she followed me out. Man I just thought of something—think she's a narc? He stands up now raking his fingers through his hair lines appearing out of nowhere in his forehead like sudden cracks as he stares down at the old black rotary phone squatting on the table next to his chair.

And suddenly it's ringing shrilling like a tripped alarm. You're in trouble you're in trouble. Probably Zeller. he wants us to get packing. Don't pick it up. But he does. His eyes go wide. With his hand over the receiver: *It's her. She wants to talk to you.*

I hoist myself up from the floor walk over and take the phone from his hand the long black cord swinging between us.

Heelloow deear. It's Duchess.

Yes?

I was wondering if you and your little friend would like to drive out for a visit this afternoon. I have something fooor yoouu. Something you might waaant.

A hiss. Then a clanking. The radiator again. *Ssssuckker, ssssuckker.*

Click.

Ms. Antje Rosekranz
855 7th Ave.
Brooklyn, NY 11215

10 January 1996

Dear Antje,

Or "Auntie," as I've come to call you in my own mind.
For though you can't be more than seventeen, you evoke the
stereotype of the "maiden aunt," of spare-fleshed efficiency
softened by a tissuey wrap of self-absorption. And perhaps
you also recall, as you scurry back and forth between your
parents' office and after school art classes each afternoon,
dwarfed by the easel strapped to your narrow back, the
spinster's insect sister. By the way, please do not be put off by
the thoughts I've expressed in the preceding sentences; you
should not feel that such associations diminish your charm,
which is considerable. With your slim form, excellent posture, and thick red braid burning down to the crest of your
buttocks, you brighten my visits to Brooklyn.

Yes, what an unexpected pleasure to discover, after
having been driven to a neighborhood I generally prefer to
avoid (up and coming or not, in my mind Park Slope will
always be a borough), by a malady I won't disclose, to
discover not only your parents' business (a business which
evokes fond, if painful memories) across the hall from my
own doctor, but you. Perhaps it was not really a malady
after all, but a melody—the unexpected song of the siren of
7th Avenue. Which is not to imply that there's anything
deliberately seductive in your manner; in fact when you
peered at me through the lenses of your granny glasses as I
stepped off the elevator behind you into the lobby last
Saturday (having had to cancel my usual Thursday appointment), your gaze felt purely aleatory, as if my cheek had
been brushed by the down of some wind-tossed chicklet. No

wonder your parents want to keep you away from life's crap shoot, safe behind the mahogany and plate glass of Rosekranz and Rosekranz.

Yes Auntie, I'm afraid I overheard the discussion you were having with your mother and father last weekend as the three of you walked to lunch at the 2nd Street Cafe. I know you want to apply to art school, to Pratt, Cooper Union, and the Rhode Island School of Design, and that the last is your preference because your painting teacher at the Jewish Community Center told you that the aesthetic of the RISD program was the closest to your own emerging artistic sensibility, although I don't think nearness is the only factor governing your preference—I think "farness" (from pater and mater) is probably a strong determinant as well. And I also know that your parents oppose your plan, although they did not go so far (or should I say near) as to forbid it. Rather, your mother set her still full lips in a firm line while your father raked his slender jeweler's fingers through his wiry and still ruddy hair, flattening it back from his temples with his palms, as if in taming it he could tame you, too. Finally, I know what they would prefer: not only for you to stay home but to become the newest adept of the craft your family mastered generations ago in Lauscha, Germany, the historical home of glass eyes.

I know all this, and I can understand your desire to escape the life they assumed you would want to live: a life dedicated to the restoration of symmetry in the human gaze. You see yourself chained to an existence of making eyes, condemned like the chicken to forever lay eggs, and you balk. Oh sure, the craft serves a noble cause, to rectify the imbalances inflicted by the vagaries of fate, those wayward rubberbands, escaping upholstery springs, dive-bombing pelican beaks, but is it fair for your parents to ask you to consecrate your talent before you've even had a chance to realize it, to become a Sister of Mercy to the ocularly impaired when you've never even tasted an oyster?

No, it's not fair, if you believe that it is a question of either/or, if you subscribe to the notion that you can become either a great painter or an ocularist. But what if I tell you that you can become both, and not only that you can become both but that each art could feed the other, in a kind of aesthetic symbiosis? The idea that your painting skills could nourish the eyeballs has no doubt occurred to you; one need only think of that shiny seashell of acrylic as a miniature canvas, upon which all your knowledge of color, form and perspective could surely be brought to bear to create tiny ophthalmic chef d'oeuvres. Or as your pop put it the other day, a good eyeball is a work of art. But have you considered the relationship between the ocularist's art and the painter's the other way around, that the painting could in fact become a kind of eye? When I ask you to consider this possibility, I am, of course, not asking you to conceive of anything so literal as an image of a giant eye; rather, I am suggesting that the pursuit of a career in ocular science could encourage you to think differently about painting, to "see" the potential of the canvas to gaze back.

Sharp little thing that you are, Auntie Maim, you may at this moment be protesting that the well-made artificial eye is not to see but to be believed. And that is true (although no doubt the relentless progress of science and technology will someday render it capable of both veracity and sight). However, I counter that belief is a powerful thing and submit that even the experienced ocularist, who knows all too well that the finished eye is nothing but a laborious composite of hard acrylic, excelsior yellow, burnt sienna, Watchung red, and cobalt blue oil paints, clear polymer and scarlet embroidery thread, still cannot help but be swept up by the exclamation of the satisfied customer ("you found my eye!"), still cannot help but to feel, examining that same customer's redoubled gaze, that another one of the soul's windows, temporarily closed for repairs, has been opened. Given the strength of that feeling, why shouldn't it carry over to other arts? Who is better prepared than the ocularist, due to the analogy between eye and canvas that her craft cannot fail to educe, to intuit the truth in painting, that the work does not exist simply to surrender itself to our gaze but also to give us a hard stare in return? Oh Anti-Maim, you can do whatever you want with your life, become whomever you please, but before you turn your back on your parents' profession please consider whether in choosing the one career path over the other, you've deprived yourself of a certain depth of field.

Of course you must be wondering (for clearly you are a perceptive creature) what prompts this exhortation. And of course I understand that I cannot hope to persuade you to follow my advice without being honest about my motivation. So time to admit that I do want to see the Rosekranz reputation for making the best falsies in town live on. For your grandfather and then your father and mother used to make eyes for (and at) a very dear friend of mind. But now your parents are passing their visual prime, having both become a bit farsighted (as you must know, the best ocularists, like the best lacemakers, are nearsighted). And while my friend long ago ceased to wear an eye and took up a patch instead, she might some day desire symmetry again—at which point I'd like to know she can still find a decent peeper.

If my friend ever wishes for a new eye, I want you to be the one to make it. But why should you oblige? To be sure, I've made a good case for "why" above. Admittedly, however, that argument is rather abstract and perhaps overly reliant on concepts such as "aesthetic symbiosis" that at this stage in your young life have no experiential correlates to give them weight. No, now I'm thinking that if I want to persuade you to pursue an ocular career, then I need to appeal not to your brain but to your heart. Yes, it is the latter organ that I need to win over, and to do that I need to show Barbara to you, to let you see her through my words. And who knows, maybe you'll feel her looking back.

So, my dear Auntie de Maim, let me transport you.
Imagine the Zeitgeist wrapping her long and timely arms
around you and carrying you back almost twenty years, to
February of 1967, over ten years before you were even born.
Imagine that she drops you (gently) in a snowbank in the
middle of a small lakeside town in upstate New York. You are
lying on your back, and so the first view you have is of the
hills that rise up beyond the vanishing point of Main Street,
the white frosted hills that hold the village and the lake
beyond in a sweetly secluding glacial bowl. Thus it happens
that you hear my Barbara before you see her, hear her soft
and rather monotonous voice insisting on a dolly. "We need a
dolly," she's saying, "we've got to have a dolly." And because
there's something flat and mechanical in the timbre of that
voice, as if one could activate it by pulling a string like the
one attached to the back of a popular talking doll of the
period, Chatty Cathy, you might think it is referring to a
children's toy made to resemble a small person. However,
when you raise yourself up on your elbows, powder snow
sliding beneath the collar of the down parka I've so thoughtfully zipped you into and down your back, collecting in a
small thrilling pool at the base of your spine, and peer over in
the direction of the voice, you see two young women much
too old to play with dolls leaning against the open tailgate of
a pickup truck, peering at a canvas wrapped block the size of
a large cow (or horse, since you've probably never seen a
cow) lying in the bed.

"OK," the taller of the two young women (c'est moi)
replies, a classic redhead with the cheekbones of a Hepburn
and the smirk of Bacall, in a green plaid mohair car coat. "I'll
see what I can do. Maybe they've got one over at Krazy
Tom's."

She trudges off through the tire-churned snow to the
furniture store on the other side of Main, leaving you to
regard the shorter woman, a compact little figure in a scarlet
turban hat (a genuine Mr. John I'd recently bought for her at

Saks) and a dark fur jacket which you'll notice, as she circles back to the cab and crawls inside, has two odd little notches in the back hem, like the cuts fishermen make in the tails of lobsters too small to keep. Through the rear window you can see her face in profile, apparently intent on something before her on the seat, and at this point it must strike you, as the glass provides both focus and distance, that she is exquisite. High bezel of cheekbone, polished point of nose, sleek plane of jaw—all are facets of the brilliantly cut head set on its supple stem of a neck, a head which, perhaps feeling your look, she suddenly lifts and turns in your direction. And as she does, she turns the full force of her gaze upon you, a gaze which in its fullness is no more than half a gaze, since where the right eye should be there is only a patch. Only a patch even though the dear girl possesses a gem of a prosthesis, thanks to your grandfather, who was able to match the matchless topaz of the remaining orb perfectly. For at least a week now, however, she's been sporting her little black cup; when I asked her the other day where her lovely falsie had gone she simply smiled and winked at me with the only eye she had to wink.

At any rate if she seems to be looking at you, she doesn't see you. Her sight for the time being is focused inward, leaving you free to stare at beauty under glass from your divan of snow. And as you stare, you gradually register the noises around you (for unlike beauty you cannot live in a bell jar), sounds of tapping, clinking, chinking and scraping, along with the murmur of voices—"a little more," "carve from underneath," "not so much," "try hot water," "careful." At last curiosity wins out over fixation and, turning your back to the pickup, you climb out of your snowbank onto the sidewalk. From the Hall of Fame past Lippit's Jewelry Store, snow sculptures line the sides of Main Street, frozen chunks of local waters fashioned into not so fantastic shapes—a hand making a peace sign, a magic mushroom, a unicorn, a love bug, a guitar, a Buddha, a melon-breasted snow woman in an

itsy bitsy teeny weeny ice bikini, etc., and so on—into the
familiar forms and motifs of the era. Gelid clichés, although
each artiste believes he or she has created an original work
worthy of first prize in the Cooperstown Winter Carnival
Snow Sculpting Contest. Indeed, these masterpieces were
probably months in the making, beginning with the tired idea
conceived during the course of some sleepless August night
or long autumnal drive to Albany over the hills of Route 20,
followed by a long gestation of surreptitious sketching and
clandestine clay modelling, until finally, the opening day of
the Carnival arrived and the labor of love began. Months in
the making, and during those months you can bet that not one
of the creators ever considered that his or her creation did not
deserve to be born, that perhaps there were enough peace
signs and love bugs in the world already. But that's nearly
always the way it is in these provincial backwaters, where
tired seeds find insensible new muck in which to take root.
Oblivious to the greater world beyond, which nevertheless
seeps in via television, newspapers and <u>Life Magazine</u>, the
citizens of such small towns are condemned to recreate it, in a
duller, weaker form. For the notion that isolation breeds
originality is, like immaculate conception, largely a myth.

Largely a myth, but not completely. There are exceptions. Giotto amongst his flock of sheep, Warhol in the
wasteland of western PA, and of course, the inimitable
Barbara Salzmann, whom you've already met in the paragraph above. Although even in each of these cases, genius did
not remain in provincial seclusion. Giotto made his Florentine
debut under the tutelage of Cimabue, while Warhol and
Salzmann simply crashed, spectacularly, into the Manhattan
art world. But after three years, Barbara, like the mysterious
guest who arrives with bells on her toes but then slips out
soundlessly at the roaring height of the party, returned upstate
to marry my brother. Hidden behind the purdah of young wife
and motherhood (no doubt she was already pregnant her last
semester of art school, as my niece appeared a mere seven

months after the June wedding), her talent invisible to our
mittened townies toiling away up and down the length of
Main, it is as if she'd never left. Oh sure, she's picked up a
new shine down in the Big Apple, so that people seem to
notice for the first time what a "looker" she is (even as they
fail to consider the nominative possibility of the term), and to
consider her an even more valuable cocktail party asset than
my brother, the dazzling "Jem" Vanderzee; however, nobody
at this point (with the patronizing exception of my dear old
dad, who'd sent her to Pratt on a Vandezee scholarship)
recognizes that she can do as well as be.

But to return to our little upstate tableau, here you are,
standing on the sidewalk in front of the Smart Shop, the dress
shop of choice of Cooperstown's fashion intelligentsia,
breathing in, for there's no alternative, the sharp winter air,
sensitive artist's hands retracted into the goretex sleeves of
your parka (so sorry I forgot the mittens), eyes once again on
the motionless woman in the car. And then there's a voice
calling from across the street, "Don't forget to bring it back
when you're done," the clatter of rattletrap wood and steel as
I reappear dragging a dolly through a narrow gap in the
snowbank, and the slam of a truck door as Barbara jumps out
of the cab and circles around to the bed.

She pulls down the tailgate, dropping it on the crest of
the bank where just moments ago you were reclining, then
turns to me and says, "You know, we should probably find a
site first."

"Find a site?" I ask realizing I'd assumed we'd just
dump her piece in the snow where we'd backed up, using the
dolly as a kind of slide. However, as you know, for the artist
the question of context, of frame, is crucial. Just as an eye
should fit its socket, so the work should fit its setting. When it
doesn't, the look of the thing falls askew. And so while I'm
not certain what it is that Barbara doesn't like about this
particular spot—whether it's the parrot-bright colors of the
Lilly Pullitzer resort wear in the window behind us, or the

shadow cast by the upper apartments of the building overhead, or perhaps the nearly finished sculpture of a
volkswagen beetle adorned with what appear to be actual
New York license plates identifying the LUV BUG to our
right—I respect her judgment.

With arms wrapped around her furred chest, she begins
walking down the sidewalk. I join her and you follow, at a
discrete distance. The other sculptors—hepped up teeny
boppers, bored housewives, prowling playboys—steal
snatches of her as we pass—a tuft of minky hair, a snippet of
rose flushed cheek, a scrap of black patch—to hoard away or
bring out and compare under the dim lights of our local
watering hole, the Pit ("what happened to her eye?") then
cover the theft with a wave or a banality: "Cold enough for
you?" I roll my eyes, but Barbara floats along with it all, "Oh
yes, it certainly is," even tossing out petals of praise—"Nice
horn you got there, Harry," "I like the V between the fingers,
June," "Hey Patti, that is too cool." A few people ask if I'm
planning to build a sculpture, but no one bothers to put the
question to Barbara, even though she was the one who went
to Pratt on scholarship, not I. And of course no one considers
that her compliments might actually be critiques; it's simply
assumed that one so pretty must be artless as well.

She stops under the marquee of the movie theater
(which nowadays announces BASEBALL SOUVENIRS &
ICE CREAM ad nauseum, but back then sparkled with an
ever shifting arrangement of Hollywood stars. Although on
the particular day I've spirited you back to, the arrangement
is admittedly rather familiar—Audrey Hepburn and George
Peppard in Breakfast at Tiffany's—having already adorned
this particular theater entrance at least six times since 1961).
Hands on hips, she backs up to the curb, where she squints
her eye at the brick facade above the marquee, at the golden
letters exhorting "Smalley's Theater… Let's-Go!"

"Yes," Barbara says. "Let's go get him and put him
here."

"OK," I say. "We can just drive the pick-up down and back it in."

But then, as Barbara points out, there's a Mars candy truck parked in the way, with a row of Country Squire station wagons flanking each side. While the upper part of Main past Pioneer is nearly free of cars, this section seems to be packed on both sides of the street, no doubt due to the fact that Smalley's is serving Breakfast, again, this afternoon. Clearly we won't get any closer than we are. Good thing we've got the dolly.

Yes, fortunately we have the dolly, the back end of which we hoist up onto the bank behind the pickup, letting the wheels sink into the snow to secure it. Now that we have a kind of ramp descending from the back of the truck, the trick is to slide Barbara's piece onto this ramp while at the same time keeping it from crashing into the sidewalk. I wipe my dripping nose with mohair sleeve and look around. You are perched on the brass railing in front of the Smart Shop, but are too thin, too intangible to be of help. What we need is muscle, and suddenly it materializes, as my brother James, along with his buddy Bucko Bielaski, steps out of Vanderzee's Wine and Spirit Shop and starts walking toward us. James, my oldest competitor. James, who boldly went where no man had gone before and still got the girl. James, who swaggers like he owns the planet. James, who nevertheless lately has begun to look expendable, more like one of those fellows who get zapped with a laser gun in the first half hour of the show than the captain of his enterprise.

And Bucko. Bucko the boyhood sidekick, who in the meantime has acquired a newly unzappable air. Perhaps we can attribute this to the fact that it is out of the bucolic snows of the Bielaski Demesne that Barbara has created her master-piece. Bucko, a doctoral candidate in art history at Columbia without, as yet, any position to milk but his standing as heir to his parents' dairy farm, has not only been lending my darling the back pasture of his parents' dairy farm but his services as a sculptural assistant. (Forgive me Auntie. I'd forgotten about Bucko when I claimed above that no one in the village recognized that Barbara could "do as well as be," no doubt a convenient lapse. We leave out what we do not wish to recollect.)

But to return to the matter at hand, now we've got the zappable James and the newly unzappable Bucko lending their manly arms to our cause. Soon the mysterious canvas-wrapped oblong (which I would guess to be at least eight feet long) has been tilted onto the dolly, slid without mishap into position and secured with lengths of rope Barbara has stashed in the cab. With Barbara and James (who has taken the handle from Bucko, insisting on his place) pulling the dolly and Bucko and I on either side giving a steadying hand as well as carrying the shovels, we rumble slowly down the sidewalk, wheels alternately catching and skidding on clots of packed snow and patches of ice. Just below the noise of the cart, I hear James asking, "Where's the baby?" but then the din completely rolls over Barbara's reply.

We halt in front of the movie theater and, following Barbara's directions, shovel loads of snow from the snow-bank to the space directly below the marquee, then begin forming and packing the pile into a kind of catafalque. As we work I can feel the looks, but when I shoot my gaze back at our neighbor to the right, at fat Patti Fleischer (né Holden) who lived in Okinawa for a year with her doctor hubby, she drops her own and busies herself with smoothing her Buddha's belly. Yes Ant-eye, everyone is watching us, but when I turn to catch them, their faces become as smooth, as bland, as the snowbanks. Undoubtedly everyone is wonder-ing, yet when Barbara declares the mound sufficient, and with my brother and his friend Bucko's help pulls the cart around to one end and slowly begins pushing and sliding the great canvas wrapped object onto its dais of snow, no one gathers round. At the moment, however, that Barbara begins to loosen the ropes securing the fabric, all sounds of artistic endeavor—

the tapping, clinking, chinking and scraping—suddenly cease. A hush as sudden and thunderous as an avalanche falls all around us as she pulls the ropes away, and echoes in the icy air as she proceeds, slowly, slowly, to peel back the canvas.

To reveal…what? Antie, you probably think that the suspense I've created in this account of that day in early February, 1967, is simply a stratagem to hold your interest, that yours truly could not have participated in the collective sense of anticipation at the moment of the unveiling since she already knew what was under the canvas cover. And I suppose it is a stratagem in that I do know now what Barbara was concealing. I didn't however, know then, and so the ignorance I've attempted to recreate via the present tense was not, at the time, feigned. For Barbara had kept very quiet about the preceding days at Bucko's farm. All she'd told me was that she was carving her sculpture from solid ice, excised from the frozen surface of Lake Otsego, rather than molding it, like everyone else, from snow made solid by alternating applications of water with overnight freezing. Further, when we'd loaded her work, with the help of a couple of the Bielaskis' hired hands, onto the bed of the pick-up, it had already been under wraps.

So…slowly, slowly Barbara is lifting the canvas and the first thing we (you and I) see is a rough hewn wedge of ice fanning out into ten thick digits which, as this lightest of labors advances, we soon recognize to be a pair of feet. These rather impressionistically carved feet are fixed to thick ankles which flow with surprising grace into slightly rotated calves, which in turn slowly, slowly clot into knees then give way again to a vast tract of thighs until at last, cradled between their upper parts, we come to a schlong as long and thick as your forearm. As your eyes linger on this anatomical impossibility, let me step for a moment outside the frame and explain what it is you are seeing. After all, lacking roots in Otsego County and a familial fund of upstate lore (my father was a respected folk historian as well as a reconstructive surgeon),

you cannot share the realization I was in fact having during
that moment in early February of 1967. For as the canvas
slowly, slowly receded, revealing inch by inch that unmistak-
able morphology, it dawned on me that I was seeing an exact,
if somewhat scaled down, replica of the Cardiff Giant. But of
course you don't know the Cardiff Giant from the Jolly
Green, and so I must elaborate further.

The Cardiff Giant was the brainchild of George Hull, a
nineteenth-century hoaxer of the caliber if not the stature of
P.T. Barnum. Playing on the public's interest in both Darwin's
newborn theory of evolution and the hoary Biblical assertion
that "there were giants in the earth in those days" (see Gen-
esis 6:4), Hull hired two Chicago sculptors to chisel a colossus out of a block of gypsum. In early November of 1868,
after "aging" the 10'4" statue with sand and sulfuric acid to
create the appearance of a "petrified man," Hull shipped it out
of Chicago on a midnight train to Cardiff, N.Y., where it
received a clandestine burial on a cousin's farm. Almost a
year later, on October 16, 1869, the giant was "discovered"
by a team of men hired to dig a well behind the barn. Within
no time, folk from every corner of New England were
streaming to Cardiff, paying 50 cents per head to enter a
small darkened tent and see, served up in a shallow tureen of
turf, the naked magnificence of their fossilized forebear. And
now a hundred years later, after a long and mostly disrepu-
table side-show career (for the "petrified man" was exposed
as a fraud within two months of its disinterment), the Cardiff
Giant rested in peace at the Cooperstown Farmer's Museum,
the gift of my father, who had rediscovered him in a rumpus
room in Des Moines, to the savvier citizens of modernity.

Well Antsy (for you must be getting a little impatient
with all this digression), when I recognized the Giant, I also
recognized Barbara's genius. In creating an exact, if slightly
scaled down model of the infamous 19th-century hoax, she
stood to capture first prize not just on the basis of technical
excellence but also on the basis of originality. For if there was

no actual Cardiff Giant, no genuine progenitor, then no one
could claim (as they could in the case of Patti Fleischer's
Buddha) that Barbara's Giant was a copy of anything. To
illustrate, picture two photographic prints derived from the
same negative, recording one original image, such as a baby
in her mother's arms. Now let us go one step further and not
only say there was never a negative but there was never an
original image—how then can one print be a copy of another?

So, stepping back inside the frame, I am certain that
Barbara's Giant is one of a kind and that it will steal the show.
Certain, until I feel someone standing behind me and turn to
recognize Dave Zeller, chief water boy at our local watering
hole, as well as stereotypist and printer's devil for the weekly
rag, and now arbiter of the 27th Annual Snow Sculpting
Contest. Yes, it is Dave Zeller with a ridiculous plaid tam-o'-
shanter perched on his flat top, green pom pom an accidental
complement to his big red nose, a man who couldn't respond
to genius if she sat squirming on his lap. And ruefully, I recall
that I am partly to blame for his appointment. Earlier, when
my father (who with his old friend Charles Boyd always
chose all the judges and referees for the events at the carnival) had asked me if I had any suggestions about who should
decide the Snow Sculpting Contest, I'd replied, thinking back
to the pathetic entries of previous years, that any bozo would
do. I had not foreseen that Barbara would enter the show, or
now, that this clown would be judging the fate of her work.

"Hung like a horse…," Dave comments. Then he clears
his throat, pulls at his wattle, and asks Barbara, who has
ceased to unveil and simply stands holding the canvas in her
mittened hands, " See the rest, little lady?"

"Why sure," Barbara replies, yellow eye glowing up at
Dave through dark lashes. But he stares off over her head in
the direction of the A & P across the street as she once again
begins to denude the iceman.

Slowly, slowly the right hand slides into view, fingers
splayed over the sunken stomach, tips just brushing the

jutting pelvic bone. Then the ribs, one, two, three, four, five.
Dave clears his throat again, looks at his watch. But Barbara
resumes the divestment at the same majestic pace as before,
and I'm sure she's blowing whatever chance she had, a
feeling I see reflected in Bucko, who is actually wringing his
hands, and even in James, who is biting his lip just the way he
used to in front of the TV set when it looked like Spanky was
gonna get it. Yes, I'm sure she's blowing it as now the smooth
curves of the pectorals swell up, then gradually roll down to
the broad bar of the shoulders. As the thick bull's neck
succumbs to the firm chin. As a subtle smile, almost imperceptible, flits about the lips like the ghost of some long
forgotten joke.

"Okey doke," says Dave, "got it. The Cardiff Giant.
Yep looks just like 'im." He starts to walk away, then
stops—arrested by my gasp of astonishment. For as Barbara
pulls back the last swatch of canvas, I see something is
buried deep behind the Giant's left lid—something which at
first I take for a stone or a shell, and then suddenly realize is
an eye. And not just any eye, but Barbara's eye, that pearly
nugget with its nucleus of amber, floating in a milky depth
of ice like an embryo in utero. If it were thirty years later,
Damien Hirst's cow parts suspended in formaldehyde would
come to mind. But it's not, which means we must give
credit where it is due and recognize my friend for the
visionary she was.

"I thought you said you lost it," James says, sounding
hurt.

"I did, but then I found it again," Barbara replies,
smoothing the Giant's great dome of a forehead with her
mitten. Bucko looks on smiling, rocking on the heels of his
gumboots.

In the meantime, Dave has retraced his steps and is now
down on his haunches, staring intently at the eye. "It's like
it's lookin out at yer, but at the same time it's sayin
'sayonara,'" he mumbles.

And indeed, Anti-Maim, as you step over to see for yourself, you find that he is almost right. The eye peers out at you, yet also recedes, draws away, as if tunneling inward. At the same time, however, it is not simply scooting off but casting a backward glance that invites you to follow.

Will you? I dearly hope so.

In the meanwhile, our little sojourn in a small town in upstate New York, circa February of 1967, must end, for I fear, seeing your cold bleached face (which has itself begun to appear as if carved of snow), that you are frostbitten. Yes, our visit is over, but perhaps at some later date, when the blood has suffused your cheeks again and the sap of art flows once more, we shall return. For now, I simply leave you with this: Yes, Barbara did win the Snow Sculpting Contest that year, for finally, as the judge himself put it, "I couldn't get that eye outter my mind."

With affection,
Judith Vanderzee

What a rush as the car rounds the bend and her A-frame jolts the woodland scene mainlining Mother Nature with high-sucrose pink and poison-apple green, what a rush of not-so-sweet memories. CAUTION says the yellow sign at the end of the driveway but it's too late I've already crashed.

Amazing house. It's like Handel and Garbo on acid.

I brake to a stop, don't bother to correct Skip—it's not my job to fix his fairy tales. The tercel shudders as I turn the keys, then dies. Will it start again? Don't think about that. Focus instead on pink and green gingerbread just choke it down and we'll be out of here soon enough.

Are you OK?

Yeah I'm fine. It just feels weird to see this place again...

But I'm not fine as we get out of the car and walk up a muddy path criss-crossed by paw prints that scrawl wildly out over the thin crusted snow like the scribbling of some immensely angry child. I'm not fine as I look away from her house toward the woods and see purple and yellow crocuses clustered beneath the trees, livid against the patches of white. What if there's nothing at all in Juju's letters about the Homer?

Get the hell out of here, a voice barks from within the A-frame as we step up onto the redwood deck.

Unfamiliar pink-velvet curtains hang behind the sliding glass doors—she must have gotten them later because surely I'd remember how they make the front of the house look blind like a giant eyeless socket. I drop behind Skip lean back against the fancy pink and green fretwork of the railing feel it stand firm even as it strains against my weight, holding me like a web. Holding me like a web as what I remember becomes entangled with what I can imagine. Yes cuz I can imagine you as capable of anything but then that's not exactly fair is it—seeing that you're no longer in a position to defend yourself? So while I can hear you announcing that Duchess Semjanov was going to do our portraits and no whining because we were lucky two very lucky girls and I can see you squeezing our knees when we wouldn't get out of the car impressing our flesh with florid red petals, I can't know that you condoned what followed.

The glass door slides open just a crack and a white head pokes through flesh-colored velvet reddened eyes peering at us through horn rim glasses.

I'm sorry, I thought you were someone else.

The door slides back further the curtains part and there's the Duchess looking every inch a gentleman from the foulard around her neck to the wingtips on her feet.

I apologize for the rude reception but as we all know it is only by not paying one's bills that one lives on in the memory of the commercial classes.

So you've got something of mine?

She fingers the knot in her foulard, rings glinting: *Well...yeeess dear. But why don't you come in and warm your bones first?*

Skip slips through parted flesh-pink driven perhaps by the monkey on his back to seek whatever heat there is within leaving me like the man in the yellow hat with nothing to do but follow.

On the other side of unremembered pink everything's familiar even hackneyed—dusty Boho charm piled on like layers of petticoats or levels of subterfuge hiding the hardness beneath. Twenty years later and heaps of nomad cushions embroidered felt donkey saddles and bukhara carpets still cover the cold flagstone floor as musk still seeps from the clay incense ball on the Turkish brass table mingling with the faint scents of bodies both human and canine as it drifts up into the Ghandi bedspreads and Persian killims that still billow from the vaulting ceiling and spirals in the shaft of sun streaming down from the skylight like the glory of god, a light which nevertheless does not lift the gloom of the back wall where the crimson candles on the black oak credenza still cast lascivious shadows on the gold-framed forgery of the *Odalisque.* When I was a kid that painting used to make me think of things soft and chewy like marshmallows and Turkish delight.

Great place, Skip says patting his pouch. No I don't think he had a chance to shoot up before Zeller came back and kicked us out but he better not be planning to do it here. I look at him hard mouth *no*—that should do it until we get back in the car then I'll pull over somewhere. He drops his eyes yes master whatever you say master he better not be humoring me as he starts pulling off his jean jacket which is slightly tight across the shoulders. No he better not be humoring me but I do love that little jacket my favorite of all his thrift-shop rags and credit card riches cuz when he takes it off he has to really scrunch his right shoulder which makes the lines of his torso all the more spectacular when he thrusts the shoulder back to slip his arm out of the sleeve. And I can see that Duchess appreciates the effect of the jacket as well as I watch her stare at how the fabric of his thermal t-shirt pulls across his chest delineating pecs he says he inherited from his father who was almost an Olympic gymnast pecs like the curving lips of calla lilies. As she reaches for his coat her lips move—maybe she'll ask him to pose for her he'd make such a great subject she could even give him an actual lily to hold. But nothing comes out.

Great place, he repeats scratching his arms and stomping his boots leaving grids of icy mud on the hemp mat. Duchess's eyes blink hard.

Thank you. Now why don't you take off the clodhoppers?
My feet will freeze.
Oh no they won't—I'll give you some nice handsome slippers.

Duchess trots over to the credenza pulls open a drawer leaving me to record the curve of his back the roll of his deltoid as he yanks a boot over his heel. Yeah she could give him a real lily—though I suppose that after what's his name he also did the bullwhip in the ass photos that would be a cliché. On the other hand so are young girls and roses and that didn't stop her from blanketing our naked bodies with a bushel of pink and white rose petals. Funny how I can remember that much the colors the staging even the feel of the flowers on my skin. But not the rest. Maybe it'd be different if they'd been forgetmenots.

Here she is again cradling two pairs of curly toed slippers like something out of the Arabian Nights fine for the boudoir boy but not for me I'm a gal on the go. Cuz it's time to get out of here I'll just run right over her with my big black hooves if she tries to stop me. Yup it's giddeyup and out the door time…but whoa…what about my knapsack?

Try these Stella. I'm sure you'll find them more comfortable than those elevator shoes. Which is not to say I don't think you're wonderful, walking around with your head in the clouds.

Wow these are actually pretty nice look at the beads and embroidery like something a Scheherazade would wear gorgeous even. Maybe I should just try humoring her putting my feet in her shoes for a while the old witch is probably lonely. Just for half an hour or so though cuz no way I'm gonna sit around here forever yakking for her amusement. Yeah might as well slide into the Duchess's lovely silken sheaths. I can imagine Aunt Juju with all her expensive boutique clothes wearing slippers like these her fancy feathers Oma called them which she gave to my mother when they got too bedraggled but never shoes cuz her feet were too small.

Come my dears. It's too draaafty to stay in here.

And mine are too big my heels hanging out the back so that I have to do a kind of tiptoe shuffle as she leads us across the room through the door down a dim low-ceilinged hall. I don't remember this part at all.

I don't think I've ever seen this part of your house.

Certainly you have, Stella. But memory takes so many twists and turns it is easy to lose one's way.

Wish I had a pocketful of white pebbles or even dry crumbs although something always comes along and eats them up. Just have to keep in mind this is only an A-frame it can't be that complicated to get back the hallway is straight even if memory isn't. If only I knew which door we came through. So many what's behind them, what does she do with all these rooms?

This used to be my studio but now I rent a space in town, she says turning a knob. The smell of wood smoke spills out.

Skip slinks in behind her blowing me an eggy kiss as she walks over to a window and pulls moss green drapes back a few inches just enough to reveal a glimpse of sun but not to dispel the gloom. I remain standing in the doorway wondering what it is now because the place is cluttered with hideous rough-hewn chairs and tables that look like they belong in a dank dark forest props for some necromantic lawn party, some Walpurgisnacht wiener roast. But there's no cauldron bubbling in the grate only a roaring fire so maybe the room is simply her study—book cases extend from floor-to-ceiling on either side of the fireplace and a green-shaded brass desk lamp sits on an antique drop-leaf table the one piece of furniture that isn't made of twigs or a cross-section of tree-trunk.

Please make yourselves at home. She motions me to a fire-side chair woven of saplings still bristling with the original bark. I sit down but it's all too easy to envision being caught in woody arms all too easy to imagine a person being trapped here for a hundred years until the flesh has fallen from her bones and the briars have woven through her ribs.

Skip slowly lowers himself into the chair on the other side of the fireplace twigs creaking as he leans back. *I love it—soooo Ralph Lauren.*

I can feel him trying to catch my eye but I'm keeping it on Duchess who's now bending in front of the fire poking at the logs. The shadowy hollows under her cheekbones seem strangely deep and soft in the flickering light...furred. And now what's that sound growling low and deep.... Shit...

Shut-up, Freud.

OK it's not her it's some sort of animal in the corner over there two animals two narrow white skulls peering up out of piles of bones—no they're only baskets. Only baskets with two pairs of coal dark eyes set in narrow white skulls staring out as I stare back. As I stare back...and see two demon dogs two drooling death's heads snapping at our heels. How could I forget it's not her it's worse. Oh sure they look all languid the way the bigger one just sighed and dropped its head back in the basket like it was too heavy for its long white neck. But I'm not fooled. Yeah I can see these fuckers even if they're not the same ones they can't be after all these years chasing us through the woods can see little ears flattened back needle-nosed muzzles gaping like crocodile jaws. And I can hear teeth clicking like camera shutters.

Or was it a camera shutter clicking like teeth? Suddenly there are two fleet pale blurs racing through shadowy undergrowth two fleet pale blurs but then the image goes dark like an emulsion of silver halides under bright light, indiscernible like a woodland path after the crumbs have been eaten. No I can't see it and I've lost my way cuz memory takes so many twists and turns Duchess said and now she's going out the door leaving us here with those hellhounds.

Turkish coffee, regular coffee, or tea?

Turkish coffee please, Skip pipes from his chair.

Sweet, extra sweet, or dental dam?

Dental dam? Oh I get it—dental dam for sure!

Stella?

Regular coffee, with cream. No sugar.

She looks disappointed with my choice as she turns away into the black of the hall but too bad it's regular coffee in a regular mug cuz I discovered when I was pint-sized that good things don't necessarily come in small packages. Cuz three tiny porcelain cups once sat steaming on the dimpled surface of a drop-leaf table. *Drink me.* Three dolly cups thin as egg shells frail as trust found by two young girls who each took a furtive sip and discovered prematurely the taste of bittersweet. One sip must have been enough. I don't think we stayed around to learn who those tiny cups were for or to see the rich brown sludge beneath the acrid brew revealed. Yes I'm sure we took off as soon as we tasted a bitterness so deep not all the sugar in the world could mask it. Surely we shot out of there as if at any moment the floor boards might explode beneath our feet. Surely I wish I could be sure.

Dental dam, that's great, Skip says as he drags his chair closer to the fire. *She's wonderful, like a cross between Truman Capote and Edith Bunker.*

Yeah, right. He's pronounced it so that it rhymes with goat and I think of a photograph I saw once of old Tru sitting with the young Kate Harrington and looking with his big round sunglasses and bloated blackclad body like a fly that just crawled out of the sugar bowl. But then I could never stomach Breakfast at Tiffany's the poison creampuffs they fed women back then if my mom hadn't swallowed maybe she'd still be alive and as for Edith Bunker well all you had to do was look in her eyes to see the only thing that prevented her from shooting her husband in cold blood was the script.

But let him discover for himself the old witch hiding behind the campy grandma act the gin beneath the gingerbread. I don't owe him anything let him find his way alone even though he can't see the forest for the trees.

I sit back in my chair and stare down at my jewelly slippers. The tops are striped with beaded bands of bright coral topaz and jet black colors you'd see on a venomous snake or insect. I never should've come in here—should've made her give me my pack at the door.

Hey what's the matter Stell? You know I'm here for you.

Is he serious does he really think he's any help? I can't really see his expression in the shadows of his chair only his white teeth floating in what is probably meant to be a reassuring smile.

I can feel him watching me though with a gaze steady as a dog's. Forever faithful in a world where grins hang about without the cat. But fido's eyes can't see me if I get up and go look at that old photograph hanging in the corner beyond his chair.

Against a background of thick leaves a girl in a hooded cape stands holding a basket one booted foot in front of the other. Have I seen this photo yes I've seen this photo I'm sure and then I'm not. I know that I know it and then again I don't as what I see pulls the rug out from under what I remember. Did the eyes glower out of the pale face like that were the lips so close to smirking? Did the thick sausage curls tumble forward so riotously out of the dark cowl was the cloth actually dangling out of the basket exposing dear grandmother's rolls to the vapors of the rotting undergrowth? And was her weight so clearly on the back foot so that it's obvious that she's not stepping out of the forest but inviting me to follow her back in?

One of the dogs hums in its sleep a sound that steadily rises thins and shreds into a series of little shrieks.

That's your Aunt Judith you know.

I turn and there's Duchess standing in the doorway holding a big brass tray of steaming drinks her lips curled in a lupine smile. Something rustles at the back of my mind flashes jewelly scales then slithers away as I walk back over to my chair and sit down. Duchess sets her tray on the tree trunk that stands between my chair and Skip's.

My Ana had one of those. Skip stares at the tray like it's some sort of miracle.

Is that so dear? How nice. I bought this in Cappadocia—in Turkey.

She kneels down rings glittering as she traces over the etchings in the brass with a yellowed fingertip, over little lines like bird footprints, hop hop hop. It's writing—possibly Greek—but then what was it doing in Turkey?

This tray tells the story of St. Onophruis. Do you know it? She's gazing over at Skip.

He shakes his head, pulls his feet up on the chair wraps his arms around his legs like it's story hour. I sip my coffee. Ugh why didn't I ask for sugar what was I trying to prove? What was I trying to prove that I'm not some sweet little sucker so the old witch won't look at me the way she's looking at Skip?

Onophruis was originally a woman, Onophruia, a ripe and comely woman bursting with beauty like a dusky bunch of grapes swaying under the noonday sun, about to fall, to fall but never falling, never falling but always swaying as the foxes stood below with watering mouths, waiting.

She lifts the tray from the tree stump table sets it behind her in front of the hearth then slowly unsteadily stands: *My legs fall sleep so easily in my dotage.* As she starts scraping the table over the bare wood floor the dogs leap up from their baskets shoot out of the room—like they know the script all too well know to leave before the show begins. I should do the same. Skip on the other hand is leaning forward half out of his chair eager to help the drama unfold but she waves him away dragging the tree trunk table over the floorboards over in front of the partially parted curtains. And now she climbs up on it starts to swing her hips in a slow heavy circle, arms curved up jewelly fingers fidgeting over her head. How weird is it a dance or a disease some kind of Parkinson's maybe I can't believe Skip is into this letting his head roll to the movement of her hips and he's not even high.

Never falling, never falling until at last the foxes grew tired of waiting and complained, yelped with dry parched mouths to the Lord above of the gross injustice of fruit that swung and swayed yet refused to fall, provokingly ripe yet profoundly out of reach.

Skip's head is rolling the flames in the fireplace are leaping like foxes over the hissing logs licking my leather coat with their heat this is really too much. I start to get up but Duchess sees waves her fingers at me and suddenly it's as if my legs don't belong to me as if she's got the strings some kind of hypnotic pull powered by the orbit of her sway.... My coat slides off my shoulders falls into a warm puddle of skin....

And the Lord assented and decreed that the grapes, that is, the woman, must be punished. But how?

Yes she's got the strings which she holds in one hand as she pauses for a moment adjusting her horn rims with the other and then straightening her foulard. I should try to stand up break the spell but it's already too late the swaying resumes.

But how? How to punish this woman who kept all her sweetness in reserve, who had never known want, who had always been satiated, replete with her own ripe self? Then finally it came to him: he would transform her into a man. And so it was that the Lord changed Onophruia into Onophruis so that he who had once been she could feel what it was like to want rather than to always be wanted, to want so badly he could die.

Something shifts and groans above our heads. Snow thunders down outside plunging the narrow strip of window with white but Duchess continues to swing her hips indifferent both to the disturbance and its cessation.

Onophruis repented, of course. Repented all his wicked womanish ways and resolved not to compound those with the offenses of man but rather to remove himself from temptation altogether. He banished himself to the Egyptian desert and lived for the rest of his days in a guano-plastered grotto, covering his shame with a loincloth of palm leaves and eating nothing but dates.

Duchess smiles at me slowly winks one true blue eye then sits down on the stump tucking her feet under her thighs like some false idol a fibbing buddha a mocking muffet on her tuffet. Or is she the spider who crouched down beside her? Surely I can stand up now the spell or trance whatever it was must be broken only my toes have started to throb inside the jewelled slippers, which suddenly feel oddly tight. Should I kick them off before they crush my feet before the bright bands of beads constrict like the scaly sides of a boa, like a big hand squeezing a small one?

Try to focus to see again what happened that day to see beyond the flowers. But all I can see is a bellows obscenely inching back and forth, copping the feel that isn't felt possessing without penetration.

The greyhounds trot back in over the bare wood threshold *clickety click clickety click* the one behind the other prancing past Skip and me like two cocky courtiers over to Duchess on her woody throne. The first dog is taller and a bit more solid than the second its sleek white back broken by a motley gray and black patch that could be shaped like Africa though I can't say for certain—geography has never been my strong suit. Red tongue dangling waggishly the dog lifts a paw and drops it heavily on Duchess's knee even as its whip tail stays tucked between its legs. The smaller dog pure white coat unsaddled by any continent watches with keen interest.

Duchess circles the dog's ears with the thumb and forefinger of each hand and peers into its eyes: *What my precious? What?* She pulls the dog's face close to her own: *OK, but you must first give me a kiss.*

The dog slides its tongue over Duchess's pursed lips then wrests it head away before I have time to gag. I can't help but think of you and Echo how Oma said he slept with you every night his purina-breath mingling with the vodka fumes as he lay with his head on the pillow next to yours. Yes he slept with you every night in your king-sized bed the only one allowed to stay all night. Wonder how she knew that...

Would you like a kiss?

I shake my head no but Skip nods even though I'm sure he once told me that angels won't visit a house with dogs in it.

Then purse your lips and make kissing sounds. Duchess turns to the smaller greyhound: *Dora, give the nice young man a kiss.*

Dora springs forward flies past me open-mouthed.

Ouch! It bit me on the lip!

Duchess walks over and with crossed arms and squinting eyes inspects Skip's face from each side and then the front. With one bony finger she lifts his upper lip exposing an eyetooth and a bit of pink gum: *That was only a taste, Skippy.*

That's it, time to go. And it's not because of Skip though I know it wasn't just a matter of tasting but of sighting as well. Let her shoot him, I don't care what develops. Let her fix him for good cuz he's a California boy a surface dude and nothing would make him happier.

I stand up thrust my arms through the sleeves of my leather jacket.

Yes you must go. But remember before you leave I want to give you something.

Right bitch. Why the hell do you think I came?

She hustles us along one hand pressed between Skip's shoulder blades the other firmly gripping my arm back down through the low dark corridor as the dogs slink along the walls like shadows. Why the sudden shift from wide-open welcome to what feels like an eviction as she shoves me over the threshold? Why do I care who knows what provokes an old witch to switch from hot to cold from Camels to Kools? She can go hex herself and I'm just grateful for the way space suddenly opens up as I step back into the main room.

Her hand drops from my arm as she pushes past the dogs swirling round her legs boiling to escape. She unlatches the front door and the dogs fly out barking madly in pursuit of god knows what. Then turning around she raises her hand palm facing outward, silently commanding us to wait.

She disappears back into the nether regions of the house and I find myself staring up at a skylight. What exactly am I waiting for—the descent of the Sangreal? Really I don't want no holy relics no sacred memories no memento moris no living legends and least of all no abreaction. Surely whatever happened here is history—herstory and yours. Dead and buried deep within the moldering folds of your brain, a treasure trove best unfound. Which is not to suggest that I'm forfeiting my claim to the family jewels: I still want that Homer.

But as soon as she returns with my knapsack I'm outta here. Where are the car keys in the pocket of my jacket no they're not oh fuck. Wait remember there's a hole in the corner of the pocket lining: yes here they are nestled in a fold of leather and acetate. And now I've got them snug in my palm it would be so easy just to walk through the door to skip out sans Skip who's snooping around over by the credenza I bet he won't even notice I'm gone.

How easy as I step toward the front door. And then I hear the dogs. Hear long deep howls uncoiling over the lawn expanding out to the edge of the wood circling round the house like enormous lassos roping space and reeling it into time so that what I remember suddenly falls backward into what I've forgotten and I can remember yesterday like it was today.

Sure and now I can see them—can see two little princesses undressing in the great hall of the Duchess's castle late one late spring afternoon the reflections of the candle flames flickering over pale smooth skin, disguising the tremors beneath. Yes I imagine you called us princesses and maybe prudes as well when we said we didn't want our pictures taken barenaked and especially not outside where bears could be watching from the woods and maybe even boys. Prunes and prisms you might've said first pursing your mouth like a piece of dried fruit and then stretching your lips wide—Ooooh Myyyyyy. What could we do but oblige? What could Anna and I do but each carry a big embroidered Turkish pillow out onto the lawn looking like ants carrying crumbs away from a picnic on the grass only we were going to one—n'est-ce pas? A picnic without anything to eat even though my stomach was probably rumbling just like it's rumbling now. Or is that the sound of Skip rummaging in the credenza?

Yes now I can see Anna and I lying on our stomachs across those pillows, now I can see Anna's plump cakes poised as if for punishment. So how could I not have been expecting a spanking? But I'm being scrupulously honest here and I can't claim you ever lifted a hand either to me or to Anna. Truth be told I can only recall the taste of the white pebble-like mints you always kept in a tin in your pocket and so I imagine you must have given us each one to keep quiet. Just candy that's all— though candy that coldly rebuked lips and tongue, like a lingering castigation.

Then the roses rained down as Duchess poured buckets of petals over our bodies bits of pink and white that must've caught in our hair and collected in little drifts at the smalls of our backs like snow or confetti. Or maybe she asked us to turn over and the petals fluttered down over budding nipples and still narrow hips filling in hollows and excavating curves. At any rate it's becoming clear as vodka that you were there the whole time helping her because I'm sure I remember the smell of it on your breath as you leaned over and kissed me on the brow willing a counterfeit serenity upon a body more inclined to shinny up trees or traverse the frames of doorways, urging bony hands elbows scapulas rib cage pelvic bone kneecaps and long prehensile toes to merge with the softbrightsexorgans of plants. No you didn't leave but stood off to the side like the magician's lovely assistant as Duchess crept round behind the tripod crawled under the black curtain and began fiddling with her ancient sheet film camera.

And then the dogs started baying just like they're baying now shredding the air with razor-edged howls shaving away the years so that once more I feel as exposed as I did that day, raw as freshly-sighted prey. It must've been then—when she saw

Anna and I start to squirm on the focusing screen like two fat maggots—that Duchess realized that this would be no still life no nature morte and stepped out from under the curtain. Yes it must've been then that she realized that this would be pure action photography as invigorating as any high-speed hijinks with Marlin Perkins or the folks at National Geographic. If you could you'd probably ask how she happened to have a portable camera with her when Anna and I started to run for the woods her wild beasties snapping at our heels. Well Gramps what I'm thinking is that she planned for that scene all along.

Hey, look at what I found in that weird-looking cabinet. He's holding out a thin album-sized book bound in black leather. The leather is embossed in gold with the initials SOS which are possibly Duchess's though I can't remember you ever calling her anything else. I take it and it's surprisingly light not nearly as heavy as it looks.

Get a load of what's inside. He steps around behind me leans over my shoulder. His breath has lost its eggy innocence has gone bad with Turkish coffee. Ever so slightly I pull away and ever so slightly he follows—one two three four one two three four as he snares me in the minutest of rhythms, one two three four one two three four as my cunt does an illicit pirouette.

My fingers trace over the book over leather soft and supple as a child's skin then lift back the cover trembling like the fingers of a pedophile—yet I'm not the one who took those pictures. I'm not the one who clicked the shutter the wicked witch who cast the spell or the dirty old devil who authorized it and surely my heart will sink like a stone when I see what you two did to Anna and I that day.

Nothing. Nothing is what I see. My eyes fall on nothing float on a page as a blank as the eyes of a senile old man as bare as institutional walls and once more I imagine you must be laughing up the sleeve of your hospital gown. Zilch as I turn to the next page and zippo on the next. Yes I imagine you'd be laughing if you could laugh cuz after all this shit there truly is no fucking pony.

You've got it upside down, Skip says reaching over my shoulder.

I turn it over and start again. And Ooooh Myyyyyy. Is that you, grandPA? I want to say that I don't recognize you without your glasses but even minus the specs that sure looks like you—the milky blue peepers naked as shucked oysters the pendulous schnozz like a snout the soft fleshy herbivore's lips hiding a mouthful of steak-eating teeth. But Ooooh myyyyyy what long and curling feet you have! What columnar legs you have got! What great arms! And what an enormous belly!

What an enormous belly and what a strange one because it doesn't hang down over your pelvis like any other grandpapa's pot but instead thrusts out and up with a decidedly maternal tilt. What an unusual belly because it isn't a belly at all but a small woman wrapped round your naked body! A small woman not a belly! The pose is extraordinarily clever... Extraordinarily clever the way her head is buried between your thighs as her arms hug your buttocks. Absolutely ingenious the way her own small round ass becomes the upward curve of your stomach as her knees clamp the sides of your torso. Why her entire body has been transformed into yours—the only remainder being the Turkish slippers on her feet, curling toes thrusting up beneath your chin like two rearing serpents.

Then again don't her slippers reiterate and thus emphasize your own? Doesn't their sigmoid curl like a beckoning finger call attention to the flourish of your own feet below? I trace the curving line of your slippers with my index finger knowing now why the ones on my own feet look so familiar. Obviously you must have had your own private photo session with Duchess that day a grown-ups' affair after the kiddies were through. Yes you must have had your own little royal ménage à trois in the studio afterwards—you and Duchess and a mysterious Lady. But who was she the Lady and why can't I see her face?

Sick, Skip whispers and his acrid breath eddies round my ear disperses across my cheek.

Yeah. And now I'm pulling off a slipper and throwing it hard at the phony Odalisque. And cuz I'm your granddaughter cuz I'm a big girl cuz I was born in the home of baseball born with a pitcher's arm and a huckster's eye the reproduction comes tumbling down flipping over the credenza gilded frame smashing against the floor. Fuck you for the photos fuck you for the rose petals like some sleazy playboy set fuck you for making us pose like little foxes fuck you for the fox hunt fuck you for finding less strenuous sport back at the manor while Anna and I raced through the woods ran for our pre-pubescent lives.

Find anything interesting, dear?

I turn to see Duchess standing near the doorway stroking her foulard with one hand, holding a dusty jar of what looks like red jelly in the other.

Here. She steps forward around the wreckage of the ersatz Odalisque waving the jar in my face. *This is for you, my last one. I had to scour the cellar for it.*

A jar of jam after all this she's got to be kidding. I cross my arms over the book hugging it to my chest I'm not taking anymore shit from her. She can keep her nasty red jissom but still she keeps thrusting it in my face: *Really darling, what were you expecting?*

And now Skip is reaching over nabbing the jar on my behalf though it's also possible that he wants the fucking thing for himself. He raises it up toward the sky light squinting as it glows in his hand bright with red clots like rubies: *What is it?*

Homemade crabapple jam. Stella remembers my crabapple trees. Once upon a time, when my trees were in bloom, two little girls took off all their clothes and let the petals fall like kisses on their bare skin.

She steps closer lifts her hand and brushes my cheek with her fingertip. Her skin is dusted with pink powder that has collected pollen-like in the seams beneath her eyes and around her mouth. I look away as she gently pulls the album from my hands.

Ah yes.... This is all that I was able to salvage from that roll. I have found photography to be a much less exact and predictable art than the layman might believe—in fact, I suppose that this is what makes it an art. If taking a photo meant producing a replica of nature there would no interpretation, no artist's vision. But even then the vision is often not what one had envisioned, despite one's attempt to realize it with light meters and f stops and so on, and all the developing room tricks and embellishments in the world don't solve the problem but only make it worse. Yes the vision becomes more and more obscure until finally it is lost. For in the end, you see, photography is as unreliable as memory.

She claps the book shut and smiles.

Well Stella, I'm afraid that's it for today. You'll have to come back sometime and let me photograph you. I remember how you and your sister used to beg me mouths ringed with the cherry Kool-Aid you drank incessantly Duchess take my pitcher, take my pitcher publeeease.... But I've never been much interested in working with children, with their apish expressions and tart little poses as simple and obvious as the imitation fruit flavors they so love. Give me adults any day, they're both more complex and more subtle. With the exception of Juju, who even as a child possessed a certain dark inscrutability and I'm sure had good whiskey on her breath the day we shot the red riding hood photos.

But you did photograph Anna and I.

What?

You did. Repeatedly.

I believe you are mistaken. The day I had your grandfather and your mother in the studio you two naughty things were outside rolling without your clothes in the crabapple blossoms. Little exhibitionists. And you got the dogs all riled. I remember how the two of you came pounding on the studio door so that I had no choice but to open it. Still naked and flushed pink you wailed

that the big dog had eaten a little mouse. Such little Sarah
Bernhardts, but your act didn't last long. William said that's
enough girls in that wonderful growl of his and sent you off with
mints from the tin he always carried in his trouser pocket. Too
bad you missed your curtain call—that night after you left my
pooch vomited up a gobbet of fur and tiny bones.

My mother was in the studio? Mom?

My mother was in the studio?

Mais oui, my dear. She pushes her horn rims up on the
bridge of her nose and peers at me like an entomologist studying an insect. *Of course—it was her idea. She arranged for every-*
thing: the session, the pose, even the body stockings special or-
dered from Fredericks of Hollywood because they certainly don't
sell anything like that in upstate New York.

She's clearly lying through her false teeth. Though god
knows why maybe just to get a rise out of me. I look over at Skip
who's now sitting on a pillow under the skylight still staring into
the jar of placenta red jam, oblivious to all this as a baby. What's
really fucked is that woman could be my mother she's small
enough after all wasn't I wearing her clothes by the time I was
twelve years old? Yeah that woman hanging from your torso like
some sort of pale heavy fruit could be my mom—the photo is
gravid with the possibility. Ripe for the plucking and I know that
Duchess's just waiting for me to grab the idea, to sink my teeth
into it like one of her damn dogs, like some thirsty little fox.

Let's go Skip.

As I pull Skip who's still clutching the jar of red jam and
looking totally spaced out down the path I fight the urge to run
because she might be watching peeking from behind the curtain. Out of nowhere the dogs appear one on each side of us
like bouncers or hit men escorting Hansel and Gretel away from
the gingerbread house and into the woods for the last time cuz I

know we're not going home. And now a bird starts chirping off in one of the trees a crabapple maybe except the blossoms are a good month away and another bird joins in and another and I look over and see a flock of black starlings filling the branches with their tuneless twittering simple and inscrutable as nonsense rhymes. I don't believe her it simply doesn't fit.

Cool, another souvenir. Skip's crouching over the ground fishing something out of the slush.

He dangles something pink and muddy in front of my face: a child's hair scrunchy patterned with tiny cartoon animals. *Look Stell, it's Scooby Doo.*

In one fluid motion he stretches it over his wrist like a clown's ruffle and dives into a flip an airborne catherine wheel spinning for a second or two only he wants me to be the martyr to cast a patient smile on this absurd animation. Screw you scooby doo I'm outta here.

Yeah I'm outta here at least I hope I'm outta here as I squeeze into the tercel and the dogs slink off to some other job. I put my foot on the clutch fingers on the keys then say abracadabra cuz maybe some of her powers rubbed off on me. And oh Lucifer my rusty little broomstick leaps to life not soon enough as Skip falls into the passenger seat but still I'm grateful. Yes I'm filled with unholy joy just to be out of there to be on the road again when I hear *hey Stell, look what I got.* Oh look what he's got bad boy a hundred dollar bill which he waves with a pink ruffled wrist in the direction of Duchess's disappearing house.

I found this underneath that book. She deserves it making us come all the way out here for her crapola jam.

Yet he still has her ruby red jar, clenched between his thighs. I return my eyes to the road to the dim tunnel of arching trees it can't be true what she said about those photos it can't but all I can see is the distant circle of light from the crossroads up ahead, like some obscure view that won't come into focus.

Dr. William Henry Vanderzee
1 Glimmerglass Lane
Cooperstown, NY 13326

19 March 1993

Dear Dad,

It's interesting how you always insisted that James and I should call you that. Not "father," for instance (in fact, I still remember how you cuffed me the day I tried that one on my tongue). And "daddy" or "dada" were of course out of the question. I can just imagine your response if I'd ever tried to call you "daddy": you would have raised one heavy black eyebrow and asked me if I needed my diaper changed. Instead it was always "dad"—modern, streamlined, as crisp and casually elegant as the Wright-minded ranch you designed to be our home, despite your deep interest in the objets of the old world. So stylistically, I suppose, "dad" suits you.

But "dad" is also unalterable. It's not like "god," for example, which when you turn it around becomes "dog." No, a "dad" is a "dad" is a "dad" is a "dad," a word as constant as the sun that rises each day—perhaps even more so. "Sun," after all can be reversed to "nus," not to mention the fact that it is also exchangeable for "son," a substitution that too many parents, especially mothers, seem to make with ease, as if the homophonic relationship authorized a semantic one. Which is not to insinuate that you ever mistook my brother for the solar principle. While our household was clearly a jockstrap autocracy, only you occupied the throne, and your rule was separate but equal (thus if the toilet seat was always up, and when my bottom was smaller I more than once fell into the bowl, you never failed to remind me that it was my prerogative to put it down again). So I'm not imputing discrimination, sexual or otherwise (especially since your view of my biological imperative as less insistent than James' provided a

convenient screen for all my early escapades and experi-
ments). Rather, what interests me is your demand for "dad,"
which like "mom" seems to promise consistency (in fact, I'm
sure she would have fulfilled this promise if she'd lived,
despite or perhaps because of the fact that I hardly knew her).
Yes, it's always been "dad," and yet I've never known what to
expect from you. Or not.

The Chinese anamorphosis, for instance—didn't you
once say that some day it would be mine? I still remember the
occasion; it was during "nap time" one muggy summer
afternoon. I must have been around seven or eight, too old
really for naps, and anyway it was unduly warm and sticky.
So I wandered from room to room, Leon, my Steiff lion
puppet in hand, always keeping an ear attuned to the roars of
Peg's hoover in the distance as we hunted for some distrac-
tion. Forays in your bedroom and dressing room proved
disappointing, except for the intriguing little silver packet
Leon found in the drawer of your bedside table, which when I
opened it later, in the privacy of my own room, yielded a
charming rubber beanie just the right size for my smallest
dolly, a beanie which in the colder months could also be
unrolled into a stocking cap. Indeed, Leon had just slipped
the foil square into the front pocket of my sunsuit when the
din ceased to pour through the French doors on the other side
of the patio, signifying that Peg would soon be making her
way into the back wing of ye olde ranch, toward the
"Master's Suite."

We shot down the hall, thinking we could escape the
back wing before Peg a leg's arrival, and perhaps even take
refuge under the dining room table until she was safely out of
sight. But the old gal's gams could go, and we only just
managed to evade her gaze as she barreled past, propelling
the chrome-plated bulk of the hoover, by crouching in the
shadow of the old grandfather clock that stood ticking by the
entrance to the back wing. (Whatever happened to that clock,
by the way? That as well was missing the last time I took a

tour of the homestead, and that as well I imagined would comprise part of my inheritance. Finally, after all these years, you would be giving me the time of day—a luxury I could now afford to ignore as I've grown accustomed to my own personal durée.) Tick tock tick tock as the vacuum cleaner and Gladys disappeared into Big Daddy's Boudoir at the end of the hall. Tick tock tick tock as Leon sighted the polished oak door to your study. Naughty lion, he wouldn't listen when I whispered we weren't allowed in there when you weren't home. Wicked creature, king of the beasties though he was, to defy your authority and grip the brass knob with his bristly mohair paws.

What could I do as the door swung open, what could I do as Leon's amber buttons bid me to follow, but go in? Pushing the door closed behind us, we surveyed your mind's refuge: the antique walnut escritoire with its neat stacks of paper and requisite skull staring from a perch atop the unabridged dictionary; the three walls of bookcases filled with books picturing the strangest things, such as a small sightless eye like an undeveloped bud on a potato fixed just off the center of a boy's face, flesh-colored fruits clustered between a lady's legs (I knew this from my one previous unauthorized visit to your study, a visit which you should know was instigated by James); the globe straddling its wooden stand in the corner, brilliant blue skin tattooed with all the places I hoped one day to visit. Leon of course wanted to play with the skull—what fun if he were to crawl in from underneath, then pop from the hinged jaw like a jack-in-the-box. But as I pointed out, he was underestimating himself—clearly he was too big a mouthful to swallow, let alone disgorge. And anyway, I had my own agenda—to taste again that book of strange produce.

As Leon nuzzled the leather spines, I searched the titles trying to recapture the big words I'd glimpsed on the book's cover during that other visit—"CONGENITAL" and "ABNORMALITIES"—before we'd plunged into its pages.

Craning my neck to better scan the works on the shelves off
to the right of your desk (since it was in that particular section
of your library that I recalled finding the book the first time),
I spotted something even more intriguing. Propped between
the gilt inscribed spines of <u>Generation of Animals</u> and <u>The
Medical Works of Hippocrates</u> was the oddest little painting.
There might be people in it: I could see a narrow eye topped
by a hair-fine brow, as well as what looked like someone's
bottom, four fingers of a hand, a few legs and several small
feet (although two of the feet looked more like hooves,
hooves with twists of cloth or tissue at the ankle, like half-
opened bon bons). Then again, judging from the flatness and
arbitrary interpenetrations of the cream, tangerine and black
shapes, it might also be some sort of map. Yes, a map made
sense, given the random couplings of the shapes, for though
only a credulous schoolgirl, I'd already intuited that the
world's boundaries were determined more by chance than
necessity.

And if a map, why not a treasure map? The brownish,
mottled paper upon which the shapes were rendered looked
very old, but maybe the prize had remained undiscovered, its
location marked by that narrow unblinking eye. With this
thought my heart began to flutter in my chest—if the chart
revealed the way to riches (and I imagined a legend written
on the back, explaining the shapes and the specific topography they signified), then why shouldn't those riches be mine?
Still, I don't think I would have had the nerve to pull over the
small stepladder you kept for reaching the highest shelves, if
it hadn't been for the encouragement of Leon, who having
given up on jack-in-the-box, was game for this latest skull-
duggery. In fact, it was his paws that were straining for the
map's black wood frame when a pair of large strong hands
seized my waist from behind and swung me down to the
Persian carpet.

For a long moment I stood staring at the hook and
diamond-patterned border of the rug, trying to lose myself in

the interstices of the lines and colors, to slip through the grid of ruby red and midnight blue. (That was a lovely carpet, by the way—a genuine nineteenth-century Iranian Beluch, according to my research. I hope the person to whom you sold or gave that treasure appreciates it as much as I would have.) And then I felt you touch my crown with your fingertips, so that there was nothing to do but raise my eyes.

To my amazement, you were beaming. Yet I didn't question your good humor, but merely took it as an unexpected portion of grace, like a bowl of blue sky when one has been anticipating rain. (Although now it's all too easy to imagine why you had returned home in such a pleasant mood in the middle of the day, all too obvious why you took a steamy shower before departing for the hospital.)

"Sorry Juju, Kinder haben kein Zutritt," you said, peering down at me over the tops of your wire rims. "But I have other anamorphoses you can look at, if you'd like."

I nodded eagerly. Although disappointed to learn that my "map" was for grown-ups (the most interesting things always were), I sensed that these "anymore feces" might offer more amusement than the usual good clean fun. You directed me over to the desk, lifted me into your leather-padded writing chair. Then you drew a large book down from one of the bookcases as well as a long silvery cylindrical object with a small knob at the top, like an elongated saltshaker. I had in fact noticed this object on the previous reconnaissance with James, but it hadn't seemed to merit more than cursory attention, being too thick to serve as a fairy wand and too short to make a convincing scepter.

Yet, as I now learned, the silvery rod was one of the more valuable curios in your study. Indeed, you told me, this "reflecting cylinder" had once belonged to an artist named Hans Holbein who had painted many famous people, including King Henry the VIII. Further, as you opened the book on the desk before me, to a phantasmagorical stew of swirling beige, peach, cream, yellow and blackish green shapes, and set the rod on a quarter-sized whitish disc in the midst of the writhing mass, you demonstrated that it truly was a kind of magic wand. For in the surface of the cylindrical mirror, the problem of color and form had been resolved, to create an image of two muscular men in turbans carrying a third who wore nothing but some sort of diaper. Wondering what was wrong with the third man—was he ill, sleepy, drunk?—I peered closer. What were those red smears and little black dots like bugs on his feet? What was that spar that rose up behind his head for? And then suddenly it became plain what constituted his problem—he was nailed to the spar, not just his feet, but his hands as well to a shorter transverse spar, and the other two men weren't carrying him but rather raising him, crucifix and all. Well, I knew that tired story—I'd heard it from Pious Peg (who was always too happy to put aside her mop and sell us on "our savior," despite your injunction against proselytizing on the job)—and thus couldn't help but feel disappointed by the rood in your rod. My disillusion only grew as the puzzles that followed, when "resolved" by the mirror, turned out to be nothing more than a Roman galley ship, a double portrait of King Frederick III and his Queen, two men fighting with foils, a monkey teasing a Pekingese, and so on. There were no maps to be read here, no treasures to discover, and my mind kept drifting to the painting on the shelf, which I was certain would not, when I crept back later and viewed it again with the cylinder's aid, disappoint like all these others.

Evidently not just my mind but eyes as well must've kept returning to that other image over yonder—I may have even been twisting in your lap to get a better look—because finally you clapped that dull book shut.

"I told you that one's not for children," you said. "You can see it when you're all grown-up. You can even have it some day. But until then, no looking."

The book of anamorphoses resumed its spot on the shelf in the "art" section of your library; the reflecting cylinder, however, no longer occupied the space beside it. Instead, you locked the latter away in the filing cabinet in the corner. And there the rod remained, R.I.P., despite my exhaustive quest for the cabinet key (how I searched—pillaged pants pockets, shook out shoes, rifled underwear and outerwear drawers, turned mattresses, groped glove compartments and rooted through ashtrays—and all for naught). Finally I could only speculate on that cartographic puzzle, could only ponder the mystery of the carnally shaded shapes, of the narrow unblinking gaze. And so every chance I got, I drank in what I persisted in calling my "map," taking long deep swallows when you weren't there, furtive sips when you were, until it seemed as if the wonder of it was part of me, until I could no longer see the thing except through other people's eyes, just as one cannot actually see one's own face but can only infer its features through the reflection of a mirror.

I had not "seen" the anamorphosis for many years the night Barbara saw it for the first time, an event you've most likely forgotten. Let me refresh your memory, DAD. It was the night of my graduation party, your reward for my summa cum laude capper at Vassar, and if I'd cared to look through the sliding glass doors off the family room out onto the velvety green lawn, I would've seen a big white tent billowing in the breeze, the backdrop for black bow-tied waiters bearing silver trays of cocktails and canapes as they wound round the clusters of madras jackets and silk sheath dresses. It was enough, however, to listen to the hot air seeping from the stuffed shirts, as the clothes hangers rattled appreciatively—I'd be damned before I'd go out there and be dressed up in back-handed compliments. "Juju got the brains," they'd say, their voices insinuating that I'd failed to capture something better. And I'd only be able to humbly agree as I caught sight of Sunny Jim in the distance, leaning against the marble bird bath on the upper lawn, his arms loosely encircling my darling's waist.

So instead of looking out, I looked in, toting my double scotch through the kitchen past the counter island where three

black-aproned young women were spreading dabs of olive
and cream cheese onto cookie-cutter stars, through the living
room past the white-damask sofa where a former high school
classmate fed already-smeared stars to her fiancé, into the
back wing beyond the grandfather clock that told me my hour
was long past, tick tock tick tock (for unfortunately I had not
yet discovered the refuge of my own durée), until at last I
reached your study. Without switching on a light, for the
candle flickering in the skull atop the escritoire provided
more than enough illumination, I settled into the leather
reading chair, my back to the anamorphosis which had
become so deeply engraved in my consciousness that outward
vision was unnecessary, indeed no longer possible.

I had just taken the last swallow of Dewars when I heard
your voice in the corridor: "There was an old philosopher
from Bel Grave..." then ice tinkling as someone slurped a
drink... "who kept a dead prostitute in his cave..." then a
muffled giggle... "he said 'I'll admit I'm a bit of nit...'" then
more giggling, a thumping noise that sounded like a hand or a
heel hitting the wall... "but think of the money I save."

The lamp next to my chair clicked on, seeming to flood
the room with light. Blinking, I peered round the padded
wing of the chair to see not just you, but Barbara as well,
citron eyes dancing, one hand smoothing the front of the
dove-gray raw silk sheath she'd lifted from my closet (a little
long, a little loose in the hips, but somehow, as always,
perfect), the other clutching the arm of your cream linen
dinner jacket.

"Oh hi Juju," she said, "your dirty old dad's going to
show me a dirty old picture."

Sloshing the bourbon round inside your glass, you
smilingly replied that it wasn't just a "dirty old picture" but
"a rather valuable dirty old picture." Then you set your drink
down on the escritoire (a ring mars the lacquer to this day),
walked over to the left wall bookcase and drew down my
beloved "map." You held it up for a moment and still smiling,

said, "But this is only half of it." Placing the anamorphosis on the desk blotter, you went on to unlock the filing cabinet (silly me, not to think of looking for the key in the copy of Keyserling in the adjacent "philosophy" section), as you told us, or Barbara at least, that the anamorphosis was from China, at least several hundred years old, and a fine example of perspectival distortion, for although any seasoned viewer could elicit a salacious subject from the fleshy tones and flashes of body parts, he or she would be able to draw no more specific conclusions without the aid of a reflecting cylinder. And fortunately, you continued, brandishing the silvery rod, you also happened to possess a particularly well-crafted specimen of the latter—a genuine sixteenth-century German-made cylinder mirror which had once belonged to Hans Holbein, and which had been appraised even higher than the Chinese anamorphosis.

Blah, blah, blah, while Barbara, in the meantime, had taken a seat at the escritoire and switched on the brass desk lamp. Intently, she peered down into the pool of white light, and though her face was cast in shadow, I could see her eyes flashing back and forth, as her right hand hovered over the surface of the anamorphosis, poising for a moment here and a moment there, as if preparing to plunge in. Shivering a little, I folded my arms over my chest—how strange, after all these years, for her to see my cryptic map, that unread-able chart that I nevertheless knew localized the only place I wanted to go. My heart skittered as I wondered if she would want to go there too, and further, if she might even be able to figure out the way, having found the legend that had eluded me.

At last she lifted her head, her face lit from below by the light reflecting off the painting, so that there was something of the seer or the oracle in her countenance, and spoke: "de Kooning. Yes, that's it. De Kooning and his bio...bio..."

"Biography?" I suggested.

"No. There's an 'm' in there."

"Biomass? Biomaterial? Biomathematics? Biomedicine? Biometrics," you reeled off.

"Mmmm...no. It's biomor...biomor...biomorphic. Yes, it's biomorphic. Biomorphic abstracts. He told me that means it's abstract, but at the same time suggests the form of something alive."

"Willem de Kooning told you that? You know Willem de Kooning?" I asked.

"Yes, who else would I mean by 'he'? I spent a weekend at the Springs." She stared at me, eyebrows raised. Who else indeed? "Although he'd be talking about someone else if he told anyone about me. I said my name was Judith Vanderzee."

"Oh Barb, you didn't."

"Ha. Yes I did."

Seemingly indifferent to Barbara's rather astonishing disclosure (although I'd noticed modern art books had begun to fill the art section of your library in recent years), you pushed aside the skull and, like some all too dynamic professor, sat on the front edge of the desk: "Biomorphic. Anamorphic. Interesting. Both words are derived from the Greek 'morphe,' which means 'form.' But biomorphic, due to its association with biological life, suggests the idea of symmetry since life tends toward symmetry, either bilateral or radial. Anamorphic, on the other hand, denotes dissymmetry, as an anamorphic form is, by nature, distorted. Yet your response seems to indicate that you see symmetry here. Very interesting."

"Maybe," Barbara said, lifting her head so that her ever so slightly off kilter gaze was now trained upon you. "I think what I like is that it looks like it's going somewhere different. Like somebody took away the directions and now you have to make them up. Yeah, you have to make them up as you go along and you have no idea where that will take you."

Then turning her wonderful yellow eyes to me, those come hither at your own peril eyes, she repeated "no idea."

No idea. I could not imagine. But because I could not imagine, I could. I felt like an alien without a home planet:

freed of gravitational and atmospheric antecedents, I could settle anywhere. Nothing was inconceivable. And Barbara had made it so, I thought, looking at the dark gleaming panes of the window beyond the escritoire where the two of you sat. All was black beyond the glass, as if some lunar sea arced over our heads, as if your study was a spaceship falling into a brave new world.

"Ah, but there are 'directions,'" you said as you leaned back, took Barbara's hand and closed her fingers around your silver rod. "You must take a look at this—it's ingenious."

I could have remained within the cove of the wing chair. For you didn't care if I looked; indeed, I think you hardly noticed I was there. But instead I found myself behind the escritoire, staring down over Barbara's shoulder. And while you gave me neither word nor glance, surely you heard me gasp when I finally saw the "true" image in your tawdry mirror stick, saw the wondrous realm of possibility shrunk down to a Sadean peephole: to a woman getting fucked in the ass.

With a trembling finger I reached out to touch the cylinder, trying to persuade myself that what I'd seen wasn't so, while the image in the silver remained, fixed, seemingly indelible, like some awful, unremovable tattoo. And then Barbara raised her arm: instantly, the image was gone.

Instantly, and it was as if it had never been, or as if someone else had seen it—for I could describe the man and the woman and what the man was doing to the woman, but I couldn't visualize the actors or the act. It was like something I'd read about in a book—something that existed in words but had no physical correlate in experience, no more real to me than a white whale.

So, despite my rash decision to gaze into the mirror, no harm was done; in the end, the anamorphosis prevailed. I'm not sure why. All I can do is speculate, via hindsight, that the unresolved image of the 'map' had taken such a firm hold of my psyche that it could not be dislodged or overwritten by a

glimpse of ruddy brown humping ivory white. Thus even as I
understood that the narrow unblinking eye that I'd thought
signified treasure in fact expressed nothing but the woman's
smiling compliance, I didn't have to <u>see</u> this. I didn't have to
see anything I didn't want to see. That is why, when Barbara
picked up the rod and said, making fishlips at her own face
swimming in the mirror, "Put your face next to mine, Juju. I
want to see how we look together," I replied "no."

Even for her, I wouldn't do it. For I knew, instinctively,
what would happen—just as the mirror reversed the unfamiliar image of the painting into a common piece of smut, so
would it render the familiar wondrously esoteric. And I
couldn't bear the thought of our secret physiognomies
suspended in your shiny silver test tube, that alien protoplasm
quivering beneath your cold and analytical eye. Which is not
to criticize Barbara—she had her reasons, I'm sure, for
wanting to turn our private paradise into a peep show. In fact,
I'm sure she had her reasons for everything, including the
decision to marry James. As an artist, she no doubt felt
compelled to explore every channel of experience, not only
"to boldly go where no man has gone before" (as they used to
say on my favorite television show), but also to revisit where
nearly every woman has been, time and time again. For her, it
was all part of the programming, fodder for the de-program-
ming processes of art. But I was not, and never will be, an
artist. I "watch" what I like.

So imagine my dismay yesterday evening in the New
York Law Offices of I.C. Yurscotoma, when instead of my
coveted Chinese anamorphosis, I received Hans Holbein's
goddamn silver rod. Imagine my dismay, and in addition, my
annoyance, as I had not been able to procure an appointment
earlier than 8:00 (age is clearly eroding your standards, for in
the past you never would have hired an attorney who con-
ducts business during the dinner hour). But don't assume
surprise. When the silk-suited Ms. Y informed me of my
disappointing inheritance, I instantly realized I should have

anticipated your reversal. For hadn't I, in the moment I turned away from the mirror, caught you staring at my "map"—not just staring, but pouring over it—as if you now knew you had been on the wrong trail for years and there was no time to lose? Thus I was not surprised, and truth be told, after a few minutes, during which I stood loosely gripping your shiny cylinder in my fist, listening to the dull roar of a vacuum cleaner just outside the law office door as the vibrations coming through the soles of my feet met the rumble in my blood, I was no longer aggrieved. No longer aggrieved, because as inside joined up with out, I remembered what I'd forgotten in the first rage of disappointment: that the anamorphosis had become part of me, as entangled with my being as my own entrails. And like a haruspex, I suddenly divined the ensuing truth: my desire for the painting proper was simply nostalgia for a modality I should have given up long ago.

Unresentfully yours,
Juju

What's with this poor but honest agrarian facade of green painted shutters cut with crescent moons and crumbling dovewhite stucco the abode of a shy romantic farmer looking for his own true love to carry up the softly sagging steps over the white trellised porch and through the steadfast oak door have I come to the right place? But he said his house was at the end of the road. And after all with a guy like Bucko the country cute setup could all be part of the act yeah he probably plays the thomashardy boy on purpose conceals the wolf beneath a sheep's grin in order to lure them over the threshold and into the sperm soaked lair of the ladykiller.

Still we're a far cry if not a moan from his old lovebus as I raise the bar of the golden calf rap once twice…thrice. Snatches of animal sounds faint yappings and lowings flap at my back like panties on a line and I turn around but there's only the tercel a flash of pink behind the windshield as Skip winds the scrunchie round his arm, a line of tall dark pines beyond. That must be where the barn is down behind the trees but no way I'm going to look there if he wants me it'll have to be in the house not the hay. Yeah I'll just wait inside—better than sitting in the car watching Skip shoot up. I turn the knob and push. Steadfast oak gives way as the golden calf stares stupidly past my shoulder.

And the nose knows where to go as I pick up the scent of pot barely musked with incense and follow it out of the vestibule into the hall and through a curtain of black beads. Voila. In a shallow ceramic dish atop a large carved wood chest there's a protopipe, bowl packed full with fresh dope au gratin just the way I like it. The brass is even still warm just a little over body temperature as I torch the carmelized crust of weed with my zippo and take a hit just one though cuz I want to have my wits about me when Uncle Buck comes back. Let it out slow.... Man I was right about the lair of the ladykiller within. There's the over-sized sofa a streamlined scandinavian affair of teak and goatskin dyed to look like zebra and lounge enough for Frankie Dino Sammy Joey and even Peter to sprawl out in homophobic bonhomie; the fine soft flossa just right for shagging ingas; bookcases packed with artporn yeah cream in your pants Mr. Congressman I can see *The Art of Karen Finley* from here; twin eggshaped robinsegg blue leather chairs with speakers built-in at ear level to lure the shyest chick out of her shell; an elephantine flatpanel TV for skinflicks to flicker over as background to foreplay.... The only piece that doesn't fit is the painting hanging between the bookcases.

Let's take a closer look who is this very serious-looking dude in the long bloodred robe and matching hat this oddly sober note in the midst of all the bacchanalian paraphernalia. Feel the surface the finely shriveled texture of the patina.... I'm no henry james but I'm willing to bet this is the real thing wonder how much it's worth. How much for this painting of the man in the bloodred pod shaped hat that stands stiffly upon his head— as if engorged? Which could explain why his face looks so pale and drained. Or maybe it's the burden of the cross dangling from his neck a cross as big as his hand a cross big and heavy-looking enough to brain someone with. A cross not to be crossed.

Man that's one spooky hombre. Even with the poofie hat.

I turn around. How'd Skip get in here he must've floated on air from the passenger seat to the zebrastripe couch I must be really stoned. Yes I must be blotto cuz it's not only Skip, but Bucko too leaning against the doorframe twiddling a strand of beads and regarding me with his famous green gaze.

That spookie hombre is my greatgreatgreatgreatgreat greatgreatgreatgrandfather, the Cardinal of Poland, Stanislaus Bielaski.

The girls called him cat eyes Oma told us and each hoped in secret she would be the next maus. But she also told us that my mother hated him because of what he once said to my Dad—why buy the cow Jem when you can get the milk for free? Sure and don't think I don't know the rest of it too how he was Dad's oldest pal cuz you were banging Mrs. B even when my grandmother was still alive from the time Dad and Bucko were just tots and so it was a good excuse for her to give Mr. B about why she had to drive into town—so the boys can play. Yeah and so he was my pere's oldest frere first the Phineas to his Gene then later the Bon to his James the Dean to his Jack two culturally impoverished preppies who traveled to Europe together after Toothpaste U and came back rich hippies hepcats who filled their hipflasks with ouzo and kept baggies of weed in the glove compartment of Bucko's vw van for getting high on the road until Bucko went to graduate school and the party was over. Sure and even now almost three decades later he'd look like he came straight from some neo-Edwardian dope-fete some high sixties Euro-trash bash in that cream silk shirt deeply ruffled at the neck and cuffs and black velvet pants if it weren't for the mud spattered rubber wellingtons he must've been down in the barn. Yeah he must've been down in the barn yeah cuz that's not just mud I smell wafting cross the room.

The door was open and so I thought I'd just wait inside. Why am I explaining when there's nothing to explain—wasn't he the one who called me back after claiming he didn't know anything about a knapsack, saying that he might have something else I'd be interested in?

He's still looking at me a faint smile playing on his lips. I know what he wants the old lech but does he know that I know? Out of the corner of my eye I see Skip get up walk across the room over to the painting.

Hey isn't a cardinal some kind of priest? He lifts a pink ruffled wrist runs his finger along the edge of the intricately carved gold leaf frame then lifts the finger up close to his eyes to inspect the pad: *How can this guy be your greatwhatevergrandfather if he was a priest?* I can't believe he's wearing that thing it's bad enough he uses it to shoot up gotta make him lose it.

How do you think? Bucko picks a piece of what looks like some kind of dried flower maybe hay off his pants. There's more of it elsewhere—bits and pieces of stalks and tiny blossoms sticking here and there to black velvet clinging to his silky shirt even a sprig sprouting out from behind his ear. He must be able to feel it scratching at the smooth skin of his bald head but he leaves it there now folding his arms across his chest and scrutinizing me with his kool kat eyes.

So what can I do for you, kiddo?

You said you had something for me?

Sure. But what can I do for you?

Nothing. I'm fine. Let him say it, it was his idea. *Why did you ask me to drive out here?*

I can't help you find the Homer—I think you know that. However, I have something else that might interest you.

Oh god not the let me show you my etchings routine again. Why can't he just say he wants me so I can tell him to fuck off?

Another painting?

Maybe. First it's milking time. Art can wait but nature can't.

Outside I light up a cigarette only three more in the pack I bought yesterday I'm afraid it's going to be a long afternoon. Etchings or no his method of seduction will probably be long and sneaky like when he took my baby tooth. Show Uncle Bucko your loose tooth you and Dad would say and each time I expected him to yank it out but he'd only jiggle it so that the day he finally pulled it I was shocked. I feel the tooth that replaced my stolen baby tooth with my tongue, feel how small and weak it is even still. And now here I am trotting down the graveled curve skirting icy puddles jogging after Uncle Buck like a dope on a rope. But I'm older now so much more experienced yeah this time he won't surprise me I'll be ready for him when suddenly he stops. I stumble on frozen earth pitch forward and he catches me with ease, rocks me upright by elbows. Stepping back he makes a sweep of his arm at the vast facade now looming before us.

Built-to-last by the best-contractor-in-the-county. This barn will still be standing long after we're dead and gone.

I drop my cigarette stomp it into the gelid mud with my hoof and gaze up at Bucko's quality cowshed. Skip slides up beside me takes my arm and I'm grateful for the support as we scan the old money green of the clapboard-covered walls rising up from the thick stone foundation the immaculate white trim edging the row of small square windows on the side the enormous bolted doors at the front a circle of stained-glass high above them depicting a scarlet cow with long forward sweeping horns against a background of peacock blue at the great silver silo standing behind the main building presiding masterfully over all. And now I'm remembering another story Oma told us: about how he tried to get Dad to drive away with him in his rainbow-painted van the morning before the wedding how he said fuck this day because time fucks all. Yeah so fuck Uncle Buck—fuck him and his built-to-last barn.

But he keeps on blathering pointing up at the stained-glass window: *That's Bos primigenius Bojanus. Also known my friends as the aurochs, ancestor to the modern cow. The last aurochs died in a Polish park in 1627, an event recorded with great sadness in the journal of my greatgreatgreatgreatgreatgreat*

*greatgreatgrandfather the Cardinal Stanislaus Bielaski, and one
which precipitated his immigration to the New World ten years
later, as the Old had lost its charm. Thanks however to the efforts
of a few dedicated individuals, there is hope that one day aurochs will frolic over the face of the earth again.*

He walks up to the entrance unbolts the double doors and
swings them open, rolling a white-painted rock in front of each
one.

And here's where I keep my sacred cows.

I grip Skip's wrist cuz surely we can miss this but he wrests
away through the doors leaving me with a ball of crumpled pink
scoobies in my hand. And now Bucko's looking at me again
eyebrows raised lips curled like he's expecting me to go wee
wee wee all the way home. I drop the scrunchie pressing it into
the mud with the sole of my boot as I step toward the barn.

Inside is a furry golden dimness the only light sources the
line of small windows along each wall and the circle of stained
glass above the door which casts a pale crimson circle at my
feet. I'm breathing the rank air of cow shit and hay cuz there's
nothing else though you and Dad always acted like it was some
kind of musky perfume or rich incense taking big deep snorts
every time we drove past a farm. Long double rows of gleaming
white stalls bisected by shallow steel channels fade into the dim
rear of the barn like lines of molar teeth swallowed by the darkness of a mouth. Over these run sets of metal tracks supported
by metal poles that like the stalls disappear into the dim seemingly boundless regions at the back of the barn. Yet these regions are no more obscure or indeterminate than the space above
which rears up over the rows of stalls and tracks like the nave of
some immense church, some holy cow cathedral. I squint my
eyes stare up through an atmosphere so charged with animal
and vegetal particles so thick with bovine effluvia that it's like
looking through a cloudy goldenish broth so thick I can only just
make out a long bristling dark ledge that must be the hay loft.
But beyond it's all shadows and confusion.

Something touches my nose and my eyes fall on Skip who's holding a stem of dried grass.

Gotcha. He's smiling.

And what's Bucko doing watching us with his cat eyes one hand cupping his chin, sizing us up or cutting us down or at the very least giving us the once over. Then again there's something vague about his gaze something fractured and scattered despite the clarity of the green. He might not be looking at us at all, he might be thinking about something else.

Your grandfather advised me on the design. He walks over to the end of the closest row points to the steel channel: *The grain goes in here and so Bossy naturally moves in head first. And she can't turn around so all her ejectamenta end up in the gutter running behind the stall. At first I was going to just let them all mill around but then your grandpa pointed out I'd be spending two hours a day just shovelling shit out of here while the cows were in the pasture. Smart man.*

Skip leaps into a stall kicks up a yellow cloud of sawdust: *So where are your cows?*

Outside, waiting for the dinner bell. Bucko calls over his shoulder melting rearward into the murk.

My boy springs up onto the low tile-covered wall that separates his stall from the next perpetually stoned yet always spry like a monkey only he's making mooing sounds:

Mooooo Moooooo. Mooooo Moooooo.

As if in answer a rumbling sound starts up somewhere in the back a kind of deep roar like the Minotaur bellowing in his subterranean labyrinth—except that it seems to be coming from somewhere above the ground rather than below. Skip flips back down into the aisle between the two rows of stalls and scampers over to my side as the rumbling at the back of the barn grows louder and louder apparently just in time as a big metal bin-like machine swings out of the darkness overhead riding on the tracks above the trough and starts spewing grain into the silvery trough saturating the air with vegetal rankness.

And now something is nudging my shoulder an even more fulsome odor a rich and tender gaminess filling my nose...I turn around to find an enormous reddish brown and white cow staring me in the face. Her eyes shine like two black mirrors giving me back my features shrunk and splayed a tiny fetal Stella while quivering pink nostrils take my scent into warm dark lungs then breathe it out again with an abortive snort. Lowing softly she drops her head and nudges me once more with her nose leaving a glistening patch of saliva on the sleeve of my leather jacket. Get out of the way she's saying get out of the way of my sisters and me their sea of brown and white flesh pressing at her flanks well I'm only too happy to oblige to step off to the side and flatten myself against the splintery wall. Without looking at me again the cow raises her snout and walks by down the center aisle her long white-tasseled tail dangling between her high bony flanks like a bell pull. Like a bell pull as she disappears around the corner at the end of the row and the rest of the cows start to file in one by one with full swaying udders, cued by her inaudible chime.

Flattened beside me Skip breathes: *I wonder how he gets them to do that?*

I don't get them to do anything. Cows are not only creatures of habit but of hierarchy as well—it is their nature to follow the leader. Bucko rematerializes from the shadows along the wall.

He moves up closer to the moving line of cows starts talking to them in a low thick voice hardly audible above the rumble of the dispenser. I follow. It's a special voice an intimate voice that seems to come up from somewhere deep in his chest as if stored there exclusively for this purpose:

Hey bos bos bos, you're a good girl Justine, yes you too Cécile, bos bos bos, and O aren't you a fine bos bos bos.

Why d'ya call them bos? As always Skip misses the more obvious question. But then isn't his innocence what makes him so fuckable? And isn't this a truth singularly demonstrated by the S & M roman? Oui, Gramps? You probably helped him pick out the names.

We farmers have always called our cows bos or bossy, as far back as anyone can remember. Most likely however the expression derives from the Latin term for cow, Bos taurus typicus primigenius.

We farmers—what crap. Maybe his parents swapped Park Avenue for Green Acres but they were never just good country people never salt of the earth Oma said he was an art history professor for fifteen years for gods sake until his dad left him a bundle or his college fired him for sexual harassment the sack or the ax I forget which. Sure they had some kind of demo farm or petting zoo when he was growing up but basically he's just a rich boy playing the rustic the Hugh Hefner of heifers the Marquis de Sod. But hey it's not like I have any other leads right now and so I might as well stay for the rest of the show. Might as well stay for the rest of the Folies Bovine as the last cow walks through the door and a huge spotted cat with a shaggy white head and long gray tail trots after her, tasseling the procession with its mews. Yeah might as well as Bucko steps outside removes the stones swings the doors shut and latches them from the inside. Yeah cuz I can leave anytime I want to.

Don't want to leave your barn door open. He throws a switch by the entrance and a row of lights mounted in the recesses above the windows blink on. Then with a wink: *Bet you'd like to watch the milking.*

Bet I wouldn't.

But hey you don't have to watch if you don't want to, he adds backing away holding up his hands displaying the smooth-looking palms. *You can wait back up at the house.*

I'd like to watch.

Some people do, Skip. Take Stella's mother for example. She loved to watch.

It comes back to me as he shows us down a dark corridor at the back of the barn a story Anna once told about how when she was very young and I was just a baby Mom and Dad and some friend of Dad's she wasn't sure who maybe Bucko took her out to see a newborn calf. She was so excited she had this little black and white fur parka that looked like cow hide and she begged Mom to let her wear it even though it was too warm almost summer. Only when it came time to visit the barn for some reason they left her behind with me, the two of us in the care of the farmer's wife. Parked her in her parka in the hot farmhouse kitchen where the old farmwoman tried to distract her with fresh gingerbread. But Anna wasn't interested and as soon as the woman turned her back to pull yet another pan of home-baked goodness out of the oven she dashed out the door in search of Mommy and the baby cow. But I couldn't find them Stell and the next thing I knew I was standing in a sort of passageway between two big buildings and in front of me there was this skunk, waving its tail like a flag.

And now we're turning a corner and it seems to me that I can smell a faint musk just the slightest hint of some long extinct skunk but then Bucko pushes open a door and it's gone. I blink my eyes in the bright light. We're standing in a small room walled with more of the white ceramic tile that surfaces the stalls up front glaring white no anchorage for the gaze except in each other. I have to look at him see him staring back at me: *Welcome to my milking parlor...*

In the center there's a waist deep pit surrounded by six stalls all shiny white and reeking with disinfectant smelling like nothing or no body which may be why they say that cleanliness is next to godliness. What did he mean she loved to watch?

Man this place looks like a gas chamber. If I was a cow I'd stay out.

No you wouldn't, Skip. What happens in here is the central event of the dairy cow's existence, the crucial Zeit of her Sein. He points to what looks like a steel elevator set in the wall opposite from where we just entered: *In fact they can't wait for me to open that door.*

He tugs on a rope dangling from a set of pulleys over the far end of the pit. The metal doors slide open and an enormous cow stumbles into the room.

Welcome Madame.

The animal lurches past Bucko without even a sideways glance like a drunk dowager ignoring the butler who just summoned her to dinner heaving her bulk into the farthest stall.

That's my prize cow, Madame Merteuil, who also premiered at the entrance to the loafing shed. And this is her inner circle, the haut monde so-to-speak of my herd he says as the five other cows who just followed her in all head for the closest empty stall.

Another small group of cows waits on the other side of the threshold gawking at the lucky six in the milking parlor while in the main section of the barn beyond the hoi polloi munch contentedly at their long communal metal troughs presumably killing time until it's their turn to get in line. She loved to watch he said but what could she see behind that black sleeping mask as she'd lie in bed til early afternoon? And even when she finally got up replaced the mask with her patch and staggered into the kitchen to lean over the sink gulping at the faucet, her good eye seemed as fake as the prosthetic one she'd lost as glassy as a camera lens. Was the shutter open? I couldn't tell.

My mother loved to watch the milking?

Bucko pulls at the rope closing the metal doors in the faces of the small band of staring cows, then turns to me:

She sure did, kiddo. She'd tool all around the countryside with a sketch pad and pencil, claimed she was seeking inspiration in her agrarian past.

He's smirking ever so slightly now smiling the most discreet of horse-trader's smiles, smiling as if he's already made his sale. But I know from Oma she hardly ever left her attic that she only started to stay out all night after we moved to Santa Monica.

And maybe I look skeptical maybe he realizes I'm not going to buy this because now he abruptly turns away and pounces down into the pit.

The stalls are arranged so that he can stand waist-deep working at the udders of each cow without hunching or stretching. He begins with the queen cow swabbing a soapy cloth over her bursting pink sack then deftly popping four hollow rubber cylinders onto each of her teats with his long clean fingers. They remind me of something what is it those little paper cylinders you can buy in Chinatown the harder we pulled the tighter they squeezed our frozen fingers and the more he laughed—but now I'm losing the image as milk starts to spurt and spatter into the clear fist-sized spheres attached to each set of cylinders the flow gaining force and momentum as it pushes up into a clear tube that runs along over the stalls and into the wall. He must have some sort of holding tank on the other side some place where he collects this deviant flow this bold deflection of maternal abundance before he sends it off to the processing plant where it goes for ice cream for yoghurt for whole milk two per cent skimmed and spilled—goes everywhere and all over the place except back into the small groping mouth that invoked it.

Skip has joined Bucko in the milking pit is peering over his shoulders eyes wide but mouth open only slightly. I squat down on the tiles along the edge between the two end stalls—there's no way I'm going to go down.

How much milk do you get from each cow?

That varies. Some of these ladies are bigger producers than others. The most abundant provide about five gallons a day. The less generous ones like Madame here only yield four. On the other hand Merteuil's milk is the crème de la crème. You'll have to try a glass when we get back up to the house, Stella.

I hate milk.

A pity, he says winking up at me. A tuft of mousebrown hair peeks over the vee of his neckline...0so soft looking what if

I were to reach down and tweak it? No. Let him make the first move then slap his paw and leave.

Four to five gallons! That's a lot of milk.

It's a hell of a lot of milk, jack, Bucko says popping off a cylinder and painting the reddened teat with blue liquid. *Especially when you consider that the average jill produces only four to five cups a day.*

And now Bucko's attaching the milking tubes to the udder of the last of the second set of cows while Skip looks on with half-closed eyes and parted lips. The milk starts to pulse then flow and as if in a trance he leans forward and reaches under the animal taking hold of the plastic tubing between his thumb and forefinger. What does it feel like with the warm milk pushing through? Does it feel like something almost but not quite alive like how his eyes look when we're fucking, cloudy and insensate as if captured in a cryonic freeze? Fuck my nipples are starting to harden. Think of something else it's just a physiological reaction what was that I read about the Folies Bergère about how someone rubbed their nipples with ice cubes before they pranced out onto the stage so their tits would stay stiff and pointy through the entire routine. Think of something else and don't look at Bucko watching us, green eyes twinkling like sequins.

While human milk is the sweetest, bovine milk yields twice as much butter. On the other hand women's milk yields an abundance of cream, which is generally whiter than the cow's.

I cross my arms over my chest then uncross them clearly the old fox is trying to unnerve me with his tacky barnyard trivia trying to break down my guard so he can raid the henhouse. Gotta show him I've still got my wits about me let's pull out old Shakehispole from Renaissance 501:

Come to my woman's breasts, and take my milk for gall.

He's leering now but he doesn't say anything. Instead his gaze swivels to Skip who has let go of the tubing and is now gently running his forefinger over the cow's nearly flaccid pink sac tracing the contours as if they are sentences of a story he can't quite understand.

Hey cowboy, how'd you like to run the ranch while I show your friend around?

Skip slowly turns his head, blinks: *Huh?*

Clearly however he is a devoted student of the agrarian curriculum certainly more engaged than he ever was in my class as Bucko shows him how to attach and detach the milking apparatus and explains the functions of various buttons switches levers and knobs. Blah blah blah as I wish there was a place to sit down and have a smoke when suddenly I see what I missed before—a little three-legged stool standing in the corner. It's old and battered-looking the flaking white paint worn thin across the seat the bare wood haphazardly scratched and scribbled over by years of hard usage. But what's this a regularity in the randomness...I lean closer. In small block letters carved in the center of the seat letters gouged deep and darkened by time is a name: *BARBARA*. And now I'm the one reading with my fingers tracing over the double swellings of *B* the bony angularity of *A* following the top-heavy curve of *R* down to the prop of its sad little tail. *BARBARA*.

Yes now I'm the one reading with my fingers reading the story that she could never tell us because you and my father took away her voice turned her into dumb flesh mute matter silent as a broken and bound foot, to be molded into the sigmoid shape of your perversions. Reading the tale that Anna would have told me if she'd been able to see what was going on in that barn—had been able not only to see but comprehend it. A tale about how Dad and a friend who must've been Bucko dragged my mom out to some old farmstead just like you forced her to go out to Duchess Semjanov's studio—about how they forced her to play milkmaid to their minotaur. And so while Anna sat up in the farmer's wife's kitchen nibbling gingerbread they already had her out in the barn sitting on that stool all Tessed-up like the last of the D'Ubervilles in pink gingham décolletage. Yes it must have been pink gingham because didn't Anna once make a dress for my doll out of that fabric, fabric which she must have cut from one of Mom's old cast-offs? Where else could the material for that little dolly dress have come from besides Big Doll's closet?

Fingers shaking I light my cig take a lungful of smoke then let it out. If Mom was wearing gingham décolletage her feet must have been bare. Her feet must have been bare her toes gripping matted straw as she tugged away at those stubborn teats trying not to tip back on her little three-legged stool her face becoming more and more flushed the harder she pulled becoming dewed with sweat her brown hair shaking loose from her pink ruffled cap and coiling into damp little tendrils her amber eyes sparking with agitation. And what were the two men doing as they sat on bales of hay, watching? I can easily see them egging her on splattering her with laughter smearing her with jeers—but I don't wanna be too Tawana. More likely they were silent more likely the only noise in that barn beyond the occasional sizzle of milk against tin would have been the deep thick sounds of their breathing a sound as viscous as honey. A sound as thick and sticky as honey as my mother felt her limbs becoming more and more leaden heavy as her own milk-filled breasts as she felt the men's eyes clinging to her like leeches draining her with their desire. And what happened next well it's not hard to imagine what happened next because human milk is the sweetest as Toni M showed us the most beloved of all. Surely they siphoned their fill leaving me and Anna nothing but a sad sack a crumpled carton of a woman, empty and inept.

So why'd she do what she did why'd she let them suck her dry? I don't blame her no of course not though it's hard to imagine how someone could possess so little self-esteem but that's what women were like back then like big docile animals with soft bare feet and burgeoning bellies animals bred to breed and housebroken by teevee. Cuz Father knows best and besides Lucy always makes a mess of things. Yeah and so she was trained to please to make him happy to make you happy and so probably would've done anything to achieve that would've jumped over the moon squealing like a pig. `No I don't blame her at all as I take one last fortifying puff off my cig then park my big but not beefy ass down on her little milking stool—you guys really fucked her over.

OK Babes, party's over.

I turn as the metal doors swoosh open and watch the cows slowly move out of the stalls like housewives dragging themselves from the afternoon soaps hopefully nosing the bins fixed at the end of each enclosure one last time before turning away. They lumber past me hoofs thudding heavily against the tiles though their udders do look smaller and lighter. I wonder if they feel relieved or robbed.

Skip calls softly to each new cow filing in *here bos bos* and even attempts to rub their noses. The animals sweep past ignoring him heaving into their stalls where they immediately throw their big heads into the feed bins.

Why do they act like they're starved when they've got all that food outside?

I spike this with honey. They're crazy for it. I've even had new mothers desert suckling calves just to get a mouthful.

What happened after the skunk sprayed her? She didn't remember who found her or took her home.... All she knew was that the little black and white parka had been ruined that the odor was so strong they had to bury it. Now Bucko's showing Skip something about some cow's udder. Does he know I've seen the inscription on the stool beneath my ass, does he know how much I know? Y'd ya do it she said, Y'd ya do what you did? Yeah I could ask him right now dig up the whole stinking mess but I won't cuz it's pointless. Cuz boys will be boys when the girl is a such a doll cuz what he needs is to be cut down to size.

Ready for the grand tour?

Am I ready for the show down ready for the old bastard to make his move now that we've got Skip out of the way? You bet I am it's time he learned he's no stud anymore time someone put the old Buck out to pasture told him his days of free range fucking are over. Yeah I'm ready for him as I slowly stand, six foot two in my tragic boots. Ready although I've never really looked before at the bald top of his head before never noticed the liver colored birthmark an irregular splotch the size of a poker chip like an unfamiliar shape on a foreign map, like a place I've never been. What's wrong with me I want to touch it trace it my fingers tingle with the urge even as my feet want to get the hell out and I feel like I did the time Anna and I found that weird book in your library. All the people were naked every misshapen skull twisted feature defective limb malformed or missing digit freakish combination of genitalia coldly compressed and framed by the camera. I couldn't bear to look but couldn't pull myself away either as Anna turned the pages pulled us deeper and deeper into the wilderness of the body. And now once again I really don't want to stay but can't leave either as I think of the photograph I saw of you and my mother the other day. I owe it to her to face the wolf man to tell him he's nothing anymore but a spotty little worm.

Given the obstacles, the first and foremost one being that the last aurochs died in a Polish park at the dawn of modernity, leaving its last supper in my ancestor's lap, a problem which I believe I mentioned earlier... He stops opens a door directs me down a dimly-lit hallway with a finger tip on my shoulder blade...

...though there are a number of others as well including the fact that, for the most part, those who drew and painted the aurochs could not copy nature in a servile way and thus anatomically accurate representations are the exception rather than the rule, the best being a pen and watercolor discovered with a scream of delight by the British zoologist Hamilton Smith in a large, well-lit Augsburg shop window early in the last century,

*although even this, I'm afraid, is rather expressionistic; the fact
that authoritative accounts of the reclusive aurochs' temperament
are even more difficult to locate and thus we must rely largely on
the fauvist anecdotes of drunken peasants out early in the morning sharpening their scythes who happened to spot him running
from the wheatfield and into the woods like a bachelor fleeing the
bed of a bride stripped bare, anecdotes recorded en passant by
their betters in letters; and finally, the fact...*

As he breaks off again I look over my shoulder at his finger
on his lips I never noticed before how full how girly soft in his
lean cold face, like the last plum in the frig before old Willy C
Willy gobbled it up. And then I hear it: a bellowing in the distance a sound unlike the rumble of machinery we heard earlier
a sound unmistakably animal. The bellowing rears up to a cre-
scendo then suddenly subsides.

*...and finally, the fact that while well-preserved skeletons
abound, one of these, a completely intact 700-year-old specimen
unearthed during the excavation of the basement of a bar in the
Folies-Bergè, being in my possession, a specimen which I acquired
in the course of my investigation of the distribution of aurochs
herds on the European continent, an investigation which not only
acquainted me with the geographical landscapes over which this
magnificent beast once roamed like a fugitive flâneur but also
provided the opportunity to explore, during frequent déjeuners
sur l'herbe, the balthusian contours of the descendants of the
dairymaids whose childish souls and other attributes were so dear
to my ancestor Cardinal Stanislaus Bielaski, we possess no fossil
record of the soft parts of the aurochs' internal organization, the
intricate collage of tiny cartilaginous and tissular peculiarities
that distinguishes the animal from the modern cow, even though
to the uneducated gaze these differences might be no more visible than the minute distinctions that separate the cubist produc-
tions of Picasso from those of Braque,...*

He pauses again as we come to a door, grabs hold of my
shoulder then slides past me brushing my breast trailing an odor

of open fields of moist cool soil and sun warmed grass. Turning the handle he resumes his tortuous monologue about the dearth of dead cows or whatever the fuck it is that he's talking about…

…my project to recreate this magnificent creature through selective breeding has not been an easy or straightforward one, though in the end, I believe, I have achieved my goal: the re-creation of history.

A wave of daylight hits my eyes but we're not outside we're standing in a kind of steel-sided vestibule in front of some kind of observation window a high plexiglass barrier which looks out into a large hay-lined shed or small barn surrounded by a fenced paddock. There's something immaculate even artificial about the scene behind the glass about the hay which looks cleaner and sharper than ordinary hay about the hoofprints too definite in the dirt of the paddock as if placed there for educational purposes, like in a museum diorama.

Bucko raps smartly several times on the glass then hollers: *hey bos bos bos, hey bos bos bos.* Nothing stirs.

She must be behind the shed. Moving to the side he pushes a broad metal knob embedded in the plexiglass. A transparent door swings open and he walks through into the paddock his rubber boots leaving big manprints as he walks away obscuring the animal's like a demonstration of human evolution. The re-creation of history he said but what if no one wants to watch?

Let's go see some stuffed animals he said and so of course Anna and I thought he meant at F.A.O. Schwartz. Wasn't it x-mas time? Wasn't he our dad's best friend our Uncle Big Bucks with the trust or slush fund Oma couldn't always remember which but whatever it was everybody knew he had a pile. Yes and so as he buttoned the gold buttons of his double-breasted red cash-mere blazer straightened and rearranged the tie-dyed silk hanky in the breast pocket which along with his black turtleneck was no doubt meant to lend a bohemian touch to the jacket while we waited for a taxi outside the hotel, the last place I thought we were going was to some old museum. Surely he must've seen our faces fall when we looked up at those sorry assed sawdust seeping mastodons and sabertooth tigers must've known we'd expected better yet it didn't stop him from giving us a lecture in front of every display. We were silent until he came to a diorama of two eskimos a man and a boy paddling a kayak on a fiberglass sea and started pontificating about how ours was the only primate species where fathers assumed responsibility for their children at which point Anna interrupted what's a primate species and when Bucko explained said well I guess that makes our dad a monkey's uncle. For several seconds her words just hung there as if frozen in midstream like a jet of piss in arctic air then he said your father has done the best he can under the circumstances.

My legs are trembling ever so slightly my blood sugar must be low I should've taken one of those day old donuts in the office at the Mohican this morning something to sop up the puddle of whiskey in my gut. A day old donut and a cup of instant coffee what a dive that place is but Discover card holders can't be choosers. Wait—it's not me it's the ground…. Yes it's the ground that is trembling as an enormous cow steps into view a dwarfed Bucko at her side. It starts lumbering toward me a cow as tall as a tall horse a nightmare out of prehistory towering against the sky like the mother of all cows. Yes it's definitely the ground not me being shaken by this empress of elsies no pink elephant but an actual flesh and blood animal, though god knows I've been drinking by the troughful.

Here she is…Bos primigenius Bojanus. Also known as the aurochs, Bucko says throwing his voice above the din over the top of the plexiglass wall. *Isn't she magnificent?*

Horrific would be better. The animal is standing within a foot of the barrier gazing down at me with big black eyes glistening like tar pits. It leans forward and I take two steps backward only now it is nudging the barrier with its great glistening black nose making the glass vibrate like a web with a fly caught in it like a ruse that is about to crack. Surely it will but it doesn't and Bucko is smiling as he reaches up and rubs its jaw. The beast cranes its neck toward him its shoulder brushing the wet print left by its nose smearing slime over the transparent surface. Why did Anna turn red why did I feel ashamed? They were the ones who fucked *us* over, not the other way around. Yeah so when Anna stole a twenty from Big Buck's billfold at the Tavern on the Green it seemed like an appropriate appropriation. Which maybe is why later on in Chinatown he never asked how it was that we suddenly had spending money.

OK baby you can go back to bed now.

He pats the aurochs' muzzle touches the tip of its nose with his finger and then begins to slowly back away. Keeping his sight on the animal the whole time he reaches behind him pulls open the transparent door with a knob on the paddock side and slips back into the observation space.

For a moment the aurochs stands there dazedly blinking its huge black eyes at us. Then suddenly it heaves its bulk against the glass. I leap back but Bucko holds his ground stares back grimly through the shivering transparency:

You know I can't be with you all the time.

The animal glowers and snorts at him for several long seconds even scrapes the dirt once with its hoof but then abruptly turns away. Switching its vast flanks with the rough tassel of its own tail it starts trudging up along the right side of the paddock less than a foot away from the wire fence. Its breath rises up white puffs dissipating in frosty blue while its reddish coat gleams dully the color of oxidizing iron in the early spring light the color of ancient history days long past yes let bygones be bygones what do I have to feel guilty about? I pull a cig out torch it with my zippo. Only one left.

A fist-sized ball of smoke floats up scatters and disappears like the aurochs' breath. What do I have to feel guilty about though he clearly saw some kind of justice in it when our fingers got caught in those fucking chinese tubes. Stuck your fingers where they didn't belong, eh? as his laughter rang like a salvation army bell through the december air.

You see what she's doing? She's flirting with the electric fence, deliberately trying to provoke me.

Bucko leans over to the wall flips a switch and there's this keening sound a highpitched wobbling electronic howl which seems to galvanize the aurochs out of its plodding course because suddenly it is standing up on its hind legs twisting the rusty hulk of its torso away from the fence stabbing at the air with its long curving horns. As it rears now bellowing in synchrony with the wailing I see the little pink sac of its udder dangling below its belly a sac absurdly small not only in proportion to the size of the animal itself but also in comparison to the great ballooning bags of the cows inside. It's ridiculous really that pink pittance on such a huge beast is it supposed to be so small or is it some kind of abnormality? Do I really want to know?

Bucko flips the switch again and the sound ceases.

My security system. She's not ready for the world again and the world's not ready for her.

The aurochs is back on all four feet once more tramping toward the back of the paddock. Maybe this was a dumb idea thinking I could turn the tables tip the cow cuz who's to say I won't get crushed? Weird how its breath seems to grow bigger as it recedes billowing up in great wordless balloons over its head as its tail sweeps back and forth from one flank to the other, brushing away some invisible annoyance. Back and forth as every second this whole escapade feels more stupid as witless as risky as Bucko's uglyass ox. Yes admit it Stella maybe this was a dumb idea and anyway whatever I say whatever I do to him won't undo what he did what all of you did to her. Really I should just go drive back to the Mohican so why can't I seem to tear myself away, why can't I help staring at that small pink sac like a child's purse dangling between the animal's legs?

Why is her udder so small? Isn't that a defect?

Not at all. That's what it should look like. By nature and design this baby was born to run...

And as if to demonstrate the aurochs suddenly patches out with a rumble and a roar kicking up cold clods of dirt in its wake swerving over to the other side of the paddock and disappearing behind the wee barn.

...even in the modern cow the lower legs and feet are long in proportion to the whole limb, with strong pulley-like joints— legs designed for running, for leaping beyond the reach of a predator's jaws, for performing la danse macabre and still pranc- ing back for an encore. Indeed if you were to look at the sprightly bovines leaping across the ceilings of the caves at Lascaux, you would realize that the image of the cow who jumped over the moon is not mere nursery nonsense, but a logical extrapolation. Unfortunately, however, the essential sportiveness of Bos primigenius has been suppressed by centuries of selective breed- ing.

Suppressed by centuries of selective breeding, he repeats looking me up and down with his bright green eyes though once again I'm not certain he's actually seeing me it's like being stippled over by a strobe light. And there's something arresting about it this being seen and not seen at the same time like being both naked and clothed totally exposed and incognito. Yes and so it must be that I've been riveted by his rolling gaze because suddenly I feel like I can't move like my legs and arms are numb. I drop my cigarette.

Although there are exceptions, throwbacks if you will. He extends one Wellington, rubs my smoldering butt into the dirt. *And further, even the most domesticated cattle become fugitives at calving time, scampering off into the woods if you let them to drop their bloody little bundles.*

But I'm numb cuz I'm cold it's got nothing to do with him. No it must be because I've been leaning against the corrugated steel wall rubbing my palms over ribs of icy metal letting the chill seep into my system like poison. I step away from the wall fold my arms across my chest tuck my frozen hands under my armpits. How did I get so cold so fast? Because it is vital to the survival of the species, he told Anna and me as he rubbed the circulation back into our fingers. The female womb maintains its warmth at the expense of the extremities. Admit it I'm not up to this I better just fetch my skipper doll and go.

I'm sorry but I have to get going.

He nods then reaches behind him in the corner next to the plexiglass wall and presses another button. Metal creaks and shivers and as I turn around the wall behind me slides open like an elevator door.

Come on up to the house, he says pulling me by the elbow out into the bright open air. *I still have something to show you before you leave.*

His fingers press the crook of my arm as he leads me back around the barn past the silver silo like a rocket ship prodding at the sky. Press the spot where they stick the needle when you give blood which is maybe why I feel a bit woozy just slightly spaced-out. Anything could happen now a flying saucer could land he could fuck me right here if he wanted to is this how my mother felt twenty years ago in that barn like the will was draining from her veins? Come on Stella get a grip.

His hand drops away a respite thank god time to regroup as he points at a row of white plastic igloos glowing in the late afternoon sun like alien ova. A reddish brown calf is chained to each one and as we approach the animals back up into their domes shrinking from sight.

These rubes around here raise their prize calves in dark barns and then wonder why they have rickets. Young mammals need light but you can't tell that to people who are still living in the dark ages.

OK he's not touching me now but what to do if he makes another move gotta remember how he treated my mother can't let him screw us over twice. Yeah so let's not forget how after the china shop it was no more bull but straight back to the hotel parking garage where he locked us up in the back of his volkswagon van while he paid the bill then drove us back to Cooperstown. Let's not forget how he kicked Anna and me our fingers still throbbing from our trip to the Big City out of the vw into the woods to play or not as long as we got lost. Let's not forget what we saw through the trees those dove white lips fluttering weak protests beneath a shame red turban his hand holding fast to a furry sleeve as he hustled her inside. Let's not forget what we heard the click of the lock as the van door slid closed. Yes let's not forget any of this as we wonder why if the young need light we had to stay outside until after the sun had sunk below the horizon?

Bucko strides up to one of the igloos and taps a light but insistent rhythm on the plastic with his fingers. I can see the still dark form of a calf inside as it resists this summons the call of fingertips pattering like spermatozoa over the surface of a cell flickering like a strobe sweeping a dance floor. Good girl. Don't let him lure you out. But then the dark nucleus of the dome shifts from the center and moves to the periphery as the head of the calf emerges into the open air and then the body. I move closer and watch the animal's pink snout nudge at the pocket of Bucko's velvet pants smearing a shining path over the fly as it moves from one pocket to the other. He reaches into the first pocket and pulls out a treat of some sort maybe sugar cubes I can't see because first it is cupped inside his hand and then it's gone.

The treat is gone and Bucko's hand is wet with cow spit as he extends it to me. I take it let his slimy palm and fingers surround mine what am I doing letting him lead me back around the barn and up the shimmering road like a length of dark sateen ribbon what am I doing fluttering down over the frosty knoll like a rivulet of syrup sliding the slippery slope of a breast or a belly. What am I doing but already I can taste his full lips feel his udderly smooth hand and there's nothing to do but go with the flow.

So I let it pull me sweep me along up to Bucko's sham-shackle farmhouse with its loose shutters and bits of brick exposed by crumbling plaster like fishnetted flesh seen through ripped denim up the artfully buckled steps and over the threshold like a willing victim floating in the arms of her tyrant lover like a little girl pretending to be too sleepy to walk as her mommy carries her up the stairs. I've never fucked an old man wonder what it's going to be like if he takes viagra the blue light special how it'll compare if a dude from days gone by might be smoother than a younger guy like the difference between 20-year-old macallans and 8. Most likely it depends on the quality in the first place after all who wants a 20 year bottle of old grandad.

The shaggy headed cat from the barn is waiting on the porch its long thick tail thrashing snakishly against the planks. But when Bucko kneels down takes the cat's head between his hands smoothing back the hair from the brows with his thumbs its yellowgreen eyes are diffident as an odalisque's. Pressing its forehead against Bucko's shin and arching its back the cat makes a chortling sound through its veil of white fur.

There there, I know you worked hard today. You're the best girl in the whole world.

The cat grins up at him the exposed teeth almost shocking in the midst of the snowy beard like some hidden perversion suddenly revealed. I can't believe I want this I've never dug old guys they've never been part of my repertoire. There must be a rhyme and a reason some Freudian rot fueling my desire some subterranean flame impossible to put out. Yeah so I just have to let it burn grip the devil by the horns. But that doesn't mean I have to be like her and let him take me for a ride. No I don't have to be like her I don't have to be intimidated just have to remember who's sitting in the saddle. Yes so what am I afraid of no one can stop me once I'm in the cockpit with my hand on his joystick. No one can stop me and no one can keep me from bailing out just before I send him bucking off into a black hole.

He pushes against the heavy oak door and his pussy trots past through the already open inner door of the vestibule and into the darkness of the hallway. Then stepping back he says: *After you.* He steers me with a tap on my arm toward the lounge and that must be his left palm sliding over the curve of my ass as he parts the beaded curtains with his right one cuz what else could it be? What else could it be that rustles up my spine and starts a tremor in my groin like the vibrations of pounding hooves but the touch of an old ranch hand? But I don't have to be like she was those days are long gone just have to remember I'm in the saddle now yeah I'm a space cowboy and this is a whole new world.

Like I said I have something for you, if you don't mind waiting a bit longer.

Without staying for an answer he disappears through the door of black beads and for a few moments I stand and watch the strands swing and sway listen to them click clicking together like ropes of pearls. Mom was wearing a strand of oyster tears when they finally called us to come out of the woods but as the Carpenter said to the Walrus the butter's spread too thick to turn back now. Besides this time I'm going to fuck him this time it's going to be the other way around.

I sit down at one end and the bearded cat hops up on the other settles down on a mound of scarlet velvet cushions. It watches me yellow-flecked eyes no longer downcast but wide and bellicose long tail beating a tattoo against the faux zebra upholstery. But if you stare back that only goads them on only gives them something to grab on to with their feeble feline brains and before you know it you've got claws in your throat. Better look away slide my eyes in the other direction to the portrait of Bucko's assholiest ancestor and start undressing him with my eyes beginning with the coneshaped hat optically plucking it away to reveal a scalp no doubt as smooth as Bucko's soft as the head of a circumcised penis though probably the forebear still has his foreskin down below then groove the grim lines of his cheeks over his jawline to the neck of his robe letting him feel what those milkmaids must've felt as I undo the heavy gold clasp seize his holy prerogative with my own unholy hole...

MmmRrrryyowww.

Of course she doesn't know what I was thinking but still her pink mouth drips with glassy teeth and I'm not gonna take any chances. Slowly I slide off the sofa slink across to one of the blue eggshaped chairs and crawl inside pulling my long legs up too cuz they always go for the ankles first. And now I'm safe with surround sound and so much more a panel of little buttons set in the curving wall of my shell like remote control from the womb buttons for vcr tv and cd for ac dc bc and ad vd and nypd or lapd for volume and disc skip and skip to my lou swap and freeze play and pause program stop go hyper scan or hyper reality random repeat. So many choices so little time what's a girl to do but close her eyes and press...

DU BIST FRÄNZE LOSGEWORDEN, JA?

WARUM SOLLTE ICH? SIE IST EIN SÜSSE WEIB FRÄNZE. SIE IST HIESS IM BETT, KOCHT UND KÜMMERT SICH UM DIE WÄSCHE.

Help Hitler a thousand krauts are roaring in my ears where's the volume control hier it is ja ja das ist besser. But what is this two talking heads on the tv screen killer closeups in afterliving color with ghostly subtitles flickering across the bottom. What's he saying the guy with the little herrbrush beneath his nose *But you promised you'd gotten rid of Fränze.* Stravinskyish piano music tinkles in the background as the camera moves to the other one to his big prolepudding of a face with its two simple little eyes and pouty lips the face of a boy schnitzelfied to ten times its normal size:

It's still too soon Reinhold. I don't want a new broad until spring. Yeah, summer clothes. I already noticed Fränze hasn't got any and I can't buy them for her. She'll have to go in summer.

You know what I say Franz? Fränze looks pretty scruffy already.

And now the camera is following Herrbrush as he strolls around Prolepudding and leans against a railing: *And what she wears ain't real winter clothes either, it's more temporary stuff. Totally wrong for how cold it is now.*

Prolepudding protests: *Weather is something you can never predict. You never know what's coming.*

Well I think there's going to be a real severe frost. That's what I think. And now Herrbrush is turning his head to gaze at someone or something beyond the camera: *And look Cilly's got a rabbit coat. Look.*

Ah so that's it. But what am I going to do with a roast rabbit? I have one to worry about, what am I gonna do with two?

What is this kraut krap I can't believe it misogyny to the tune of modernist schmaltz how totally offensive. I should turn it off not watch as the camera moves to a woman leaning against a lamppost a woman wearing a black fur coat with a zebrastriped collar a little cardinal red hat perched on her head and suddenly it doesn't matter whether the tee vee's on or off cuz the image on the screen is supplanted by another entirely—an image of Bucko shoving my mom into the back of his van. Chuffing her off like a Jew. And although Sylvia says every woman adores a Fascist it's more than just an image that bloodred turban being swallowed up by the volkswagon it's also a record documentation of what they did to her a glossy photo illustration of how to make roast rabbit.

I tap the filter of my last cigarette against the hard plastic rim of my egg then place it between my lips. Now let's take a deep breath watching the tip glow red in the zippo flame as we try to reconstruct their recipe the pièce de résistance created by Chef James and his assistant Le Bucko. Begin with sweet young bunny. Knock her up twice then when you get tired of her ask your assistant to take bunny's babies away for the weekend so that you can tell bunny you don't love her anymore. Let bunny stew for two days in her own tears; when assistant returns she's soft and yielding as meat falling off the bone. Have assistant take over this tasty dish from here on add creamy words of comfort blended with spicy gestures letting her simmer until finally the silly rabbit is cooked and the air is filled with…smoke.

Yikes my egg is thick with smoke not another fire no flames it's just second hand smoke but they say that's the worst and I'm too young to catch the big C. Eyes streaming I stagger out of my shell stumble over to the chest and stub my butt out in the bowl of the protopipe.

Ahhhem.

Le Bucko. Yes it's le Bucko and he's got something in his hand what appears to be a large sketchbook what he's cooked up now what's next on the menu? Cuz I haven't lost my appetite nosiree my mouth is watering as my tongue strokes the tooth that replaced the one he stole.

I see you've been enjoying a little Berlin Alexanderplatz. A wonderful film—Fassbinder's finest.

I think it's awful… Shut up Stella save the feminist critique cuz god forbid we should get into a discussion—I don't wanna talk I wanna fuck.

But he merely smiles as he saunters over to the zebra couch plunking the sketchbook down on the wooden chest as he sits next to the bearded cat. Stroking the stripes of the cushion on the other side of him he winks at me. This is it now he's thrown the gauntlet here's my chance to fight on my back to beat him at his own gametes slay the swordsman with his own sword. So be brave crawl out of your shell suck in your gut and get over there.

I plop next to him sinking into the cushion but not falling in love again though wouldn't it be pretty for him to think so. Yes wouldn't it be perfect if he thinks I'm his little snugglebunny his velveeta rabbit only to learn too late that this is no cheesy story of the old dude debauching the young chick—that I wasn't hatched yesterday that I'm the one who has something to teach *him* about how to make a tasty stew. Leaning forward so that my hair screens the tiny smile on my lips I look over at the teevee. Prolepudding and Redhat Mama are in someone's dingy apartment both stuffing their feet into an enormous boot. Laughing they attempt to hop together across the floor but end up in a pile. He makes me gag old Footbinder and his stinking art farts what am I doing grabbing a scarlet pillow and lobbing it at the screen. Shit.

Stella, Stella. And now he's leaning across me lifting up a fabric cover from the arm of the couch to reveal another small control panel.

He presses a button and the boobtube blips off. As he draws back he lets the smooth underside of his forearm brush ever so lightly over the top of mine making the fine blond hairs stand erect. I gotta give it to the creep—he knows what he's doing. I'm tempted to sit back go massive passive and let him keep on making all the moves just to see an old pro boner at work. Yeah maybe I'll just let him strut his stuff wait until we're in bed or better on the floor to pull the rug out from under his feet.

And now he reaches forward and picks the sketchbook up from the chest. Oh what a treat a bit of vintage venery at last the hoary fucker is going to show me his etchings. I settle back into the cushions stretch and hear the snaps on the crotch of my bodysuit go pop pop pop. But that's ok cuz it's bedtime for babygirls time for Daddy's pillowtalk. So it's thigh to thigh shoulder to shoulder no mistaking the message as he sits down next to me as close as he can possibly get and lays the sketchbook on my lap.

What art is she good at, but hurting her breast with the milk-teeth of babes, and a smile at the pain?

Excuse me?

What the hell is he talking about what does he want he's looking into my eyes cat eyes they used to call him and suddenly I find myself thinking of that horrible unearthly screaming sound that cats make when they fuck. Better grip the pommel hard...

That was of course a rhetorical question, as you'll see for yourself.

His arm slides around me and I get a whiff of Old Spice just like you and my dad used to wear the smell of our fathers who aren't in heaven but then there's more than one set of pearly gates isn't there pop pop pop ?

At first we were both pretty uptight. And cold. As you know upstate New York even in late summer can freeze the balls off a brass monkey. Yet as autumn came and the days grew even colder we warmed up. I like to think that in those last few weeks James and I were more than a couple of shivering stooges—that we became collaborators.

Evidently he actually wants me to look at his etchings to play along with his antiquated act I'd rather lick the top of his bald head slide the tip of my tongue around the waxen petal of his ear until it blooms pink but what the hell. I cast my eyes down at the open sketchbook on my lap.

Oh isn't this charming a charcoaled manger scene only Mary is a cow with Papa Joe sitting naked on her back and baby J is no baby no look at him now. Look at him now lying supine on a pile of straw his face in shadows but his crotch lit up like a christmas crèche his soft penis cradled between his thighs. Look at him now because Mama is looking somewhere off to the side her neck craned away from the viewer so that she appears to be headless and Papa Joe's face is too dark and smudgy to tell whether he's gazing down at his boy or musing about bovine anatomy.

Uncle Fucko reaches across me turns the page flipping through several more variations of naked men and moocows.

This is all early work of course but already you can see the obsession with the body even as that body is being aestheticized into an abstraction…

Aestheticized into an abstraction? I don't think so. I mean I know nothing about art but these drawings are just porn plain old porn smuttily pencilled by some cornholer with a good eye and a sure hand. So why is he showing me this shit is he trying to tell me something like sorry Stella I don't shuck girls no more?

They look pretty explicit to me. I'm looking down at yet another depiction of the manger scene only this time the penis isn't soft but fully erect and penciled in red bright as Cardinal Bielaski's hat.

Come now, use your eyes.

His finger hovers over the dick and though I'd rather look at his finger at his long and supple finger and imagine it snaking its way up my thigh I look down.

See what she's done here.

She?

Not only has she created these exquisite pencil studies of the nude male body an object too seldom studied, but she's gone one step further and rendered something even rarer in the history of art: the hard-on.

Who?

The hard-on. Thirty years before that new blackbanged brit twit Cecily Brown. Years even before Mapplethorpe who anyway worked mostly with flaccid. The true genius however is in the way she handles the boner. So easily she could have satisfied the viewer with a few rough strokes but instead she proceeds with deliberate delicacy, fattening the tissue with the most subtle hachure. Instead of the common cock of the walk we get a penis that is both tumid and dainty, etiolated and extravagant, a hothouse florescence that could only exist within the rarefied atmosphere of pictorial space. To be sure, recently we've seen something akin to this rich and raunchy artifice in Lisa Yuskavage's impossible bimbos; however, given the long tradition of the female nude, the subject par excellence in western painting, can we really credit Yuskavage with the same level of innovation?

I grab his hand as it flutters again over the drawing:

Who do you mean by she?

His fingers rear up out of my grasp and lightly rake the underside of my chin:

Your mother, kiddo. The artist Barbara Salzmann.

Bucko reaches across me again this time without the slightest brush of skin and turns the page:

It was an honor to work for her although I think it was tough on James. But art happens—no hovel is safe from it...

What am I looking at. What the fuck am I looking at it could be a squid or a tangle of vines or even a nest of vipers. I lean forward squint my eyes there's a thing in the middle a globular sac like a drawstring purse from which sections of precisely cross-hatched tubers radiate then disappear into smudges of graphite. Closer and I see a tuber dive then rear up again out of carboniferous foam emerging thickened into a long cylindrical bulb that reminds me of something I can't think of what some machine I saw in a dream. Then closer and the foam rolls forward an inch or so then recedes again revealing a little tuft of rootlike hairs and I realize what I'm looking at is the stalk of somebody's dick jammed into one of the bulbs of that thing I saw out in the barn.

I push the portfolio away and stand up. My temples are pounding as I catch the faintest whiff of the pipe on the coffeetable like the hangover of some sick hayseed joke. The cat leaps off its mound of cushions strolls over and peering up at me eyes gleaming through the rough fringe of its brows begins to rub against my legs.

Enough Mietze, Bucko says pushing the cat away from me as he rises. He holds out the sketchbook: *These are yours Stella, all I've got to give you. Maybe I should've tried harder. Who can say?*

And now he's looking down at his shit-spattered wellies green eyes almost hidden by his lids cracks of light beneath closed doors. I really don't want to ask but it's like I'm a girl in a horror movie who hears a noise and just has to get up and see:

Tried harder at what?

Well... and suddenly there's this weakness in his voice a wobbling as if we've reached a place he doesn't want to go either. ... *Well I knew he hadn't been able to convince her to stay with him as soon as she opened the door. Sure she was wearing his anniversary gift but nothing had changed. Nothing had altered except for maybe the pearls themselves which had looked like such a sure thing in the jeweler's display case, so pretty and regular, and yet now were clearly baroque. Not just baroque but somehow unconscionable so that what every good woman pretends to forget could not be ignored—that the nucre is an animal secretion triggered by an alien prick. Of course it was hopeless— even he knew that. By the time I dropped you and your sister off he was already gone...*

And now Bucko is standing with his back to me before the portrait of his assholiest ancestor like it's time to confront the past or maybe just because he doesn't want me to see his face.

Sure it was hopeless but I was your father's best friend. Maybe it would help if I talked to her. So I invited her to step out to the van for a cup of ovaltine. But as the water was heating on the hotplate she pulled a fifth of 151 out of her brown fur jacket and well that's one poison I shouldn't have picked. Next I knew we were mashed up against the back of the driver's seat coupled without shame on poppyred shag.

No.

Without shame but without pleasure either and afterward she just slid her wide flat hips back into her levis like a bandito slipping his knife back into its sheath grabbed her fur coat and split. Left me nothing but her scarlet cloche, camouflaged by the carpet until finally some chick pecked it out of the shag a couple of months later.

No way I don't believe a word of this not a single word but when I open my mouth all that comes out is *ovaltine?*

Bucko's hand smooths over his gleaming crown comes to rest for a moment at the nape of his neck then falls to his side as he turns away from the painting:

Without pleasure and yet I couldn't stop thinking about it for days afterward, as if my mind was a kinked pizzle knotted to that hour in the van. Couldn't stop thinking about white painted lips like alabaster or the bared gums of a bleeding beast, couldn't stop thinking about golden eyes like a Venetian sunrise or the onset of mortification, couldn't stop thinking about the darkness of a diminishing perspective and how it can open up a world. Without pleasure and yet I learned more about the art of fucking in that one afternoon than I've learned in my whole life.

    Where is he? Nobody in the milk room just miles of tiles white as rolled up eyes staring into space and an empty stool standing in the corner. And he's not in here either nobody in here but cows. Cows moaning and groaning in their stalls like lunatics in an asylum. But I'm not crazy I know what I know you old geezer that you and my dad and probably Uncle Fucko too rode the golden calf until she got too ornery and tough so then you herded her out of town. I bet he drew the pictures himself but there's probably no way to find out no one left to ask. No one but a bunch of old cows and they've all got their backs to me all lost in their secret ruminations brown tasseled tails idly stroking flaccid pink udders. No I don't believe a word he said this was just another cul de sac. Time to blow out of here.

    SKIP, I yell up into the rafters. *LET'S GO!*

    No answer just the mindless moaning unless you count the sudden shower of liquid dung that hits the gutter behind a stall just as I'm walking by. I jump back but still get sprayed splattered with cowcrap and specks of hay from my thighs down though it could've been worse. Lucky I had Bucko's dirty drawings to help shield me from the shit. Holding the rung of a long ladder propped up against the wall of the barn with one hand I scrape the wool of my sailor pants with the hard cardboard edge of the back of the sketchbook. So sorry Uncle Buck I'm adding insult to injury although the spots of shit on the cover are sort of interesting, like an animal action painting like Pollock on the Farm.

I lean back against the ladder look up into the golden darkness above—what's that story about the woman who loses her leg in the hayloft? He cons her out of it then skips off leaving her stranded up there. Skip would never do that to me. Not my trusty junkie my faithful little fuckup. No if I was stuck up in the rafters of some old barn he'd climb up to me. Like a prince scaling a castle wall like a fireman shinnying up a tree to save some nasty puss. Gripping the steel struts I step onto the first rung feeling the ladder tremble slightly but hold firm against my weight which anyway is not so much about ten pounds more than his as he lifts his wafflestomper to the next one. The muscles in his back ripple like Rapunzel's hair as he pulls his princely bod up rung by rung the ladder vibrating just a little but still steadfast and strong just like him. Up up he climbs into the dim and dizzying heights up up and onward my sweet chumpion goes not knowing whether he'll receive a kiss or a bite because I'm his bitch goddess his hissy cat queen. Which is what he loves about me.

But uh oh now look where I am my power over him has taken me to the top. Don't look down Stella no don't look down. Best to haul myself up into the hay rest for a few minutes and get my bearings before I attempt the descent. So yo ho heave ho and now I'm sprawled across a gritty wood floor in a pool of sun. I roll over squint my eyes against the bright and see hairy bales of dead grass heaped up to the rafters hemming my little alcove and if this were a different story maybe I'd be worried about how I'm gonna spin it all into gold. But it's not and as soon as my heart stops pounding I'll climb back down that ladder scamper up the hill to my car and drive away either with him or Skip free. Just a few more minutes in the sun a few more minutes to breathe and I'll go.

What the hell was that noise a snort or a chortle—some porker rat or maybe just a gargantuan pigeon. There it is again. I prick up my ears follow the sound as it smooths out and trails off into quiet breathing coming from somewhere just beyond the hillock of hay behind my head. I sit up twist around draw up onto haunches and rock oh so quietly back and forth on my hooves as I survey the wall of hay that rises up before me. The center stack of bales stops short of the others creating a ledge like a pharmacist's window and if I stand up I'll be able to peer over and through to the other side. Slowly I stand raise my eyes cautiously to the open space in the hay because who knows what's over there some cow rapist or rustic killer sleeping off his dirty deeds or maybe even wide awake. I blink into the sun. And blink again. It's Skip.

It's Skip awash in the bath of golden light pouring through two small windows under the eaves. Skip floating like baby Moses on bales of hay his eyes locked tight the ends of his twotone hair charged with the current of the late afternoon sun. He's never looked so good so utterly remote so unavailable so where is it the secret of his charm? Where is it the needle in the haystack no sign only this bunched in his hand: cardinalred angora what does the label say *a hat by Mr. John.*

James Henry Vanderzee, Esq.
Setting Sun Estates
Elysium, USA 00000

13 September 1998

Dear Brother Mine,
You must forgive me for not responding sooner. Unfortunately a dilatory attitude toward the non-immediate fuels the fast pace of city life, and truly your situation has not been pressing for some time now. And even when it was, I don't believe I could have been of much help. You know our father never played favorites, at least not with his own flesh and blood. So why would he give to me what he would not give to you? No, I could not see the point in importuning our parent on your behalf; thus your letter sank to the bottom of a wicker basket already overflowing with parking tickets, overdue notices, and other sundry annoyances. Out of sight, out of mind.

Today, however, as I sit picnicking in Christ Church cemetery, I suddenly feel the need to put pen to parchment, to, at long last, address you. Whence this urge? Perhaps it has arisen simply out of my being here, in Cooperstown, the longstanding arena of our filial competition. Like a soldier revisiting a former battlefield, I find myself assaulted by images of fallen foes. That, however, does not explain why, though I've been back in the village for two days, securing our father's admission to Lakeview Lodge, where he now lies as peacefully and nearly as still as the Cardiff Giant, you only came to mind just now. Only just now did I think of you, whilst sprawled on the stony catafalque of old Judge Cooper, nibbling at my sandwich of goat cheese and arugula on a stale but still tasty baguette.

There must be something peculiar to this specific spot, Brother, the resting place of our town's founder, that has

returned you so abruptly, so unexpectedly, to my attention.
What could it be? Not these winged seeds, these cellulose
apostrophes, strewn over the pocked and blackened surface of
the Judge's granite bier. For whilst such seeds fall on the
lawns of the Vanderzee Estate each September, they also
annually litter the sidewalks all over town. In fact they've
been a nuisance, slipping beneath the balls of my feet as I
walk, although perhaps I should have known better than to
wear mules upstate this time of year. The same could be said
of the moss that muffles the contours of earth and stone with
its moist jade pall. After all, this very same vegetal material
upholsters tree trunks, stone walls, and even roof tops
throughout the village, its ubiquity no doubt a consequence of
the cool terrarium created by the lake and surrounding hills.
Yes moss thrives generally here, not just in the shadow of the
grave. Indeed, one could say that the dank velvet of the
boneyard adorns the entire town.

What could it be? Not the maple seeds, not the moss,
both of which I've already become reacquainted with during
my hikes back and forth between the Phinney house (for our
dear old ranch has already been sold) and the Lakeview
Lodge. Perhaps it would help to cease thinking about form for
a moment to think about function—to consider not just what
this spot manifestly is, but what it is for. That is, we must
consider its explicitly sepulchral capacity. (I qualify with
"explicitly" because while one could attribute such a capacity
to the village as a whole, only here, in our local ossuarium, is
the reliquary foregrounded.) And voilà. Suddenly it is clear:
we must examine the gravestones.

Let us begin with my picnic table, this slab of blackened
granite that marks the final resting place of the esteemed
Judge William Cooper, "who departed this life on the 22nd of
December, 1809, aged 55 years and 20 days." Here our own
father William, the equally esteemed Dr. Vanderzee, comes to
mind; however, no aspect of this granite marker suggests his
son James—other than its inertia. For it is true that like this

stone (and the bones beneath), you no longer possess the
capacity for motion. That, however, is a capacity we all
eventually lose: clearly death is no distinction.

Let us turn then to the graves which flank old William's.
To the right, we find "Elizabeth Cooper consort of William
Cooper, Esq., died 13 September 1817, aged 66." Noting that
the Judge's consort outlasted him by almost a decade, I think
of Doc Vanderzee's, she whose existence was considerably
less tenacious. I do not, however, think of you, though you
were left as motherless as I. Then I recall the 1816 watercolor
by George M. Freeman at the Fenimore House, in which one
can see the pudding-faced Elizabeth seated in her salon, a
potted plant squatting at her feet like a favored pet, while
behind her at the far end of the room, a flock of additional
plants bask in the sun. And still I do not think of James
Vanderzee, despite a not dissimilar image I have of you, circa
my sweet sixteenth. Enthroned in the velvet wing chair that
ought to have been the birthday girl's (it was my party), you
gaze mildly into the camera, as little Marigold Parsons
perches upon one arm, and a nosegay of several other homegrown sweethearts clusters behind you. Yet while you clearly,
like Elizabeth Cooper, possessed a talented thumb, the rarest
rose is missing from the photograph. Yes your bouquet wants
the only flower worth having. And while she was most likely
in the bathroom when the picture was taken, or in the kitchen
negotiating an extra slice of cake, I read her absence here as a
prelude to her absence later; the fact that you briefly managed
to cultivate that bloom in between in no way attenuates your
failure.

But that's all by the by as I stare over at the mostly
blank surface of Elizabeth's grave, a surface like a page from
the notebook of a lazy diarist. While the train of thought
could lead to you, it does not; my mind simply idles, only
picking up momentum again when I shift my attention to the
third grave in the triad. Here, beneath this stone to the left of
William's lies the sloughed coil of Hannah Cooper, died 10

September 1800, aged 23. As you can see from the text I have
so thoughtfully provided below, the page of Hannah, old
William's daughter, is as full as his wife's is empty. While
Elizabeth is his consort, a word suggesting someone less than
a wife, Hannah, "gentle, pious, spotless, fair" is the "more
than daughter of [his] fondest care." To his more than daughter he is more than a father, anticipating in heaven, as he
pounds on in iambic pentameter, a coupling forbidden in life
once death has "waft[ed] [him] Purer to [her] kindred Soul,"
while in the meantime finding surrogate satisfaction in
orphan annies and merry widows whom "thy bounty fed"
(bababoom) and their explorations of thy "lonely spot" (pant,
pant) until finally, in the penultimate line of his premature
sonnet (he just can't hold back any longer), "thy hallowed
shrine" is showered with "grateful tears."

> Adieu! thou Gentle, Pious, Spotless, Fair,
> Thou more than daughter of my fondest care,
> Farewell! Farewell! till happier ages roll
> And waft me Purer to thy kindred Soul.
> Oft shall the Orphan and the Widow'd poor
> Thy bounty fed, this lonely spot explore,
> There to relate thy seeming hapless doom,
> (More than the solemn record of the tomb,
> By tender love inscribed can e'er portray,
> Nor sculptured Marble, nor the Plaintiff lay,
> Proclaim thy Virtues thro' the vale of time)
> and bathe with grteful tears thy hallowed shrine.

Yesirree the Judge was hot hot hot for Hannah, and that
supple flame swelled the pinched purse of plain frontier
speech into the blimp of his almost sonnet (although otherwise William Cooper remained a tight wad; rather than
demanding, given that botched final line, that the whole
inscription be done anew on a fresh stone, our thrifty founder
accepted the engraver's crude correction). Still he was hot for

Hannah to the point where all the others—his wife Elizabeth, his six other children including the future novelist coincidentally called James—must've felt a proportional chill. For given the thermodynamic principle that energy is constant, Hannah's gain surely was the others' loss. And it is as I reflect upon this loss, brother mine, a loss so abundantly signified by the grandiloquent lines etched into the surface of the left lying slab, that at last my thoughts turn to you.

Like that other earlier William, ours had his favorite, his darling, the non pareil of his great appraising gaze; and like that other long ago James, you were not the chosen one. But neither was I. No, because our father kept us both at a distance—let us both graze in the outer pasture of his affections, like two old hackneys he just didn't have the heart to send to the knackers. Yet another parent would have found much to please in such a pair. Weren't you the golden calf of Cooperstown High, worshipped by girls and boys alike for your springy step, your curling lip, your perfect sang-froid— the attaboy forever safe from the sharp tongues of that teenage abattoir, for who would've dared to touch a hair of your sleek hide? And wasn't I, although less popular with my peers, the perennial pet of every teacher as I pranced from one class to the next, mastering concepts and spewing out facts, balancing complex equations and dashing off treatises with a toss of my wavy red mane? Another parent would have been delighted to call two such fine young creatures his own, and would've reinforced the blood tie with the strings of approbation. Ours, however, just let us trail off…as if there was no bond at all.

No bond at all, although we were well provided for, with an abundance of toys and books and old Peg Phinney to serve us home-cooked suppers and bind our beds with crisp cotton sheets. No doubt you, lacking discernment, mistook that material comfort for love, and conflated the gingerbread-scented ease of our household with the Old Spice of his embrace. But I could smell the truth, sterile as the smells of

Phisoderm and gauze he brought home in the folds of his
white coat, and knew that you and I, though we belonged by
birth on the inside of his circle, were perpetually outside it.
Only one person ever stepped within, with the possible
exception of our mother (so difficult to say, as he never spoke
of her, and I was too young when she died to ascertain the
degree, if any, of his devotion to her), and that person was
your wife.

Oh come now, for I can feel your agitation just as I can
feel the breeze that is ruffling the grass and stirring the russet
flushed tree tops overhead, raining winged seeds down on the
remainder of my goat cheese and arugula sandwich. One
moment please, as I set my pen down and slide my baguette
back into its brown paper bag.

Now, as I was saying, I can feel your agitation, just as if
you were perched opposite me on Hannah Cooper's tomb,
and to be frank (since it is too late in the day to be anything
less), I'm exasperated. Surely, even if you did not know the
exact nature and degree of his involvement with her, you
must have intuited something. Really, you must have seen the
way his normally steady surgeon's hand trembled when he'd
light her cigarette, making the flame wave semaphores any
fool could read. You must've heard the tiny growl in his voice
when he said her name, the last syllable vibrating in his throat
as if he didn't want to let it go. You must've smelled the way
his spicy musk clung to her for the rest of any social evening
at his house, in the wake of that too enveloping greeting at the
door. Yes, even one as obtuse as you must've perceived the
signs of his infatuation—for how could you miss them?

What was beyond your ken was why. Why should the
good doctor, a man who saw life as an operating theater best
observed through a lorgnette, a man of die Weltanschauung
who liked to say that everyone looks the same under the
scalpel, give or take a pound of flesh, suddenly have a
favorite? Really, given our father's famous analytical detachment, the signs of this prodigious partiality to Barbara must

have seemed incomprehensible to you. In fact, while I'm sure you must have seen, I can also conjecture that you may have chosen not to see what you saw, like the villagers in a story I read in the newspaper about a Sierra Leonian boy who gave birth to a baby. When the young man, a hermaphrodite who'd been declared male at birth, became pronouncedly pregnant, his neighbors looked past his burgeoning belly, for there was simply no place to put it in their compact little world.

Likewise, there was no room for our father's passion for his daughter-in-law in the narrow space of your conceptual schema. No room for his passion because there was no room for her, at least not the whole of her—the artist as well as the woman. For you she was just the one girl you could never really get, even when it seemed you'd got her, the coquette who always seemed to have a sexy new trick up her sleeve, a stiletto hidden in her cleavage. She was a woman you'd seen in a film, some elusive fraulein, a pencil-skirted silhouette thrown against a wall, the lady in red, perhaps. You saw an image, not an image maker, the icon rather than the iconoclast. Thus as you stood before the idol you called Barbie, palms pressed together in a logogram of supplication, you never noticed the rubble all around you, or the new forms she was cobbling out of the wreckage.

Brother, forgive me for the long pause at the end of the last paragraph. Once again, nature superseded the flow of my ink, this time in the form of a flock of geese flying overhead. Then, drawn heavenward by the honking (which somehow seems louder and more raucous than when you and I lived here), my eyes fell upon the silvery steeple of Christ Church and followed it to its dissolution in the saturated blue of the autumnal sky. For a long moment my perception simply dangled there, suspended from the vanishing point of human endeavor, and then slowly, slowly, it slid back down over the face of the clerestory inset with its dagger of stained glass depicting the ascension, to the great arched doorway that opens on Sundays, holy days, and other sanctified occasions, into the dim paneled interior of Cooperstown's oldest wasp nest, est. 1810, with the generous help of William Cooper who, though a lapsed Quaker himself, felt that an Episcopalian church would provide a most gentile refuge for his swarm.

How could I not be reminded of the last time I saw those dull red doors (red like the color of a faded blood stain; a choice both morbid and boring) wide open? It was late May of 1965, Saturday the 24th, to be exact, and although the lilacs were in full, livid bloom, the damp cold of early March still clung to the town. And yet there was Barbara, standing on the steps of Christ Church with her smooth olive shoulders exposed in the white spaghetti strap and tulle creation she'd stitched together one warm spring night while she was still living in the city. Oh sure she looked lovely, and trés chic as well (perhaps too chic: anticipating the deconstructionist designers of the nineties, she'd left the seams of the satin sheath beneath the tulle turned out, so that shreds of satin fiber had littered the church like dandelion spoors as she'd glided up the aisle. Fortunately, the bride is always a spectacle, and like all spectacles escapes close scrutiny. I'm sure no one noticed this unraveling besides me). Yes, she looked as if she'd stepped off the cover of <u>Vogue</u>, but she also looked chilled, goosebumps pebbling her arms from shoulders to wrists, and for the life of me I couldn't figure out why she hadn't worn the brown mink jacket by Schiaparelli Paris you had presented to her the previous evening before the rehearsal dinner at the Sportsman's Tavern—the maternal mink buried for years at the back of our mother's closet and recently unearthed by Peg Phinney who, after brushing out the flecks of seventeen-year-old blood, had handed it over to you, suggesting, "This'd be nice on yer bride."

Why, I asked myself as I stood leaning back against the brick facade, maid of dishonor in the apple green dress Barbara had chosen to go with my red hair but which somehow didn't flatter, watching her perform kisses and hugs upon

the guests streaming out of the church, while you stood,
proud consort, pumping arms at her side. Even from six feet
away I could see she was covered with goosebumps, and my
own skin pricked in commiseration. Why, I mouthed and for a
moment thought she'd seen my silent question as her right
eye met mine over the back of old Jack Bielaski, until I
realized it was the fake. My gaze dropped in disappointment,
and it was then I noticed, as a gap opened in the forest of
trousered and nyloned legs, the small dark furry thing peeking out from beneath her satin hem. Something sparked red—
a little eye? a bloody tooth?—and then the gap closed.

Pushing through the flow of guests, I managed to align
myself with the wall on the other side of the great arched
doorway. Now just a few feet away from my dear friend, with
an unobstructed view of her right side, I crouched to get a
better look. Not just one, but two furry things sheltered
beneath her dress, two scraps of some soft dark pelt which
she'd stitched or glued to the tops of her white satin pumps,
affixing in the center of each a bit of red paste like a pome-
granate seed. Yes two bits of ruby bedewed dark fur blinked
from under the overhang of Barbara's hem, like shy creatures
who had crawled forth out of some obscure concavity, some
speleological profundity, drawn not by light (for I imagine
that recess to be encrusted with flickering red jewels) but by
simple curiosity.

And as I gaped back at those two tiny furballs, I suddenly knew their source: our mother's coat. Had I not gone
many a time as a girl to her closet and fingered it, thrilling at
how its glassy smoothness succumbed to a deeper denser
plush, then wondered, after I'd drawn my arm out of that
napthalene night, over the powdery rust that floured my skin?
Knowing that source, I marveled over Barbara's boldness,
and also, though at the time I couldn't put this thought into
words, admired her visual audacity and the displacement it
had effected, at the way she had coaxed forth the fetish and
set the maternal mink, if not loose, then into a less predictable

circulation. But then, as if threatened by my stare, the pome-
granate-eyed mites retreated. They retreated and stayed in
retreat for the remainder of the ordeal outside the church,
including the photo session with the wedding party. When I
next saw Barbara, at the Cooperstown Country Club reception, she'd exchanged her white tulle and satin for navy silk
and a perfectly conventional pair of spectator pumps.

It was as if they'd never existed, and yet I knew what I
had seen. I studied your face as you stood with an arm around
your new bride, trying to discern if you had, too. She was
chatting away with one of the poor Vander cousins, those
ne'er do wells who'd not only lost all their money but also
their zee, and as you looked on, smiling, I suddenly realized
you not only hadn't seen a thing—you were blind. Yes, your
eyes had the exploded look of someone who has suddenly
stepped from bright sun into a dark room, of someone who's
been staring too long at dazzling snow. If your eyes had even
traveled below the white expanse of her gown, I was sure
they'd seen nothing, their gaze having been suspended by a
darkness they could not meet.

My own gaze returned to the spectator pumps. I could not
believe the tiny creatures they'd displaced had crept back to
their ruby-lined lair. At any time one could shoot from beneath
the long white cloth-covered table centered with the five-tiered
butter cream cake from Schneider's Bakery, or pop out of the
pink and green upholstery of the wicker chairs on the veranda,
or perhaps spring off one of the hors d'oeuvre trays shouldered
by the black-skirted waitresses, abandoning its sheltering grove
of parsley in one bold leap. At any moment surely one or both
would break out, either now or later, and so I waited for the
next twelve years. Waited as she bore one of your children and
then another, yet worked steadily at her art. And it seemed to
me that all the while I could see them just below the surface of
her works, never quite blending with the brushwork as they
peered through a scrim of paint, betrayed by bubbles as they
floated beneath a layer of emulsion.

Yes, I could see them, but whenever I tried to persuade Barbara to abandon the stuffy hidey hole of life with you, the upstate tidy bowl of the petit bourgeoisie for the breezy space of a lower Manhattan loft or a Parisian atelier, I always met with the same response: a blank yet somehow fixed yellow stare that made me feel as if I was the one taking shelter, that I had best think twice before I stepped out. Still, I would've left with her in a second if she'd ever accompanied that stare with the phrase "let's go." Oh I would've been ready in a flash if just once she'd uttered the golden words that hovered over the marquee of Smalley's Theatre, those words that floated on the dull brick facade like the grin of a cheshire cat, like a mockery of my desire.

Yet she did finally leave, as you well know. She did at last leave, and, dimwitted as you were, you must've wondered how. How, when you had trotted over to Wilber's Bank and closed the joint account the same morning she said her final sayonara? How, for if the strings of sex had frayed and snapped, didn't the bondage of economics remain? And yet she had stepped out of those other shackles with houdini-like ease, had gone on that very morning to pay cash for a Country Squire station wagon at Smith Ford which she'd packed up not only with art supplies but also Anna, Stella, and the old world mother-in-law you thought you'd charmed with your jazzy new world hey Batty Baby ways. How did she get the moolah to finance their mobility and, once they'd reached Santa Monica and Batty Baby had secured a job at Sacred Heart Hospital faster than a boob can say bababoom, to put forty per cent down on a pink stucco bungalow?

Perhaps it is better not to ask—better to let the past rest in peace, like the bones of old William Cooper beneath my picnic table. Better not to inquire why our father did not support your decision to sell the liquor store and chase after her in a deluxe winnebago, armed with the stack of Harry Belafonte records with which you hoped to lure her back. Better not to pursue his failure to endorse your pursuit, than to be blinded, again, by the strain of staring at what you could not see. Thus your letter begging me to beg him to further fund your quest, as if I was the more than daughter of his fondest care, sank under a pile of papers, like a coffin beneath the shoveled earth. For while I must admit I was flattered by the intimation of paternal favor, I also felt you needed to know Dad wasn't going to give you a dime, and the most effective means to convey that message seemed to be silence, just as the best way to block an entrance is to build a wall.

By the way, I hope you'll forgive me for nevertheless removing a brick or two in the lines above, and I assure you that the dislodging was selective. Because you must know position and angle are everything—he who only sees a small patch of hide need not know it belongs to an elephant.

Your Sister,
Juju

So Chubby Boyd is going to meet us here on the hallowed ground of her ancestral deer park. And then she's going to buy drugs from you.

Sure. Why not? Better than that sleepy-time syrup you were drinking the other night. I told her she's too cool to do the same shit my old ana did back in Turkey.

The moon's thinned out tonight tightened her belt but still I can see him slouched against the chain-link fence that along with three crowning cables of barbwire protects the cloven-footed from the adidas shod. He's wearing the red turban hat squashed down and rakishly askew. I ought to rip it off his head. If ought tos were horses they could pull him away. Pull me away.

Instead I flick off the lights of the tercel cross ground still soggy from today's thaw. Funny how fast the snow will go this time of year. Funny how the firmest resolve melts away how horny I was this morning nothing could stop my hands my lips my hips from meeting his. Must've been the cheap motel room the beetles in the bathroom the grit between the sheets like the irritants that goad the oyster to secrete her glistening bead. Must've been only I can still smell our juices on my fingers even though I scrubbed them after with that powdered motel soap scrubbed until the skin shriveled.

Squelch squelch and now I'm beside him flopped against the fence my stinking hands clutching the steel mesh like limpets I won't open them again. I won't open them again but oh I can smell his sweetsalt breath and oh oh I already am hand floating away from the wire drifting over the firm shoal of his fly slipping beneath his thermal shirt flattening against his smooth warm belly oh. Sliding down cold metal running over my spine as my coat slides up and then his warm hands. My shell is dissolving and now I'm long long like a snake the slush seeping through my jeans slicking my scales greasing our coil as he rolls over me then I roll over him each trying to swallow the other whole as the wasting moon looks away. Yeah might as well do it here no one can see us no one comes out to see the deer at night especially not at the back gate not this time of year least of all the mighty Charlotte Boyd. Where's his zipper my hands are numb but I'll find it. When suddenly he goes still.

Hear that?

What? My fingers find the tracks climb for the tab, then slip away as he pulls himself into a crouch.

That.

I raise my head. A dog barking. The distant hum of a car passing out of town, but then I see the lights have swiveled onto the back road that leads to the rear entrance of the deer park.

Come on we gotta get up. She thinks we're just friends. He stands over me, silhouetted by approaching headlights. I can see his breath dissolving against the starry sky but not his face as he reaches down and touches the scar above my lip. The only person who knows where that came from is dead.

She what?

Thinks we're just friends. That's what I told her.

You what?

Don't be jealous. He leans down grabs my hand and pulls me to my feet. Now we're eye to eye I can see his again, large moist and imploring. Don't shoot me.

I'm not jealous.

It's just for one night, OK?

The car is slowing, pulling off the road. I turn my back to the lights, pulling him by the arm. *Just one night? One night of what?*

Quickly, under his breath: *She wants me the old cunt wants me. So here's the plan: I drive her home in her very expensive car, mmmm looks like a jag, sweet, give her another lovin spoonful for free, an investment, and while she rides the white horsey far far away I clean her out rugs paintings silver you name it except for the car that's too risky. Then we tear outta here down to Queens where I got a cousin who will fence for just a tiny cut. A mere puhrick.*

NO!

Shhhh. It's pay back time. Just be cool.

He falls back against the chain-link fence, pulls my mom's hat down low over his forehead. With arms folded across his chest dope pouch slung over his hip like a holster he waits, my life-sized action hero my wind-up vigilante.

The headlights flick off. A car door creaks open slams shut. It's too late to argue but I sure as hell won't wait around for him to get nailed just check out and leave before the hammer comes down. Yeah cut my losses and go. Leave all this shit behind the whole huge useless pile. Cuz there's no pony, not even the goddamn bones.

No pony but it sounds like she's got spurs that jingle jangle jingle as she comes squelching merrily through the slush. Jingle jangle jingle and now the light hits my eyes again. Two blind blinks before it falls enclosing our three pairs of feet in the circle of a flashlight beam. My black hooves Skip's waffle stompers and her shiny riding boots. No spurs. No spurs but above the boots more leather an entire calf skinned flayed and stitched into a pair of tiny-assed jodhpurs flowing frockcoat snug gloves and closefitting cloche, a completely epidermal ensemble that ought to make Skip's own hide twitch with disgust but instead

he's grinning at her like she's the purtiest little thing he ever saw.
Veggy boy plays the ham.

Good evening Mrs. Boyd. He extends his hand.

Hello Scoop darling. She draws him to her gives his cheek
a peck.

It's Skip.

Skip. Of course. She traces a finger down his chest: *Like
Skip to my loo.* Then she turns directing her flashlight beam at
the locked gate of the chain-link fence. In her other hand she's
dangling a ring of keys and she jingle jangle jingles them like a
tiny tambourine like she's applauding herself for being 55 years
old and fit as a flamenco dancer like she's saying just watch me
steal your boyfriend olé olé.

*I thought we could continue our little rendezvous inside the
park. Believe it or not our local boys in blue do occasionally cruise
by here looking for wayward teens.*

Great. I love deer. He's smiling at her back glazed eyed like
he just shot up like she's the drug he's thinking of. He really
thinks he's going to score off her.

She throws a glance over her shoulder at me as she fumbles
with the lock: *Are you planning to walk through the fields in
those Stella? Careful you don't fall.*

Careful you don't fall. Fuck her. But maybe I should say no
I'm going back to the motel I'm really tired. Cuz I am tired and I'll
need to get some sleep if I'm going to drive the getaway car when
Skip comes back with the loot. Ha. What fun imagining ripping
her off the daughter of your old buddy Chip it'd be a kind of
poetic justice, olé olé. Cuz who says you can't rob peter to pay off
paul especially when the money should've gone to mary. Yeah it
should've gone to mary as compensation for that sicko manger
scene for the nasty photos for the way they just used her. Cuz she
was just a dabbler a housewife making half-baked art projects in
the attic a pretty monkey imitating the big daddyos at MOMA, she
never would've thought of stuff like that. Just a ditz with paint on
her nose trying so hard not to fall on her ass.

Why is it that I can never begin with the right key? Why do I always have to go through every key on the loop before I get it?

Maybe it's one of those laws? Skip suggests as the bolt slides out of the lock.

Like the law of gravity? she asks unwrapping the chain.

Trying so hard not to fall, and then Anna and I were always underfoot.

Or the law of Reilly.

I don't think I know that one. You'll have to teach me. The chain slithers to the ground on the other side of the fence.

She smiles for Skip's eyes only planting her flashlight in the small of his back like she's inserting a key then directs him through the gate pulling it half closed behind her as she goes so that I have to sidle. Did she feel me behind her slipping through the attic door? Did she see me snatch a paintbrush from her toolbox? Did she know how softly the bristles could kiss my skin? She never did…. Fuck.

Boot must have caught on that damn chain. I bet someone's happy to see me sprawled face first in hoof-churned slush. I told you so. I knew you wouldn't be able to walk in those silly shoes. Is she laughing? Probably. All I can hear though is the rattling of the chain links…like casters rolling over hardwood…. Maybe she knew I was in her studio but still I'm sure she couldn't see anything from behind her easel, couldn't see me dancing brush clutched in my hand trying to get out of the way as she pushed her canvas across the paint and birdshit splattered floor. She couldn't see me didn't know she'd backed me up against the attic stairs. I know she couldn't see I was going to fall cuz she was just a fall guy herself. Yes can't forget how they all fucked with her can't let this last week get me down, just gotta pick myself up sluice the mud off my leather jacket and move on.

Yes and so its onward ho my subhuman right to follow as Mistress Boyd leads my boy into darkness her flashlight beam skittering over sloping ground pocked with cloven hoof prints yet still bristling with tufts of last year's grass. Why haven't they gobbled it all up by now? They must get other food maybe bales of hay forked over the fence. It's the good life probably if you're a deer no hunters to hassle you a steady supply of grain plenty of room to roam within the confines of Charlotte Boyd's barbwire seraglio. Yeah and if you were one of the wild ones your gums raw from gnawing bark off trees and the gate was open you might not only scamper through to snatch a bite but even try to stay.

Where's the deer?

Good question, Scamp.

It's Skip.

I'm sorry. Skip. Like pip, sip, dip. Like my father, Chip, who stocked this park with a herd of European red deer culled from the countryside around Brugge. That's why mine don't look like those white-tailed clodhoppers that trample cornfields and total cars. As you'll soon see.

She trains her flashlight at the copse of trees directly before us, scooping out the darkness between the trunks: *Funny, this is where they usually settle at night.*

Maybe they're further in.

Beneath the trees slush turns back to icy snow mixed with slick clumps of dead leaves. Treacherous footing. Let them scamper ahead without me, I won't be her fall guy. Does a deer think about falling about slipping or catching a hoof about twisting and snapping its long skinny legs? I know I wouldn't sleep here wouldn't risk it just to lie down on a slimy bed of snow and leaves my warm hide a magnet for creeping toads and sluggish centipedes, a sudden Florida in the dead cold damp of winter. Or California although the nights still get cold this time of year the days are brilliant hot sun bouncing off chrome and white concrete sinking into your bones. I miss it. I actually miss Lala Land and the Discover card won't get us back, too many places won't take it.

No and we can't get back the way we came my Visa is finished, kaput. I never should've left it wasn't a bad life the life of a hack for hire a freeway flyer I had enough to eat money for cheap booze a firm new futon to crash on at the end of the 405. If we ever get back I'll let Skip move in. So what if he sponges off me as long as he cleans up the kitchen after he makes his veggy surprises. It'd be nice to come home to the smell of something hot even if it's only roasted eggplant zucchini fricassee not as good as steak but better than the nothing we had today. God I'm hungry.

Look at her the sleek puss in her handmade boots I wonder what she had for supper veal maybe and tender asparagus tails no matter that they're not yet in season that I saw them the other day at the Great American for six bucks a bundle. Wonder what she's thinking as she leads Skip into that little dip like a leafy saucer between the trees. I still haven't had my dessert? Wonder what she's saying her lips to his ear as she pulls him down. I need a new mouse boy, would you like the job?

He's a creep but he's my creep all I've got left since I need to put a stop to this. No choice but to follow this trashy plot, let the big cheese above be my guide. Yeah that's ice there you can't fool me my pal the moon showed me your shine. Just have to pick my way with care lift my feet and place them squarely a step at a time this snow patch here looks safe and so does this one foot in front of the other and soon we'll be flying just like Rudolph out the door heading toward 90 west. They probably won't take Discover at the toll plazas but maybe we can find some sleazy motel restaurant Best Western's Jackpot Lounge that will and I'll order a big t-bone for me the salad bar for Skip. And when we get back maybe Oma will take me in let me sleep in my old cot bed with my feet hanging over the end until I get on them again. What about Skip though I can't bring him no boys in your room she always said. We'll have to dress him up as a girl my friend Sue then he can take Anna's place at the breakfast table the chair of the fuck up who poured orange juice on her cereal and salt in her milk. She was out of her senses Oma said after Mom disappeared. Out of her senses like there's a way to get back in again if you can just find the right path figure out which is the proper door.

What I like about when I'm high is that I don't have to be me anymore. My old ana used to say the spirit of Allah is not only in the body of man but also in the worm in the shrub at the edge of the forest. When I'm high I go with that.

Yes but who would want to be a worm?

There they are in their cozy hollow sitting in the cocoon of the flashlight beam on a tree stump half-submerged in leaves. I can see them but they can't see me. I can see how she's gripping his thigh with her claw. If he really was a worm he could just wriggle away leave her clutching the tail. At least I'd still have the best part the torso and arms inherited from his dad the gymnast. No more backflips though I'd have to get him a wheelchair though or better yet a cart I could pull around on a string. Then I could tell Oma that's no boy in my room that's just a toy. Just a toy I can't stop playing with, why can't I let him go?

Really Skimp, why would anyone want to lose himself? Why would I not want to be Charlotte Boyd?

Yes why would she want to know how the other half lives can't he see she has no interest in his dope that she's an old boozer through and through so besotted with herself she assumes he must be as well? She doesn't see herself as a joy of sex relic as a totaled woman nosiree but as still totally hot. So in her mind this is no drug deal but a lover's tryst.

It's Skip but good question. I mean I'd like to be you a beautiful rich woman, a power babe, a queen. But why would you want to be me?

Man he's really laying it on, what's he thinking? If he can't get her wasted he might actually have to do the nasty with her be the worm in her shrub and no wriggling afterwards until she's sound asleep. Yeah I bet that's his plan to go home with her and then after he bonks her he'll rip her off. That's really low and if I help him return to the Mohican now get the tercel and

park it on the street outside her gates I'll be low too, can I sink
that far? Heigh ho, let's do the limbo.

Is that you Stella?

Shit she can see me.

*What are you doing standing over there in the dark by your-
self like a lonelyhearted moose? Come join the party.*

Come join the party I don't think so but what's that she's
pulling out of her frock coat, something silvery and flat. A pocket
flask. When did the Bells last toll after the Bucko fiasco I must've
killed the bottle. I could really use a swig just something to
warm me on the walk back to the motel a little lube for going on
the lam.

OK.

*Watch your step. The leaves are slick and there's mud and
ice underneath.*

Don't need her to point out the obvious that I can't trust
the ground beneath my feet. Yeah it's a shaky proposition that
I'll be able to get over there without breaking an ankle I never
should've worn these shoes but what was the alternative I didn't
bring any others how was I to know what a slippery slope this
would be? How was I to know but soon enough we'll be on the
highway trusty asphalt under our wheels. Soon enough my legs
will stop trembling once I've had a good meal yes a juicy steak
will straighten me out get me firmly on my pins again. Soon
enough but right now they feel really weird all wobbly and throbbing as if there's a bass beat pounding up through the soles of
my boots, where's it coming from that beat like the drum roll of
a quake? Is it really just me?

No it's not just me the earth really is rumbling amazing in
upstate New York I can't believe it can't believe the way she's
clutching him she's really got nerve. Who would've believed it
we're gonna be swallowed up unless somebody says something
makes a sacrifice throws a bone. I should yell take her even
though she's not a virgin and close to 60 years old I bet she's all
pumped up with estrogen that her skin's softer than mine. Only

then Skip will go down too. Gotta get over there and pull him away tell him to forget his silly scam we're just going back to L.A. where at least if we fall through the cracks we'll fall together.

They're here.

Who?

My deer.

Stella! Stella!

Shit they're gonna trample me can't run in these just crash and burn no more standing tall sometimes you just gotta roll gotta roll like a loser with the punches like a baby down the attic stairs but I'm not gonna make it to the hollow better just wedge myself here against this log she didn't mean it and let them fly over my head now dasher now dancer man they stink but not like you'd expect like old furcoats and paintrags now prancer and vixen ouch something scraped my ear on comet and cupid the hard edge of a wooden step no it must've been a hoof on donner on blitzen got to keep my head down press my face into spongy moss like the wool carpet at the bottom of the stairs so I won't see her stop to pick up her brush on the way down but that was a long long time ago so dash away dash away dash away all…

Stella? Stella?

I can feel her crouching over me but I don't open my eyes don't want to see what's in her hand. Something soft touches me just above my upper lip. A fingertip? A paintbrush? I don't think I'm bleeding.

Stella?

A honk in the distance. A car horn? A goose? Then a click and the inside of my lids go red. Might as well wake up and see what Santa's brought me.

Chubby?

As I open my eyes her flashlight beam clicks off. But the moon is out again and I can see her face see that her lips are pursed and she's pinching the bridge of her nose like she's trying to gather her thoughts. Like a hoof scattered them. Ha. But where's Skip?

Where's Skip?

I don't know.

Excuse me?

Her hand drops inside her coat, pulls out the flask. She unscrews the lid, swallows. *I don't know. One minute he was sitting beside me, the next he'd sprung off into the darkness shouting your name.*

She hands me the flask, then reaches again inside her coat. *I found this on the ground over there.*

What is it a bandaid no a label: *a hat by Mr. John.* Dash away dash away dash away all.

Ms. Stella Vanderzee
Humanities Department
Irvine Valley Community College
Irvine, CA 92717

14 February 2001

Stella,
   As you may have noticed, I've dropped the "dear."
While most people employ this term casually, mindlessly
adhering to formal convention, I cannot help but think of its
Old High German root, "tiuri," which meant costly. Deep in
the heart of "dear," a word that the guy and gal on the go use
without a thought, addressing collection agencies and discarded lovers indiscriminately, lies the idea of great value,
and even, perhaps, a price too exorbitant to pay. Knowing
this, I can't bring myself to apply "dear" to someone who is
not dear to me. But please do not then assume that I dislike
you. I don't. I bear you no ill will. No ill will, although I must
admit that initially I saw you as yet another wedge between
your mother and I. Yes, you were just one more wedge of
flesh forcing us apart, filling the fissure that was once just a
hairline crack (for the initial split must've been nearly
imperceptible; how else could I have failed to notice I was
losing her until she was already gone?), like some kind of
human cement so that the growing gap soon became a wall.
   Over the years, however, I began to realize (and I'm not
sure when or how; this knowledge snuck up on me, creeping
into my consciousness as quietly as cancer) that nobody stood
between Barbara and I. No body stood between us because
every body was grist for the bloody mill out of which she
cranked her art. Human beings were simply material for
her—yet this is not to imply that they were immaterial. On
the contrary, from the beginning, even as the bands, bars,
grids, helixes, pixels, splatters, tatters, and whorls of the

Abstract Expressionists seemed to have blotted out the human form for good, Barbara's work exhibited that it was deeply indebted to the body and all those defining gerunds—eating, shitting, sleeping, fucking, birthing, dying, decaying—that give shape to its existence. Your mother's art was bound up with the body, or perhaps I should say bodies, since the singular perhaps implies some immutable marmoreal ideal, rather than the ever shifting junk-strewn sludge of corporeal experience.

Yes, her work was bound up with the body, yet no body stood between us. No body but the body of her work. Unfortunately, that was body enough—one that was ever growing, reaching, sprangling, twisting, tangling, inverting, diverting, dallying, and surging, swelling the attic studio of the Leatherstocking Street house like some ineradicable rhizome, or endlessly resourceful tumor. For much as I admired her art, I admit I also found it increasingly alienating, an invasive presence cutting off whatever flow of feeling there had been between us. Especially as the years went by and I began to understand that there were no others, no tangible and thus defeatable rivals, only it. No others and yet by the winter of 1970, I'd ceased to be not just her lover and patron, but even her admiring audience. She didn't want me in her life, let alone her studio. Can't I come in, I want to give you something, I'd beg from the other side of the door, bearing my offering for the bin full of found materials I knew she kept in the corner of her attic—cradling some little contribution such as a piece of scrap wood pulled from the dumpster behind the Guggenheim or a Polaroid camera plucked from a bench in Central Park while its owner took a whiz in the shrubbery. Trembling, I'd wait despairingly for her reply, hearing nothing in the interim but the sounds of her activity behind the attic door, sounds of scraping, hammering, something slapping against something else, wait like the condemned for the guillotine of her refusal to fall. "Sorry, but I don't like the way you look at my stuff," she'd finally call out, the razor sharp edge of her words scarcely dulled by the door, "Like you wish it had never been made. Just leave whatever it is on the landing."

And so I would, and then I'd drive back to my apartment in the city and my little editing job at Schocken Books, tearing down the Taconic swerving around the curves half wishing I'd lose control entirely and fly off into the stubble of last year's corn. Last year's corn because why would Barbara Salzmann ever again want anything to do with a maudlin old (for hadn't I just recently turned 26) dyke like me? Yet a month or two later I'd be off as usual tootling northward in the tired old Triumph I'd inherited from your father (which I'd always coveted, but could scarcely bring myself to accept when he told me he'd outgrown it now that he was a "family man") like some off season goose or brainless scarecrow, unable as always to counter my life's lack with some other lode star—and thus powerless against its pull.

So it was, exactly thirty one years ago today, that I found myself standing on the porch of the Leatherstocking Street house with a box of chocolates in my hand. Oh I'd resisted that last tug, so inauspiciously timed, with all my might. How degrading to succumb to the Valentine's Day tide, to be one of love's lemmings floating amongst the fleet of Russell Stover candies, bobbing along in a sea of salable emotion. How demeaning to be swept along by the stream-lined gush of sentiment through the doors of the Belgian confectioner (though at least I still had sense enough to seek quality sweets) on the corner of Madison and 73rd and then out again clutching a gold foil wrapped heart full of chocolate covered cherries. How humiliating now to be here on Barbara's door step holding my cardboard organ like some low rent romeo, oozing the sticky sweet of manufactured feeling as if I had no more say over this surrender to schmaltz than over my monthly menstrual flow (which likewise had always mortified me, ever since it first began in the June of my thirteenth year, just as my pop and I were about to cycle

off to the Country Club for the Father-Daughter Doubles
Tournament. Feeling the sudden wetness as I settled on my
bicycle seat, I ran back inside to the bathroom and discovered
a smear of berry brown syrup. Well I knew what it was, being
a doctor's daughter, and also that I would not let this trickle
stand in the way of sport, even though I hated tennis and had
only entered under paternal pressure. So I stuffed my lace-
trimmed tennis panties full of toilet tissue, and was pedaling
resolutely up the hill, when I heard my father call from
behind me, "Juju, what is that strip of white dangling like a
banner between your legs?").

I rang the bell. Silence. Silence which told me I should
just drive back down to the city, even though it was already
late in the afternoon and the light was nearly spent. I rang the
bell again. More silence, and then, just as I was about to press
the button one final time (before I tried the back entrance), I
heard someone call "return to the bath you bad girls, you ruin
the nice floor with your drips." The door swung open—no
one. And then Batty Salzmann glided out from behind, white
as an iceberg in her sleek nylon nurse uniform. Her broad
Nordic features were blank, her blue eyes cold. Would she let
me and my chocolates in, or would she not?

"Oma we wanna come down."

I looked up and saw two pale little bodies pressed
against the railing over the landing, faces sandwiched between the rungs. Your face. Your sister's. And Barbara's too,
yet with enough of James' to mar each one, to blur its pure
features with the feathers of my brother's native petulance, so
that they seemed to belong to another species entirely. I
wanted nothing to do with either of you, and dreaded that you
would come scampering down and press your bath damp
flesh against me, that you'd clamor to paint the slime of your
plump lips on my cheeks. Fortunately, just as I was tensing
for this onslaught, Batty turned toward the stairs, shook her
fist above her head, and cried "GO! NOW! OR I WILL
SPANK YOU WITH MY WOODEN SPOON!"

As your shrieks thinned away in the upstairs hall, she
turned to me, one hand on the door knob and the other braced
against the jamb, seeming to fill the space between with her
solid white form, although I suppose I could have ducked
under her arm: "Hallo, Judith. What do you want?"

I told her I had a valentine for Barbara and that I would,
of course, like to hand deliver it.

She flattened her right side against the frame, pulling
the outer edge of the door flush against her left, so that now
there was no way past but to knock her down.

"You know she is working, you know she cannot be
disturbed. She is a great artist so the Doctor says. Who am I
to question only a nurse even if sometimes the nurse knows
what the doctor does not."

Well then I'd just leave my gift before the threshold of
Barbara's studio.

"Oh no you will not, Miss Judith Vanderzee, I am aware
that my daughter was your special girlfriend and that she is
no more. But you can give this so-called gift to me. I will
give it to her."

She extended the arm that had been wedged against the
door frame, and as she did, the smell of something hot and
cheesy slipped through, no doubt the odor of her famous bread
and velveeta casserole baking at the back of the house, a dish
which had been a staple of Barbara's youthful diet, and which,
I imagine, was also a principal component of yours. Suddenly I
couldn't stand myself—I was behaving like a character in a
dime store potboiler, a pulpwood butch sprung from the
tobacco stained fingers of some pimply hack hoping to make
enough money to finance his novel about a sensitive young
writer forced to write trash to finance his novel. I handed Batty
Salzmann my gold foil wrapped heart and walked away.

But instead of cutting through the grounds of the
Courthouse over to Main and the top of Nelson Avenue where
my little Triumph sat under a "NO PARKING AFTER 6:00
pm" sign, I found myself rambling up Leatherstocking, along

Railroad Avenue, down Main past Nelson, left onto Pioneer, right on to Lake to where it curved into River Street, up to Beaver all the way over to Chestnut Street, at which point I turned back towards town. Now dark had fallen in full and my feet, sleek but ill-insulated in new designer boots, felt as if they'd been shod in blocks of ice by Jack Frost rather than stretch suede by Beth Levine. I stopped and stamped them on the pavement, arms folded across my chest, benumbed fingers tucked beneath my elbows: it was a five hour drive back to the city at best, if I took 87 instead of the Taconic, and I had to make a decision soon, to either get on the road or present myself at my father's door. Neither prospect warmed me—neither the four-lane toll-way back to urban swingerdom nor the narrow shelter of my girlhood's canopied bed. What to do, what to do, how to choose between two brands of such cold comfort? I did not wish to wander the streets of Cooperstown all night, stumbling along on block feet beneath the black ice-splintered sky, but the alternatives seemed even bleaker. And then something on the other side of the street caught my eye, a vague white shape emerging out of the dark outlet of Leatherstocking, a shape which turned left onto Chestnut and as it glided swiftly past the softly glowing display windows of the Victory Supermarket, cinched into the distinctive hourglass silhouette of Batty Salzmann.

This time I did not knock, but I did not simply burst in either, for it occurred to me that my brother's arrival home from the Vanderzee liquor emporium could have coincided with Batty's departure. No, I made my entrance stealthily, absorbing the creak of the parquet floors through the thin soles of my suede stretch boots as I tiptoed over to the closet beneath the stairs. The parlour to my left was dark, and the glass of the French doors discreetly reflected the disappearance of my long arm behind the closet door and its subsequent reemergence, along with the small smile on my face. Through my probing I'd established the absence of James' Burberry trench, and hence the absence of James himself.

So far, so good, as I stepped into the dining room. All was still, the heavy sideboards like massive sleeping dogs or drunken guardsmen indifferent to my passage beneath the tepid light of the chandelier, which Batty had no doubt dimmed to low upon her departure. While I knew Barbara would not be happy to see me, I saw no reason why she should be unhappy either, especially once she understood I had given up all hope of competing with her work. Yes, I've given up all hope, I repeated to myself feeling the phrase descend over my shoulders, a mantle of invisibility. Because if I wanted nothing, it would seem as if I was nothing. And if I was nothing there was no reason now why I should not be with her in her bower of art—no reason now that I had become as imperceptible as air. As imperceptible and perhaps as necessary, for once she grew accustomed to my presence might she not come to regard it as integral to the atmosphere? Unobtrusive but utterly vital, I pressed my palm against the swinging door that led into the breakfast room, which in turn led to the kitchen and the back stairs, the first of the two flights to her studio. But just as I was about to push it open, a volley of giggles burst from the other side. My hand fell.

"Look at me look at me I'm so stinky heeheehee!"

"Ohhhhh Stelly that's naughty it looks like poo and guts ahahahaha!"

"Now you try, Annie!"

"Nuhuh. Mama's gonna be mad."

"Mama don't care!"

As you may recall, there was a service cupboard built into the wall between the dining room and the breakfast room, an architectural relic from the turn of the century designed to keep the kitchen and all vulgar laboring within a mystery. No dinner guest need know of the grease scummed soot smeared matrix out of which the beef wellington had been born, for there it was resting on a silver charger in the magic cabinet, fully formed in its pastry shell and ready to serve. But those more squeamish times were long gone—I

had no qualms about sneaking a peek at what was on the
other side of the wall. Crouching, I pulled open the outer door
of the cupboard, and then as I poked my head forward into
the recess, cracked the inner door...

Anna sat, naked, at the head of the breakfast table, small
splayed hands slapping the edge of antique oak, her wide-
open mouth foully berimmed with brown paste. Wretched
child—what had she got into? I nudged the cupboard's inner
door out another inch, and saw that whatever she'd got into,
you'd got into more. You were standing on a chair and like
your sister were without clothes. Yet I could not describe your
flesh as devoid of covering: all over it was slathered with a
pale pinkish slime clotted with dark gobs of brown and
globules of bright red. And then suddenly I realized what
those little red balls were. Cherries, I gasped as my eyes fell
on the heart-shaped box lying open on the table. Crumpled
gold wrappers were strewn all around it—still as broken
butterflies at first but then, as my eyes filled with tears, they
began to flip and flop like shiny little fishes dying in the air.

I flung open the cabinet door and sticking my head in as
far as it would go, screamed, "GET YOUR GODDAMN
PAWS AWAY FROM THAT CANDY!"

It must have been terrifying, the sight of my disembodied
face in the service cupboard, and if you retain no conscious
memory, I am sure it haunts your dreams. Then again, maybe
I'm just projecting into your nightlife the specter that frequents
mine, a specter whose countenance I drew from the reflection
in the window as I entered the now empty breakfast room.
How awful it was, bloated with rage, blotched with tears,
stretched and streaked by insupportable cacoëthes like some
monstrous pod on the brink of irruption. Yes it was monstrous,
that face. My face. I turned away from the dark windowglass
and the alien yet all too familiar visage planted within its
panes, to gaze down at the remains of my gift on the table.

To my surprise, the box was not empty. Indeed it was
still more than half full with the foil-wrapped candies, despite

the copious mess you had squandered on your insensitive
skin. Not empty and still more than half full, yet I could not
present my unreplete heart to Barbara, like a beggar seeking
alms. No because then she would think I wanted something,
when really I wanted nothing. I wanted nothing, I was
nothing, and somehow I had to prove I was nothing, to erase
the insatiable desire reflected in the glass. But how? Trembling, I shed my stretch suede boots, fitted wool flares, snug
cashmere turtleneck, silk camisole, and matching panties
until I stood naked on the bare wood floor, nipples cinching
in the underheated air (no doubt Batty had turned down the
thermostat when she dimmed the lights). I half-turned to the
window, regarded myself in profile as the heat from the vent
along the baseboard rode up my left side, making the right
feel even colder. The body I saw was long, white, hungry
looking. As if to confirm this last impression, my stomach
rumbled and I realized I'd had no lunch, let alone dinner.
And now I could smell bittersweet chocolate and maraschino cherries, a twofold solicitation both insolent and
cloying, yet impossible to resist. I found myself plucking
one of the stemmed bonbons from the box on the table,
found myself unwrapping it, sniffing it, raising it to my
lips…when suddenly I recalled you standing on the chair,
dripping with the wreckage of my gimcrack heart, and
retched. With the thought that I'd sooner eat crow, I
smashed the chocolate against my chest.

It felt good. Icy but soothing, like a balm or poultice.
Like the camphor oil Peg Phinney had massaged into my
fever-flushed skin when I was a child. I stuck my finger in the
center of the mash, drew a plume of syrup down between my
breasts, traced the curve of a rib. A piece of cherry became a
jewel burning in my navel, while dark flecks of chocolate
clustered round it like a tribe of scarabs. I took another
bonbon and flattened it against my hip, another against my
inner thigh, my fingertips all the while stroking and swirling,
marking my body without thought, without shame, as the

wind ripples the sand of the Sahara, patterning it with bold
and unforeseen designs.

"I like that."

I turned around to find Barbara regarding me from the
entry into the kitchen, the Polaroid camera I'd scavenged for
her loosely cradled in the crook of her arm. Unlike Batty, who
had filled her doorway like an impregnable wall, Barbara
slouched into its side, softening the rectilinear lines with the
curve of her body, transforming the frame, or at least one half
of the frame, even as she melded into it. What if I were to
station myself inside the other half, to touch my fingertips to
her fingertips, my toes to her toes, so that the hard wood
rectangle became an elliptical portal of flesh: what might we
not usher in?

But I could not move. And even if I could have, I can't
say that I would have. I was too much enjoying the novelty of
her attention. Had she ever looked at me so intently, had the
black of her pupil ever so completely eclipsed the amber of
her iris as it did now, blotting out the cautionary rim with an
all embracing darkness? No, to be honest, not even in the
earliest days of our acquaintance had I felt her awareness so
completely enfold me as it did now, plush as a new mink coat.

"Yeah, I like the textures. Do you mind if I take a few
pictures?"

I shook my head, feeling my flesh tingle even as I
remained frozen in front of the window.

"Good." She walked over, took me gently by the elbow,
and led me into the kitchen, flicking the switch for the
fluorescent lamp overhead as we entered.

I expected that she would back up against the wall or the
counter, to get as much distance as possible from where I
stood in the middle of the floor, directly under the buzzing
fluorescent tube, so that she could fit all of me into the picture
frame. But instead she drew right up close, exploding the
flash over my breasts. She pulled out the square of exposed
film, placed it on the counter. Then she zoomed in three more

times—first on one side and then on the other and back
again—blasting the inside of my thighs, the curve of my
buttocks, the slope of my belly, pausing only to lay the film
on the formica countertop between each shattering kiss of
light.

After she was done I continued to stand in the midst of
the tiled floor feeling the places where the flash had caught
me, as if shimmering nets of photons had been cast over my
skin. But as the sensation dwindled and decayed I gradually
became aware of her standing over the counter with her back
to me. I padded up behind her and peering over her shoulder,
saw that the protective developing layer had been prematurely peeled back from each image. Not only this, but the
straight pin she now held poised over the last of the photo-
graphs had apparently been used to stir the still liquid emulsion of the preceding three, rendering the topography of my
flesh unrecognizable. The pin descended and I winced.

Yes, I winced at this wanton abortion of pictorial
potential. For though I had only seen the last of the photo-
graphs intact, I'd immediately comprehended what I'd
already intuited whilst massaging the chocolates into my
flesh—that although the close-up rendered the body less
recognizable as such, it opened up the body's potential to
gestate other images and associations, to develop beyond the
preconceived forms, the imprinted imagos. If Barbara had
photographed my candy-coated curves from the standard
distance, I would have become a stock figure of feminine
degradation, a Karen Finley smeared with yams, a Kiki Smith
trailing a rope of turd (although even still, Barbara's stock
figure would have preceded theirs by more than a decade).
Without that distance, however, those curves need not assume
their expected outlines: a navel could, for instance, become a
sheltering hollow keeping alive a sacred flame, the expanse
of belly surrounding it a sloping sandswept plain. By daring
to relinquish perspective, Barbara had birthed new visual
actualities. But then, before their natal fluids had even had a

chance to dry, she'd unmade them with her sharp yet unperceiving pin. What a pity, what a shame.

Of course, however, I kept these thoughts to myself. I turned away, walked over to the sink, and leaning over the stainless steel basin, clutched the edge with my hands. The black rubber maw of the garbage disposal gaped up at me, but my lips were sealed: it was her right, her prerogative to undo what she had done, the artist's right to choose. Still, she must have sensed my dismay, because after she had finished destroying the last of the polaroids, she stepped up behind me, and lightly grasping my upper arm, held up a vertiginous mess of bluey white ivory dun pinkish brown and vermillion before my face.

"Isn't this great? There's so much movement—the whole thing is spinning whirling twirling like nothing's yet become anything like anything could become nothing, you can't say where it's going because it might already be gone. Or not."

I nodded, rendered speechless by this unprecedented descent into the inchoate depths of abstract expressionism. Or maybe it was the warm weight of her hand, which had, incomprehensibly, settled on my shoulder. Or the inexplicable fact of her fingers stroking the hollow over my collarbone. Or the paradoxical way her breath, blowing softly against my shoulder blade, seemed both to yield to my trembling body and draw away from it. I had nothing to say about what was happening, nothing to say about what would, for these gestures had no incubating context (at least that I could discern) and thus no narrational viability.

And I have nothing to say still, since some events are best left in the shadowy lacunae where language fails to shine. This is not to imply that I could not dig up words if I needed them, words which would undoubtedly fall short of that night but which would nevertheless launch the imagination with thrilling force; however, because I am your aunt and your elder, I won't. For I am well aware that no child wishes to contemplate the sex life of the parent; indeed this subject may be the modern mind's last prohibited zone, the dark chamber where thought not only refuses to go, but which it cordons off with thick curtains of flannel nightgowns, having first pushed two twin beds against the door. And as I sense your deep-seated fear and avoidance, my protective instincts are aroused, here manifesting themselves as self-censorship. So enough of that night at 7 Leatherstocking Street, and let us instead focus on an entirely effable aftermath: my gratitude.

My gratitude, which extends not only to your mother, who in allowing me to accompany her that night on her aesthetic adventures took me to the very height of the sublime, but to you. Yes to you, my stinky Stella, for would she have allowed me to tag along if I had not had the requisite gear, which I probably never would have thought to don had it not been for your smooshed and smeary example? I think not.

In short, I owe you one. And thus it is that I'm now inspired to dissuade you from flying off on a silly goose chase—even though I'm the one who laid the golden egg that is now lodged in your frontal lobe like an idée fixe. (I do so love mixing metaphors, although it is a pleasure, like mixing alcoholic drinks, that one must pay for later, for who can reread without feeling queasy after the intoxication of writing wears off?) Yes, I not only laid, but lobbed it with my letter of a month or so ago when I claimed the Homer was here waiting for you. And now I must admit I misled—the painting is long gone.

I imagine you mouthing those last two words over and over—long gone, long gone, long gone—your curls writhing as you stamp your little foot in furious accompaniment. Only it is not so little anymore, to judge by the size of the rest of you in a photograph (the date 1987 is pencilled on the back) Batty Salzmann must have sent my father. I came across it yesterday afternoon, as I sorted through the sundry boxes Heidi Phinney has so obligingly stored in her attic since the

sale of the Vanderzee estate. Against a background of shore-
line, you stand swimsuited with your arm draped over Anna's
bare shoulder, leaning into and over her, your shadow swad-
dling the contours of hers. Even though she was your big
sister, you were clearly the bigger girl by a head and maybe
even a foot, which may account for the protective quality of
your posture. By virtue of that altitudinal mandate, perhaps,
you saw yourself as her defender, and thus you went on later
that same year to blast the good doctor with the righteous
missive I found tucked in the same file as the seaside snap-
shot. How could he, the scion of Vanderzee Dairy Products,
whose own grandfather had bought him an alphabet's worth
of degrees at Johns Hopkins, deny Anna financial aid for a
simple A.A. at Santa Monica Community College? Or, to
quote sixteen-year-old Stella, "What kind of selfish old
bastard are you not to care if your own granddaughter gets an
education?"

   Perhaps the doc was simply being pragmatic; rumor had
it that the A.A. your sister needed was not to be found in
academe, even if that establishment often serves as a launch-
ing pad into the twelve step program. And anyway, she
apparently went on without his aid to earn a terminal degree—for didn't she O.D. just two years later? But to be
honest, I don't think my father's failure to finance Anna's
schooling stemmed from the belief that she was a poor
investment; rather, I believe it followed from the fact that his
funds were tied up elsewhere. Elsewhere being with your
mother.

   I imagine your eyes widening, the white scar above your
lip fluttering like a tiny moth in the light of the preceding
paragraph's disclosure. Oú est la mere? Elle est dans la mer,
n'est-ce pas? Because much as you wanted to believe she
wasn't gone for good, you did, the hope in your face when I
came out to California looking for her the hope of a child
who clings to her belief in Peter Cottontail (or the goose who
laid the golden egg) long after the bunny trail has gone cold.

But now you must feel as if that long lost rabbit has crawled out of the hat, dripping wet and wriggling its little pink nose. Yes Stella, it is true: she did not drown herself. She only made it look that way (for like Claes Oldenburg, she was "for an artist who vanishes, turning up later in a white cap, painting signs and hallways"). And after she sank out of sight, it was my father who helped her keep afloat.

Just as he always had, ever since she captured the Vanderzee with her cartoon triptych of paternal denucleation. From the first he had felt her talent, his aesthetic inexplicably stirred by her anti-aesthetic, so that he could not help himself: no choice but to become her sugar dada, for reality would never be the same. And so it all went to Barbara, the whole candy store, and when the kookie jar held nothing but crumbs (its contents depleted by the various causes and collectives Barbara launched, incognito, on both coasts—such as the Women's Building in Los Angeles and then later, when she returned to New York, the Guerilla Girls—as well as her own projects and maintenance), he began to sell off all the bric-a-brac he'd accumulated over the years. The Homer was, I believe, one of the first things to go.

So there you have it. Or, perhaps, you don't. Which is my grateful gift to you, a nothing that might very well be something, or a something that may be nothing, like the quivering lump beneath the magician's scarf, forever fort, forever da.

Not yours,
Aunt Judith

P.S. She does resurface now and then, if only in submerged form. Every time truly interesting new work appears in one of art's forums, you can be sure it is hers, even though the name attached to it—say Takashi Murakami (for she never abandoned figuration, despite her flirtation that night with abstract expressionism)—sounds nothing like Barbara Salzmann. And if you're afraid I'm pulling your leg, perhaps you should try standing firmly on your own two feet.

Lost. All lost. Even Skip. I don't have anything and she's got everything even marble lawn furniture who has marble lawn furniture maybe the president and the pope but otherwise you only see it in cemeteries a luxury only the dead can afford. I wonder if she ever sits there if she brings a pillow for padding or if she prefers the hard chill of stone. Probably the latter I bet she even gets off on it the solidity of marble against her ass like some kind of mineral endorsement of her familial right to sit on this town. Not that anybody around here minds no they want to be sat on like that woman I bought the Bells from at Dad's old store the other day when my visa was still good. What was it she said something like *where would we be without Charlotte Boyd*. She didn't mention the Vanderzees though we're gone and forgotten like the days of picking cotton. Even Gramps lying in his bed up at the Lakeview Lodge. He's like some old rusty relic some ancient farm tool that nobody quite remembers how to use. Nobody remembers and it doesn't matter just leave it there hanging on its hook in the barn and move back to the future pick up where you left off like none of this ever happened none of this ever happened.

Yes so just turn around Stella you don't need to see old Chub a dub who cares if she was lying when she said she didn't know what had happened to him who cares if she's got your man in her tub. Or not. Let him go. Let it all go. The painting. Mom. It doesn't matter anymore, what anybody did or didn't do. It's done. Too late for Sharon Tate but not too late for me. Sure I'll just leave I don't have to park here I can just turn the key step on the gas and follow the curve of the circular driveway right back out again on to River Street over to Main on to the Lake Road north to Route 20 and eventually 90 west. I'll just follow the signs I won't even have to think just read the words do what they say and I'll be fine. Fine.

So what am I doing standing in front of these tall black double doors when there's no sign of what I'll find on the other side? Or who. No sign just the feel of the finish beneath my fingertips slick as a casket or a frisco seal. She died before I had time. She died before I was old enough to tell who was hurting whom and now I don't really want to know. I don't want to know anything not one more thing not even how that big brass ring will feel curled against my palm. Anyway I can just as easily imagine—a hard dense and tingling coldness. I also know the sound of metal striking the solid wood of the door panel will be deep and resonant, brimming with possibility. And I'm done with hermeneutics. Yes I'm done with trying to figure it all out time to stop thinking just follow your nose back home Scooby Doo. No more sniffing around.

But what's that someone's talking the tentacle of a voice stretching through the fissure between the two big panels which is widening widening as the double doors swing open and I ought to turn and run helter skelter back to my car. ...Too late. I'm stuck.

Stella. Just a moment please, Gregory...I've got someone at the door...No, Carrie's off today, just like you.

She's wrapped in a black silk kimono a cordless nestled in her whiteblond bob like the worm in the shrub. Bitch I bet she's got him up in her bed, a succulent tidbit swaddled in Egyptian cotton.

Where's Skip?

Resting the phone on her shoulder she looks me straight in the eyes: *Well that's what I'd like to know. Last night when I returned to my car I found it odd that my Hermes was under the passenger seat and not the driver's—where I thought I'd stashed it. Still, I assumed I'd misremembered. Until this morning, when I couldn't find either my wallet or my checkbook!*

Goddamn him. *How do you know who took it? It could've been anyone, anyone who happened by....* Goddamn him.

Maybe... She plants the phone back in her shrub with one hand, hooks me round the elbow with the other pulling me over the threshold. *Gregory? Yes darling, I'd like you to close the Visa Platinum account.... No that's ok, I've still got my Mastercard ...yes, thank you...*

Yes probably it was him the shifting shape of lack I should have known better you can't count on anyone or anything it can all come crashing down that chandelier for instance swarming overhead like a cloud of crystal locusts could drop any second destroy us both, better not to look up as she drags me over the parquet. Better not to look up but oh it's so bright so myriad filling the room even the floor with droplets of light. Yes must close my eyes shut brightness out let it slide down my cheeks instead. Oh fuck.

Oh come now Stella, what is this. He's not worth crying over...Gregory, hold on, I'm afraid the pipes just broke. No no you don't need to send anyone over, I was speaking figuratively.... All right my dear, through this door. Just take a seat here next to Puff, there's a box of tissues on the little marble-topped table. I'll be with you as soon as I finish speaking with my secretary...

Must get a grip must get a grip there's no point in this no reason to break down he was just a roll in the hay a lightweight a strawman but not the last one and anyway I'm not a camel. I'm not a camel but man I'd sure like one any old c-stick would do just a little fire to dry me out so I won't look like this when she comes back. No can't let her see me looking all smeary eyed and snotnosed still like some little baby who fell down the stairs gotta pull myself together stand up and walk out of here as if none of this ever happened and I'm just dandy. Yeah a smoke would be nice a little ride with the marlboro man to get me out the door but if I can't have one I can at least wipe the tears away so I can see where I'm going. Where'd she say the kleenex was?

Ah here.... That's better. Now I can look around. Nice place. This must be what they call a solarium one of those words you read but never use let's try it, darling shall we serve cocktails in the solarium? Oh yes I do so love to sit and swizzle a pimms cup amongst the calla lilies. Me too though what I'd really like is some whiskey funny how I'm not hungry anymore after two days without eating just a little tired. Maybe I'll at least sit here a minute or two just a few moments in luxury's floral scented lap. Then I'll split. And drop the adieus like those fuchsia petals scattered over the marble I'll simply slip slide away over her parquet floors, maybe take off my boots first so she can't hear me. Just another minute or two though it smells so green in here is it plants or money yes another couple deep breaths let me fill my lungs like pockets then I'll run back to the Mohican and pick up my stuff. Or maybe just leave it, why bother to check out? Skip didn't. And neither did Mom. Leave em' hanging I say— closure is for pussies.

Sure cuz I can walk off the stage anytime I want who says I have to be in this show, I'm nobody's gull nobody's glass-eyed marionette. Anytime I want but right now I'm going to sit and enjoy the setting for a bit a few moments longer before I climb back into my tin cell. Wonder what's behind that lacquered Chinese screen over there in the corner it looks old and expensive probably it's just to add ambience a touch of oriental opulence to the Boyd empire. Yes so let's luxuriate a little enjoy our pimms cup like that fat tabby curled up on its cream damask cushion I guess Chubby doesn't care about the hairs and why should she Oma would say, she's got someone else to vacuum them up. No cats in the auto she said the pelts make me sneeze and so we had to leave Tigger behind. I should take this one, kit for kat since last time I had to leave my fur baby behind. It'd be nice to have some company on the road.

Hey kitty kitty wanna come with me?

Shit that's no cat it's that raccoon again yellow eyes blinking through its black domino what's it doing here. Yikes it's opening its mouth what sharp teeth you have you little mother fucker yes all the better to gobble you up if I wanted but right now I'm merely yawning. Merely yawning thank god and now rolling over on its back presenting the plush of its belly like an invitation to feel the charmin, so irresistably soft. No way I'm going to take it. Yeah it can lie there and flail its stubby legs all it wants I'm not going to fall for this I'm just another purina loving household pet act I saw those polished canines the calculating click of the lids. Yes Puff I've called your bluff.

I've got its number and it knows it as it trundles off our loveseat onto the floor. No more of this little honeybear shit it lands on all four paws with a thump like a gavel like let's get down to business. Something's started up inside its furry skull some animal racket some primitive reel it's clearly got an agenda in mind as it lumbers away then stops suddenly in the middle of the room turns rocks back on its haunches and raising its hand-like paws opening its mouth starts spewing out a stream of staccato noise...

reeeki rreeeeeki reek reek reeeki rreeeeeeki reek reek reeeki rreeeeeki reek reek reeeki rreeeeeki reek reek reeeki rreeeeeki reek reek reeeki rreeeeeki reek reek reeeki rreeeeeki reek reek reeeki rreeeeeki reek reek reeeki rreeeeeki reek reek reeeki rreeeeeki reek reek reeeki rreeeeeki reek reek reeeki rreeeeeki reek reek ...reeki reek...reeki reek...RIK.

God that was so obnoxious it just went on and on worse than a telemarketer like it was never going to stop. I wonder if Dame Boyd puts up with this if it pulls the same shit when she's around I don't think so I can't imagine it jabbering at her like that she'd lock its jaw with the remote control of her stare. Yeah it's taking advantage of the situation seeing what it can get away with doing its crazy varmint shtick for the visitor while the mistress is out of the room. And now it's just sitting there waiting for me to applaud like they did back at the Bump to say Bravo Puff way to go.

You suck.

Uh oh. Looks like someone's a little miffed I've gotten the finger before but never the tail. Anyway good riddance whatever it's gonna do behind that screen maybe take a crap but what do I care this is not my house. No this is not my house and I really ought to be going I've got three days on the road ahead of me probably four without Skip to share the wheel. God I hope the Discover card works I can sleep in the car but I'm still going to need to pay for gas and food. Maybe Oma will wire me some money I'll call her from Buffalo the city of no illusions think I've got enough in my tank to get me that far tell her you were right I did drive off on a fool's errand now will you help me get back home.

C l i c k. . . . . C l i c k . . . .
. . . . . .Click. . .

What's it doing back there clicking to itself might as well see what kind of nasty mess it's making maybe I'll tell Chubadub on the way out and maybe I won't...

How cozy a little computer nook her own microsoft nest with a jewel of a mac glowing emerald in the soft lacquered light they're not that expensive a little over a thousand I could have afforded one easily if I had my Homer to sell. Yes and she must have been back here not too long ago cuz this mug of coffee is still warm she must've been sitting in this padded leather chair now taken over by Puff. Man the animal's got a sense of entitlement its black paw hand clutching the mouse like it's daring me to take it away. It was probably trying to open it up that's what that clicking noise was it thought it had a clam.

GET DOWN FUCK HEAD!

Hey it worked like Oma always said if you make a big noise at a strange dog you can scare it away. Even though puff daddy's no dog. No dog and it looks pretty pissed with its ears flattened down like that its lip curled up but still it's backing off turning tail disappearing around the corner of the screen. Off to squeal I bet someone's playing with your computer someone's playing with your computer twitching its tattle tail. But I'll only be a minute just long enough to check my e-mail it's been weeks after all maybe there's a message from IVC maybe they wanna hire me back. Ha.

Hmmm...looks like someone's been poking around on the Online **Auction** Site an online market place what are **you** looking for? Yeah what was she looking for this could be interesting let's press the back arrow and see...

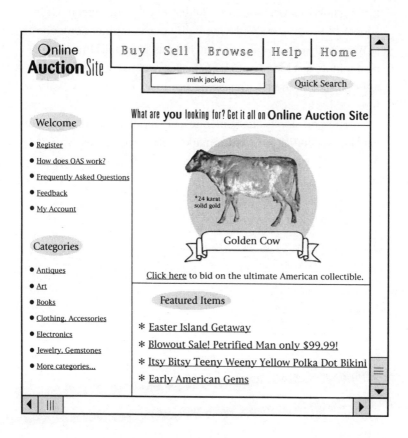

Online Auction Site

Buy | Sell | Browse | Help | Home

mink jacket   Quick Search

What are **you** looking for? Get it all on **Online Auction Site**

Welcome

- Register
- How does OAS work?
- Frequently Asked Questions
- Feedback
- My Account

Categories

- Antiques
- Art
- Books
- Clothing, Accessories
- Electronics
- Jewelry, Gemstones
- More categories...

*24 karat solid gold

Golden Cow

Click here to bid on the ultimate American collectible.

Featured Items

* Easter Island Getaway
* Blowout Sale! Petrified Man only $99.99!
* Itsy Bitsy Teeny Weeny Yellow Polka Dot Bikini
* Early American Gems

Online
Auction Site

| Buy | Sell | Browse | Help | Home |

Auction Information
Clothing, Accessories

| Item: | **L@@k Pink Scooby Doo Scrunchie** |

Current Price: $1.95
Quantity: 5
Time Left: 1 day, 2 hours +

Auction Started: 4-05-01 12:35:27 PDT
Auction Ends:　4-12-01 12:35:27 PDT

First Bid: $1.95
Number of Bids: None
Location: Show Me State, St. Louis, USA

✉ mail this auction to a friend
 watch this auction

Seller: **whereareyou?@aol.com**
　　(view seller's feedback, view seller's other auctions, ask seller a question)

High Bid: None
Payment: Credit card, money order/cashiers check, other
Shipping: See item description for shipping charges
Other seller information...

Item Description:

Pink Scooby Doo Scrunchie: This cotton
hair accessory is printed with a pink floral
background highlighted with images of the
big dog holding a yellow bouquet in his
paw. It suggests innocence combined with
resourcefulness. The girl who wears

Auction Information
Clothing, Accessories

| Item: | **Vintage Mink Jacket-Schiaparelli Paris** |

Current Price: $42.00
Quantity: 1
Time Left: 2 days, 13 hours +

First Bid: $10.00
Number of Bids: 1
Location: Bellflower, California, USA

Auction Started: 4-06-01 23:42:19 PDT
Auction Ends: 4-13-01 23:42:19 PDT

✉ mail this auction to a friend
👁 watch this auction

Seller: **maternalmink@earthlink.net**
   (view seller's feedback, view seller's other auctions, ask seller a question)

High Bid: None
Payment: Credit card, money order/cashiers check, other
Shipping: See item description for shipping charges
Other seller information...

Item Description:

Schiaparelli Mink

This is labeled Schiaparelli Paris. The fur is top
quality but slightly damaged along the back
hem. Rust colored stains are visible in the lining

Online **Auction** Site

| Buy | Sell | Browse | Help | Home |

Auction Information
Clothing, Accessories

Item: 1950's Mr. John Red Angora Turban Hat

Current Price: $8.00
Quantity: 1
Time Left: 6 days, 17 hours +

First Bid: $8.00
Number of Bids: 1
Location: Coney Island, New York, USA

Auction Started: 4-10-01 16:23:54 PDT
Auction Ends: 4-17-01 16:23:54 PDT

✉ mail this auction to a friend
👁 watch this auction

Seller: **nights@thecircus.org**
     (view seller's feedback, view seller's other auctions, ask seller a question)

High Bid: **barbieredux**
Payment: Credit card, money order/cashiers check, other
Shipping: See item description for shipping charges
Other seller information...

Item Description:

 I believe this is a Mr. John Hat from the 1950s (it has no label). It is a rich red angora (top quality yarn) in a sort of turban style. It could be worn either squashed down like an accordion or fully expanded as shown in my view. The bottom circumference is 22 1/4". Height is 9". Hat is slightly soiled but a good dry cleaning should work wonders. Winning bidder must confirm within 3 days and pay within 10 days of auction close. Buyer pays $3.50 shipping, plus optional insurance. Seller assumes no responsibility for loss or damage if insurance is declined.

Auction Information
Art: Fine Paintings

Item: **Winslow Homer, *Girl with Cow***

Current Price: $85.00
Quantity: 1
Time Left: 2 hours +

First Bid: $85.00
Number of Bids: None
Location: Show Me State, St. Louis, USA

Auction Started: 4-05-01 12:35:27 PDT
Auction Ends: 4-12-01 12:35:27 PDT

✉ mail this auction to a friend
 watch this item

Seller: **wildgoose@chase.com**
      (view seller's feedback, view seller's other auctions, ask seller a question)

High Bid: None
Payment: Credit card, money order/cashiers check, other
Shipping: See item description for shipping charges
Other seller information...

Item Description:

This is a fine reproduction painting of Winslow Homer's 1874 painting *Girl with Cow*. This reproduction painting is the same size as the original painting. Size: 15 1/2 X 22. This reproduction painting is like a genuine painting. It is on canvas with wood stretcher bars on the back. The image shown here on the scan is poor due to the shrink wrap that protects the painting. I did not want to remove it. I originally paid almost $200 for this about 5 years ago. I never had it framed and kept it stored away. High bidder pays $8 shipping and handling. Thank you for looking at this auction.

Dear Barb,

Yes because a barb is "a sharp projection extending backward, preventing easy extraction." But that's just wishful thinking. Truth be told, I am rid of you, and what my mind keeps coming back to, like a tongue obsessively searching the socket of a lost tooth, is your absence. And to be more honest still, that void offers its own reward: as my mind retraces my loss, defining its contours and then filling them in, what I've ended up with is only your likeness—a cast of you so much more flattering to me than the original.

Thus when I think of you and your mother living up on the hill at the end of Grove Street (for where to start but at the beginning, at the very root of our relationship), living like hillbillies in the poorest house at the end of the poorest street in town, yet only a walk through the woods away from one of the richest, this is what I imagine: that it was not I who climbed over the window sill, to tramp in the twilight through dead leaves and bracken, but you. Consequently, I see you molding a pile of dirty clothes under the quilt on your bed, shaping a form that your mother would take for her daughter's when she finally came home from her shift at the hospital, in the so-called wee hours of the morning (after all, for some these are the fullest hours of the day). A form that she would embrace as yours—mentally at least, since I don't believe I ever even saw you so much as tap each other on the shoulder—long after you'd slipped out the back door (so that no neighbor would see your departure) and into the crepuscular forest.

Do you have sneakers on your feet? Or are they wet from the dew of the overgrown lawn you've just dashed across, welted round the ankles by the lashings of the long coarse grass? I imagine that you don't, imagine that as you step into the woods, bats in the dusky air overhead receding like voices, even you feel the fragile cushion of leaves under your calloused heels, the powdery crumble of decayed plant matter seeping up between your toes. Lowslung branches

catch at your hair and scrape your bare arms, while through
the treetops stars blink out a code you'll never crack. Perhaps
a length of spider's web, suspended between two trees, wraps
round your waist like the sash of the prom gown you never
returned to me, perhaps a plastic six-pack holder from
someone else's party catches at your foot. But you stumble on
because you know that I am waiting for you.

Yes, you stumble on, past the cherry Naugahyde recliner
that sits in a small clearing, its redness cozy as a campfire in
the dim light. Although, in fact, this chair provides no comfort—a spring has pushed through the seat, and even if you
were to perch on one of the padded arms instead, the gnats
and mosquitos would soon be flying about your head, covering you in a swirling, stinging veil. Regardless, you keep on,
dodging branches, springing lightly and quickly over the
leafy mulch so as not to sink into the loam beneath, that dark
loam teeming with beetles and centipedes, beckoned by the
ruddier glow of the setting sun through the pines beyond.

And soon you are standing at the edge of the woods, at
the top of a bank that sweeps down to the curve of the private
road to our house, and I imagine that for a moment you just
stand there, admiring the view in the clearing below. For how
could you not be impressed by our gleaming white neocolo-
nial ranch, that architectural chimera of east coast tradition
merged with western ease, sprawled out over the sloping
green lawn like a Puritan sleeping it off? How could you
resist taking a few imaginary springs on the great canvas
trampoline set off to the side of the house, on the level ground
just beyond the French windows of my father's study? How
could you fail to admire the dark background sparkle of the
Glimmerglass in the valley below, as the sun's last rays
bounce off its waters?

When your eyes have taken their fill, you make your
way down the bank, steadying yourself by grabbing hold of
the smooth trunk of a sapling, toes gripping the dirt, trying to
make it to the lawn without falling on your ass, without

tobogganing the backside of your little white jockies (cast-offs, no doubt, from some farm-boy cousin) over the raw dark soil. And perhaps you do slip just once, just once as you reach the bottom of the decline, the earth crumbling away beneath your feet, just once so that white cotton becomes smeared with reddish brown before you lurch forward and spring onto the dewy lawn like a toad. No matter however, as you stand up and lifting the back of your skirt, brush off your buttocks. No matter, because you know that in the darkness I'll still kiss you, that in the night the most surprising transformations will occur, regardless of the woodsy stink clinging to your clothes.

Knowing this, you creep around the perimeter of the grounds as if skirting the sleeping immensity of a dragon, keeping close to the woods as you pass the trampoline backlit by the glow from my father's study, until you reach the window I have so surreptitiously opened for you. Knowing this, you place your two hands upon the sill and leap up and over—landing lightly on the Aubusson. Knowing this, you step over pale imitations of courtly life, rendered in dull golds, wan blues and insipid pinks, to the bed where I await you, ready to restore your crown.

Yes, because then the reversal would be fait accompli, the switcheroo complete. Then I would have been able to claim that just once you came to me, rather than the other way around, that just once there was another side to the story, a diptych with a second panel that shows you running through the dark forest past the red chair with its broken spring coiled like a snake in a nest of split vinyl and foam, and not I. Yes, I would have been able to assert that just once you had to creep along the edge of the lawn, the dew feeling like cold sweat beneath your feet, until at last you reached the sanctuary of the bedroom—a sanctuary that was not, however, a reprieve, as the terrifying pleasures between the sheets far exceeded those found beneath the unreadable stars. Because you never cut me any slack, did you? You never gave in to my whimpers and

pleas, or rather, understood them for what they truly were—
invocations to press on, further and deeper into the woods.
And for that I worship you.

Piously,
Juju